The GIRLS

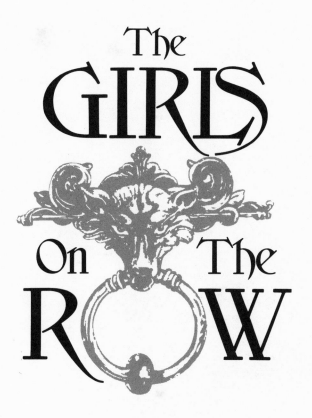

On The ROW

Also by Carolyn Banks

Mr. Right
The Darkroom

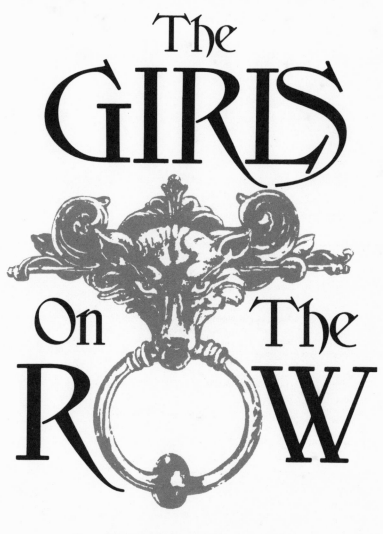

The GIRLS On The ROW

CAROLYN BANKS

Crown Publishers, Inc.   New York

For Kathleen O'D. Walton

Grateful acknowledgment is hereby given to
WARNER BROS. MUSIC for permission to reprint the
lyrics from EMBRACEABLE YOU by George & Ira
Gershwin on page 140, Copyright © 1930 (Re-
newed) NEW WORLD MUSIC CORPORATION. All
rights reserved.

Excerpt from "PLANET CLAIRE" by Keith Strick-
land, Fred Schneider, and Henry Mancini
© 1980 BOO-FANT TUNES, INC. (BMI) & NORTH-
RIDGE MUSIC CO. (ASCAP) All rights for Boo-Fant
Tunes, Inc. administered in the U.S.A. and Canada
by ISLAND MUSIC, INC. (BMI) All Rights Reserved-
Reprinted by Permission.

Published by Crown Publishers, Inc., One Park
Avenue, New York, New York 10016 and si-
multaneously in Canada by General Publishing
Company Limited

Manufactured in the United States of America

Library of Congress Cataloging in Publication Data

Banks, Carolyn.
   The girls on the row.

   I. Title.
PS3552.A485G5   1983   813'.54   83-10076

ISBN 0-517-55038-5

Designed by Dana Sloan

10   9   8   7   6   5   4   3   2   1

First Edition

PART ONE

PRELUDE

For as long as anyone in Washington could remember, the little stand of houses across from the playground had been called the Row. No one knew why or how the designation came about, but it figured in directions people gave, and somehow even newcomers understood. "Eastern Market? Sure. You just walk on down the Row, turn left, four blocks and you're there." Or "The post office? Let's see. Go up the Row, turn right at the corner, and it's maybe three blocks. You'll see the flag."

In the old days the Row wasn't even part of Capitol Hill, but gradually that neighborhood expanded to include it. Houses near the Row—whole blocks of them—were costly now, with many restored to their former elegance.

Singles rented apartments in these houses, whole floors of the two- and three-story buildings. Couples bought what was called a "shell" and set about removing siding, pointing bricks, and clearing litter from the tiny yards front and back. Everywhere stained-glass transoms and polished brass trim caught the light and gleamed. And everywhere that residents met they talked of restoration, comparing the grained oak woodwork they'd found under layers of chipped enamel paint, or the condition of once-elaborate crystal chandeliers. They talked banisters and knobs and hinges and, of course, dollars and cents.

No one had yet considered the Row for a major overhaul. Facing the buildings, it was easy to see why. Of the five houses on it, the one farthest to the left was mainly rubble, with no doors, no windows; indeed, no roof. Its walls, on the unsupported side, had crumbled in places, and bricks spilled into the street.

Two among the remaining four were eyesores. The house next in line had been covered with artificial stone and was unlike the rest— squat, two stories, with a flattish roof and a front porch. A very ordinary house that would have been much more at home in the blue-collar sections—out Rhode Island Avenue, say, toward the District line, or across it, in Mt. Rainier, Maryland. The center house was owned by a black family, who had painted the brick a bubble-gum pink.

The fourth was plain—two stories, but tall ones. The lower floor was given over to storage, but the upstairs and the brick-floored basement had been rented, and at a decent sum.

It was the place on the corner that had brought the Row its flurry of fame: an elegant turn-of-the-century mansion with plywood boards still nailed across its windows.

A murder had taken place there. The victim, Faye Arensberg, had been young, beautiful, up-and-coming. Hers had been a spectacular death, a death that even major magazines—*Time* and *Newsweek*—did not ignore.

"Police still have no leads," area broadcasters would begin in the several days when the bloodstains were bright and the fear was fresh.

The small knot of people who had watched Faye Arensberg's shrouded body being taken away, the ones who had seen those ply-wood sheets going up over the windows—the ones who asked each other, "Did you see anything?" and "Did she scream?" and "Who would have done such a thing?"—formed a community of sorts now.

They had their dread in common. And they'd been badgered, questioned, interviewed by the press.

Jessie Wood Trotter, who lived in the tall house right next to Faye's: "I prefer not to think about it."

Rita Puleo, from the downstairs apartment in the squat house: "Well, one good thing, it'll keep the rents from going up."

Jay Reynolds, who rented the basement of the house where Jessie lived: "Great subject for a book, don't you think?"

Margaret Speidel, Rita's upstairs neighbor, who had just moved in a week before Faye was killed, commented with her tears.

Before the murder the Row had been a stopover, a section of the city where people on the rise could pause, plan, save some money, nod to neighbors whom they knew by sight but not by name. And all the while, boast a Capitol Hill address.

But murder makes that sort of insouciance impossible. Murder—particularly when the death house stands empty and waiting—marks those near it, some indelibly.

PART TWO

LATE FEBRUARY

Claire sat on her deep-pile sofa looking out at the panorama of the Blue Ridge Mountains. The room in which she sat was exquisite: modern, but not offensively so, its effect achieved through symmetry and understatement. It was a sitting room, and it jutted from the body of the house into a large rye meadow. Three of the four walls were glass, floor to ceiling, so that when the rye was green it might appear to a visitor that he'd entered Eden.

She propped the telephone against her shoulder and finished her breakfast of brioche, sections of mandarin orange, and tea, balancing the tray on her lap, while Aubrey spoke.

Occasionally, she managed an "Mmm-hmm," so that he would know that she was listening. Otherwise, he might have begun to repeat.

This time it was a house.

Claire could easily rent such a house, he was saying. To a secretary, perhaps, or someone's speech writer. It would be a good investment and she ought to, really, start thinking along those lines.

"Fine," she agreed, dabbing at her lips with a napkin and then laying the cloth atop the tray. She had been as patient as could be, but now she was eager to get off the telephone and down to the stable yard. If she didn't hurry, Steve would feed the horses and drive off without her, she knew. "Fine. Do it," she told Aubrey.

But no, that wasn't enough. She would have to see the house herself. And quickly, before someone else came along and bought it. Could she come that very morning?

Well, of course, Claire thought, that *would* be the point. If she weren't in such a rush, she might have said what she was thinking, although softly, with her voice curled around the words as if around an endearment. She would speak so that Aubrey would conjure the swell of her lips forming the words. Oh, he *was* a transparent old fool.

Outside, Steve gunned the truck, spinning the rear wheels in the gravel and making the engine whine. *Sorry, babe. Waited long as I could.* That was what Steve would call back to her if she could manage to get outside now. But that would be impossible.

She heard Steve pull away.

Claire examined the silvery polish on her fingernails. She'd awakened half an hour earlier than usual to apply it. She sulked but allowed Senator Aubrey Denton to ramble on.

"You won't have any trouble whatsoever finding tenants," Aubrey continued, his voice more solid now, as if he knew her attention was no longer elsewhere. "There's a firm up here that will handle all the details." He cleared his throat. "One more thing, darling, in case you were wondering." He snuffled a bit, as he always did when he called her *darling,* to take the edge off. "Let me read you a bit of this article. . . ."

Claire leaned back to hear him read what some real estate agent had to say about the dwindling crime rate on Capitol Hill. A real estate agent. You'd think even Aubrey would have known how ridiculous that was. As he spoke, Claire recalled a newscast she had seen. The camera had swept along a row of houses on the Hill, the voice of the announcer calling attention to the decorative wrought-iron bars laid over every accessible window. "But here," the man said when the camera halted and fixed on one with no such protection, "*here,* the young and beautiful Faye Arensberg met her death."

The house disappeared and the face of Faye Arensberg flashed onto the screen. Claire had watched with an ache that she could not name as they described Faye's life. Envy? Then Faye was gone and the camera was back at the scene of the crime.

"*Mise en scène,*" Claire said now, and it seemed appropriate. The Arensberg girl had been a set designer at the Folger.

"Pardon?" Aubrey asked. He had finished reading.

"Nothing," Claire said, "go on."

He launched into a fuller description of the house he hoped to persuade Claire to buy.

It was at the end of what was called the Row, and easily the most attractive house on it. Three stories tall, with a charming—well, he didn't quite know what to call it—not a turret, exactly, but a roundish area . . .

Something alerted Claire, and she listened more closely than she would have ordinarily. Could it be that Aubrey's description would mesh quite completely with the house the news camera had locked onto? It had been a year, at least. Why *would* she remember?

But she did. She even remembered the way the image had jerked a bit as the camera drew back and away to show the murder house whole. The Row, yes, the announcer *had* called it that: the Row.

Aubrey finished his recitation and waited.

"What did you say the address was?" Claire asked, taking care to sound reluctant. But she was standing beside the table again, fully as impatient as before. She found a pad, but not a pen. When Aubrey answered her, she gouged the number into the page with her frosted thumbnail.

She jiggled the phone for a dial tone the minute she was able to get Aubrey off the line. She said she was calling from Aubrey's office and yes, of course, she'd hold on.

The librarian's voice was so wonderfully monotonous, so bored:

. . . The body sustained numerous puncture wounds, including fourteen to the face. In addition, police found what one officer described as "fistsful" of hair, with portions of the scalp still adhering, scattered around the body. According to the medical examiner, Faye Arensberg was alive when these wounds were inflicted. . . .

Claire had been right about the address. She almost giggled when she thought of it. The irony—Aubrey with all that business about the crime rate dropping. If poor, stupid Aubrey only knew.

. . . Cigarette burns on the woman's breasts and shoulders, though these, police say, were not in any way related to the cause of death. Nor were they linked to the killer. Saliva deposits indicate—

"Thank you," Claire cut the woman off. "If you'll send a copy of those . . . yes, to the Senator's office." She spelled her name, then Aubrey's, resenting the time that it took.

There was a hitchhiker standing on the ramp to the Interstate. *Standing the way they do,* Claire thought, weight to one side, hip jutting forward, head tilted. Claire tried not to laugh when she passed him, but she couldn't help it, not with the way he looked at her, the way he made his eyes big and round and beseeching. Exaggeratedly, the way a character in a silent film might.

She pulled to the shoulder and watched him in the rearview mirror, watched the way the fact that she had stopped finally registered, then watched him scramble. If he was like the others, he'd get in, out of breath, and make some remark about his good luck. For a change. They usually added that, that their luck was good *for a change*.

She had met Steve this way, on the road. But Steve hadn't only pleaded with his eyes. He'd seen her coming a long way off and gone down to his knees, his hands folded as if in prayer, and his eyes looking up at the sky. Even so, Steve didn't run to the car, he—what was the word he always used?—he *moseyed*. And then he'd stood on her side of the car and leaned in, eyeing her up and down, and not just her, but the car, too. "Jesus Christ, I don't believe it," he said with that gradual smile of his. "A girl in a Jaguar."

Steve opened her door and held it and Claire got out, as if the whole thing had been rehearsed. He slid into her seat and found the lever that moved it back, and then he stretched his legs and rubbed his hands along the wheel before he looked at her again. "Well?" he asked, and Claire came around to the passenger side and got in, looking straight ahead until she heard him laughing.

"This is real nice of you, ma'am," the hitchhiker said now, gasping the words out. "I been standing there, seems like a couple of hours." He reached for the door handle, and she looked at his hands and saw that they were dirty. Really dirty. So was his hair and so were his clothes. When he got in she could smell him, and it was awful; it numbed her.

"I'm only going as far as Manassas," she lied. It was the very next exit. "I probably shouldn't have stopped." That part, at least, was the truth.

She had picked him up, she supposed, to get even with both of them—Steve for having driven off without her, Aubrey for forcing her to come to him.

She pushed the Jag to over eighty, hoping there weren't any troopers up ahead to stop her. She figured she could have the man out of the car in less than ten minutes that way.

10

"What's in Manassas?" he asked her. He had rummaged through his knapsack and was pulling raisins out of a little box. "Here." He gestured toward her with a little clump of them. "You want some?"

Claire shook her head no, and felt her stomach turn at the thought of it.

"Sugar," he explained. "Gives you energy. So"—he put the box back—"what do you, live there or what?"

"Oh no," she said. "I'm meeting someone." She smiled at the thought of the Senator, his posture and grooming impeccable, watching this horrible man emerge from her car.

What had possessed her to pick him up? She hadn't needed to. She couldn't *be* more excited than she was already.

But if you think he's something, Aubrey, she ought to say, *let me tell you about this house you've chosen. Let me tell you what I plan to do there.*

Claire squirmed against the seat, just imagining.

Oh, if she knew Steve, he wouldn't need much coaxing, he wouldn't be able to resist this. He wouldn't say no to her this time. He would go there with her, he would want to go. He would want to find the very room where Faye Arensberg had died.

She and Steve would spend the night there, maybe many nights, and everything would be the way it used to be.

She remembered the librarian's voice. She would have to read those clippings to him.

"Portions of the woman's abdomen had been removed with a sharp instrument, though the lack of hemorrhage, the coroner said, indicated . . ."

"Hey, what's funny?" the hitchhiker asked, and waited. When Claire didn't reply, he let it drop. They rode in silence until Claire pulled to the bottom of the Manassas ramp.

She cloverleafed back to the highway. He could see her do it, but she didn't care. His smell lingered in the car, and she had to pull into a rest stop a few miles up the road to air it out.

She stood in the ill-lit bathroom and arranged and rearranged her hair in front of the mirror. Long and thin and pale, her hair swept down her back to a point below her hips. She coiled it atop her head, then released it, curled it over her right shoulder. Then, deciding anew, her left.

A woman and a small child entered the room and paused, involuntarily, to watch her.

Claire was accustomed to the way she momentarily arrested those who encountered her. She'd been doing it all her life. It was as if they'd found a single, perfect flower—a calla lily, perhaps—unexpectedly in their path.

It wasn't just her hair, which she almost always confined in some way, but the whole of her. Willowy, someone had once said.

She glanced at her watch and decided more than enough time had elapsed. She placed her hairpins hastily.

This would make her late, and Aubrey was always not just on time, but a few minutes early. Always. It had been a joke in her family, Aubrey's more-than-prompt arrival. Her father said it was a vice, because it made the rest of the world scurry so. Aubrey answered that that was precisely the idea.

Mustn't keep your Uncle Aubrey waiting. Even Harnette, the maid, recited it, straightening out Claire's skirt. *No sirree, you know how that man is.*

None of them knew. Only she, Claire, knew.

She started the car again and pulled onto the Interstate behind a tractor-trailer. She pressed the accelerator and surged forward and around it. The driver honked. Claire honked back. *A girl in a Jaguar,* she thought excitedly, nearer the Row now. And, thanks to Aubrey, she would be Steve's girl again.

Rita groaned and groped toward the knobs on the television set, knocking a wineglass to the floor in the process. The sunlight made the tiny screen look blank, but Rita knew it was on. She had just been wrenched awake by the maniacal laugh of Woody the Woodpecker, which meant she had fallen asleep again with the damn thing going full blast. She tried to pinpoint the exact moment when she'd conked out. She remembered seeing Wolfman Jack, but only for a second or two. Then she'd thought to close her eyes, just while the commercial was on. . . . My God. That meant she'd slept through all of *Midnight Special*, as well as the after-hours buzz. Who would believe it possible?

The smell of the wine that had spilled really got to her, stale and yucky sweet, like dead roses. *I'll clean it up later,* Rita thought, remembering that the glass had been full. She'd poured it and carried it into bed with her, and then had set it on the nightstand without taking even a single sip. Well, at least no one could call her a wino.

She found her bathrobe at the foot of her bed, half stuffed under the mattress. She couldn't find the sash, though she even got down on her knees and peered under the bed. No sash. Just a lot of dust, some of it in those little balls that rolled like tumbleweed. She really ought to vacuum. She couldn't remember the last time she had. Christmas? Maybe. It was February now. Her mother would croak if she knew.

Not that the place looked messy. Rita was good at what she'd grown up calling "straightening." But Rita couldn't afford a regular maid, and she had better things to do than spend all her time cleaning the place.

Actually, that was one thing she hated about men. They always held it against you if your place was a mess, but their places, God. The pits, even the ones who had someone come in and do it. Especially the bathroom, those creepy little hairs from the razor always sticking to the sides of the sink. But God forbid your place should be dirty!

Rita didn't mind vacuuming; what she minded was getting the vacuum out, that stupid tank and all those cumbersome hoses and pipes and attachments. That was the part she could never face. But if the last time really had been Christmas, she would have to admit that the place was overdue. So maybe tomorrow. If she felt like it, tomorrow.

Rita poured herself a glass of Ginseng Express, a blend of tea and apple and grape juice that she'd bought at the health food store, and downed a vitamin and a spirulina. Her New Year's resolution—one of them, anyway—had been to lose five pounds or so. She'd been putting off her diet and, well, you had to start sometime.

She squinted at the window. If she got herself and her gear together

13

in a hurry, she could run down to the Eastern Market and photograph those cornices she'd been thinking about. Bright sunlight was what she'd been waiting for, and here it was. She put the Express back in the refrigerator, and while she was in there checked to see if she had enough film. Good. Now, if this almost-white light held out, she'd be all set.

Rita had tried to explain to the others on the Row—Jessie, Jay, even Margaret—about this architectural stuff she wanted to shoot. A whole series. But talking about it, even to people she knew, was a lost cause. "I want it to be, um, very contrasty," she would say, "and grainy. And the pigeons, um, will be up there in the eaves, all fat, with their feathers blown up the way they get? Real close up, so you'll see the way the paint is peeling on the wood, you know. Like some temple in India or something. And, um . . ." And so on. No damn wonder she couldn't talk to art directors.

She knew she'd better learn, though, because the bullshit game was what got you ahead. You couldn't just show them, you actually had to go into the galleries and magazine offices and sit down across from these jerks and say something. That was where Rita really fell apart. That was where she um-ed them to death.

Why did photographers have to talk? At least, why did they have to spiel like traveling salesmen? Weren't the pictures enough? She even knew one guy who included a philosophical statement with his stuff. He sold big, naturally.

But shit. In college and graduate school she had accepted being poor. She'd felt okay about it, even expected it. All along she had thought, really believed, that her status would change once she was out. Especially given the way everyone—her teachers, her friends— pumped her up, told her she'd go far, whatever the hell *far* meant. Easy for them, her teachers; they weren't out there trying to hustle their work. Come to think of it, when had she ever seen their work? And yet they were the ones who kept saying, *Go for it, do it, Rita.*

She ought to hit her old teachers up for money, that was what she ought to do.

It had taken Rita eight years to get her M.F.A., and now that she had it, where was she? On the Row. It was better than the place she had lived in before, but still, she'd expected to be in this apartment maybe six months at most. Now, the way rents were going up all over the place, she'd probably die on the Row.

"I take that back," she said out loud. She didn't like to let herself think about dying. Not after Faye.

She hadn't known Faye, really, except to see. But she hadn't known anyone then. She—and everyone else who lived on the Row, it seemed—had held back, as if to affirm, if only to themselves, that they were just passing through.

Jessie was a more-than-temporary resident, though. The Row was plenty good enough for her. It was Jessie who made Rita see how it was when you didn't have to scrimp.

Rita copied Jessie, buying the stuff that Jessie bought: unsalted sweet butter sliced in chunks that had to be weighed. Olive oil in gilt-trimmed bottles. Pepper that got ground in a mill, and coffee that did, too. Not just any old coffee, either, but brown-black nuggets so shiny they looked glazed.

Jessie was as old as Rita's mother, but there the similarity ended. God. Rita's mother was a classic nothing housewife all her life. Rita never talked about her, not even to Rosenberg, her shrink. Jessie was in charge of all the displays at a Washington department store *and* its many branches.

When Rita got old, she'd live the way Jessie did. She didn't want any part of the way it had been, growing up. Her mother slamming the dishes on the table any which way and not bothering to pour the milk into a pitcher, but just putting the carton out, plop. And using the cheapest margarine ever made, like yellow lard.

No wonder that in restaurants Rita would ignore the you-have-exceeded-your-limit letters she'd received from the credit card companies. In department stores they checked before they gave you the package, but in restaurants, when the bill came after dessert, what could they do? Rita loved feeling as though she could afford it, loved the crisp tablecloths and heavy silver and real cut flowers. She loved turning her back on the way things had always been.

Shit. Why didn't she get some kind of job, be a GS-something for the government? She'd make a bundle. Or, hell, a cashier at the supermarket, for that matter. Even a cashier made more than she was making now, as Rita, who'd part-timed it through school that way, well knew. The Safeway Scholarship, she'd called it. But, oh God, the thought of somebody seeing her behind a cash register now. The thought of admitting her failure that way.

Rita closed the blinds on the sunlight, and was about to crawl back into bed when she heard, not exactly a tap, but a vibration at the apartment door.

It had to be Margaret, since the vestibule door was locked up tighter than the door in a crazy house. Why couldn't Margaret knock instead of rattle?

"Margaret?" Rita crouched down by the lock.

The vibration came again, a little louder, a little panicky. Rita opened the door, and Margaret almost fell inside.

"What's the matter?" Rita asked, and Margaret shushed her, making her way to the window. She was denting the blinds by pulling at them like that, and Rita had to fight to keep from yanking her away. "These blinds cost a mint," Rita said, "so just pull the cord, okay?"

But Margaret was still holding a slat to the side to look out. She motioned for Rita to join her.

"Give me a break," Rita said. "I haven't even brushed my teeth yet."

Before she went into the bathroom, Rita gave Margaret the once-over, though she could have drawn her from memory if she'd had to: hair bobbed like a British schoolboy's, no makeup, black tights, and lace-up shoes. And, as always, wearing one of her three A-line skirts—her navy, her camel, or her gray. They were decent skirts, but still.

Nevertheless, wouldn't you know it? Margaret, not Rita, had a boyfriend. Even if it was only Jay. Margaret had managed to snag Jay by crying all the time in the weeks right after Faye. Jay's had been the most convenient shoulder. Rita even had to stoop to borrowing Jay once in a while, when some occasion called for an escort and she couldn't dredge up anyone to take.

Rita gargled without tilting her head back at all, so that she could watch herself in the mirror. Even in this awful mood, she liked what she saw. Dark circles under her eyes, but she'd always had them, thought them dramatic. Hair that was black and blowsy. *The French Lieutenant's Woman* with a dye job.

16

Still, men didn't seem to like it. Some of the government types looked at her as if she'd just climbed out of a pink Corvette. *Fat lot you know, shmuck,* Rita would think.

She spat.

She did her lips a deep magenta and then squeezed a curling device over a length of black lash. It was a bit much for a Saturday morning, but so what? While she counted to ten, she caught sight of the sash she'd been searching for. She entered the living room knotting it at her waist.

"Oh, Rita, not your bathrobe," Margaret said.

"Why not? Who's out there?" Rita jerked the slat back herself. "Hey, wait just a minute," she said. "You're not expecting *me* to go *outside!*"

"But it's the Senator," Margaret said.

Wouldn't you know? A United States Senator would shlep over to the Row to see Margaret? "Not my type," Rita said, and he wasn't. He was rolling his lapel back, making sure the Burberry lining showed. "Look, why involve me in this?" Rita told her. "Go on. Go on out and say hello."

"Ri-ta," Margaret pleaded, "I can't! Not by myself."

"Why not? You go to work by yourself." *And earn a lot more than you're worth,* she wanted to add. Rita knew because she'd peeked at Margaret's tax forms. Twenty-four thousand dollars a year, almost. What did she spend it on? Not clothes. Not her apartment. *God, what I could do with twenty-four thousand dollars a year!* There really wasn't any justice in the world.

"But he wouldn't do that," Margaret insisted. "Not to see me. He would have somebody call me. He would never . . ."

That was some relief. But damned if Rita was going to go out there. She wondered how she'd get herself off the hook.

Aha! Rita slid into a pair of high-heeled mules with big maribou puffs at the instep. When Margaret started to protest, Rita told her, "Look, if you don't like my outfit, you don't have to take me with you." She hadn't figured the extent of Margaret's desperation, though.

"Okay," Margaret said, "let's go."

"Well"—Rita eased her own mind as much as Margaret's—"it isn't a bathrobe, really. It's a kimono."

Rita slammed the door, then regretted at once the clatter that she'd made. The minute she'd crossed the porch, she glanced toward Jessie's window, hoping that Jessie wouldn't see her out there, dressed—or semidressed—that way.

Jessie Wood Trotter gave up trying to guess at the time and switched the radio on. ". . . On this glorious Saturday morning in our nation's capital," the announcer said, in a far-too-cheery-for-morning voice. This was followed by a selection from Vivaldi—the one Rita called "the theme from *Kramer vs. Kramer.*"

Jessie grunted her approval at the music before attempting to get herself ready to go to the Market.

She was stiffer than usual. So stiff, in fact, that only slowly had she managed to stand up perfectly straight. Crick. She had a crick in her back. Nothing to fret over. But it wasn't until Jessie had finished making up the tall antique bed that she was able to bend and move about freely.

Maybe it was damp outside. Or maybe she was getting old, really old, at last. Or maybe—this was what Rita would say—she'd dreamed about something unpleasant, about her job or something from her past, and all the tension had tied her muscles up. Lately Rita talked about something called body-mind, or maybe mind-body. Body-mind. Such craziness.

Jessie stretched her arms up over her head until the movement hurt, and then she bent down, knees straight, and let her arms dangle until *that* hurt, and thought, *So much for the morning calisthenics.*

She put her scuffies on and padded up the long hall toward the kitchen. It was so bright in there, she thought for a moment she'd gone to bed with the lights still burning. But no, she could remember switching them all off in the order she always followed. It had to be the sun. Sunlight in the kitchen. Sunlight after nearly a month of gloom. No wonder the radio announcer had called this Saturday morning glorious.

Time to buy geraniums, she thought, looking at the sill and mentally picturing the plants she would put there. Small pots, four of them, plain clay pots precisely aligned. The smaller the pots, the more they'll bloom, she reasoned. And maybe she would paint the sill itself, one of those bright enamels that look wet even after the paint had dried. A bright blue or a bright green. Some color that would make both the clay pots and the coral blooms of the geraniums stand out.

She pressed the lid of the coffee grinder and listened to the raucous whir. The smell of freshly ground beans filled the air. On weekdays she was not so patient, settling for a coarser mix, even though the difference meant less than a minute. Jessie poured the coffee into a paper cone and waited for the water to come to a boil. When the brewing was done, she put her cup and the mottled enamel pot on a wicker tray and started back toward the bedroom. With all that sunlight in the kitchen, she had begun to think about the yard again, and the thought still saddened her.

Odd. Can't let anything go. Can't let anything go anymore. Old wounds, new wounds, it didn't seem to matter. *Can't let anything go.*

She raised the bedroom window a crack to let the fresh air in and heard, or thought she heard, a man clearing his throat. *The way Edward used to, in the mornings. Edward, in this very bed.*

Edward. She couldn't even remember his face, not completely, only the gray of his eyes and the way the stubble on his cheek felt against the palm of her hand. If she stood up, she could recall his height exactly, an inch and a half taller than she, once she'd taken off her shoes. Jessie groped in the drawer of her bedside table for a pencil. She stood in front of the wall and marked the spot where the top of Edward's head would reach. *There,* she thought.

But then she was ashamed of having done it. She smudged the spot with her thumb, but couldn't erase it. There was a gray smear now. Appropriate, she thought.

What if someone knew of what she'd just done? Rita, say. Rita would draw on that battery of psychological terms she'd learned since seeing that doctor of hers. Psychiatrist. Not a practicing psychiatrist, but someone Rita had found and hounded into taking her on as an ersatz patient. Imagine wanting to be a psychiatrist's patient! Things had certainly changed since Jessie's day.

Jessie slipped into well-worn jeans and duck shoes, her standard weekend outfit. She pulled a nubby sweater over her head. She wondered about her string bag, the one she used for groceries. Where had she left it?

She was about to go into the kitchen to look for it when she heard the motorcyclist in the distance. And voices, too. She switched the radio off and tried to sort out what she'd heard.

The cycle was coming closer. She hurried to the window, hoping she could shut it in time.

She saw Rita first, then Margaret, making their way toward Faye's. No, making their way toward . . .

That must have been the man who'd cleared his throat. She pulled back from the window, but couldn't force herself to turn away. Taller than Edward by far. Gray, but then, Edward would be gray by this time, too.

Jessie eased the window closed, so that none of the people below would hear the sound. By this time, the motorcycle was so close that it wouldn't have mattered.

The roar of the motorcycle drowned out Margaret's words, but she went on with the introduction in what seemed pantomime.

When the bike passed out of range, the Senator looked at Rita quizzically. "I'm sorry . . . ," he said, indicating that he hadn't caught her name.

"Rita Puleo." Rita shook his hand. Manicured nails, she thought, watching him withdraw it. Despite herself, she was impressed.

In part, it was his size. He was larger than he seemed on television. Or even, for that matter, than he had when first she'd seen him through the window. Tall and broad. Taller than Jessie, Rita thought, and about the right age.

He was smiling at Margaret, a smile that befitted campaign posters. He told Margaret he was meeting a friend. "My, uh, friend," he said, "is interested in real estate." He gestured at the boarded windows of the house at the end of the Row.

"Oh, how wonderful," Margaret answered.

They heard the bike again in the distance. "Oh Jesus," Rita said, "not again." Margaret scrunched her face at Rita, pouted mouth, furrowed V above her nose. Rita called it her human chipmunk expression. Rita ignored this sign of disapproval and went on. "I can't believe it. He's out already. On the first goddamn warm day of the year."

Margaret was scrunching like mad. At the swear words, Rita guessed. It was probably Margaret's reaction to the *Jesus* that made Rita add the *goddamn*.

The Senator, however, didn't seem to notice. "The motorcyclist?" he asked.

"Yeah," Rita said. "The mad biker." She looked at Margaret. "Can you believe he's out *already?* God"—she turned back to the Senator—"last year he drove us crazy. All summer long."

Margaret interrupted, almost stepping in front of Rita to do so. "Rita is exaggerating," she said, "really." She stepped back and gave Rita another scrunch.

Oh, I get it, Rita thought. *I'm not supposed to queer this little real estate deal.* "Exaggerating?" Rita flailed her hands at both of them. "Exaggerating? Listen. It's like . . . like . . . Did you see that Cocteau movie? The one where Death is this woman on a bike? Except, wait a minute, maybe that's wrong. Maybe *she* isn't on it, maybe it's these two guys on bikes, who are sort of her bodyguards. They're on these bikes, see . . ."

Margaret's voice rose. Rita couldn't tell if she was deliberately trying to change the subject or if she actually believed this was relevant to the conversation. "In *Snows of Kilimanjaro,*" Margaret stated, "Hemingway describes Death as something that sounds like bicycle tires on a wet pavement." She stood proudly, as if expecting to be congratulated.

"Not *bicycle,* goofy," Rita said with some venom. She didn't like to be interrupted, particularly when pursuing some dimly recalled train of thought. She especially didn't like to be interrupted by Margaret. "Bike as in *motorcycle.* Anyway," she went on, "the way this guy, the mad biker, works is—"

"Ri-ta. Really!" Margaret all but stamped her foot.

The Senator looked at the women, then past them, then at them again. He felt as if at any moment he'd be called upon to referee. If only Claire would arrive to spare him.

But Rita appeared to have won. She continued. ". . . So you'd be waiting for a bus or something, see? And he—the biker—he'd pull up beside you and stare. Well, at least you had the feeling he was staring, because you can't see him. He has this mirror thing that comes down over his face, right? I don't even know how he breathes."

"Visor," Margaret explained.

"Visor, right." Rita separated her hands as if they rested on handlebars. "Anyway, this bike is so big, the whole sidewalk is shaking under it, you know what I mean? And here's this guy, staring and staring and staring until you do something. Run away, or scream, or something. The thing is, it's like a challenge. You think to yourself, 'Boy, I'm gonna do it, I'm gonna stare him down.' But then you look into that mirror face of his, and you can't. It gets so creepy, you just can't."

The Senator was still wearing his campaign smile. He nodded as if interested. The nod spurred Rita on.

"No kidding," she said. "I've seen him do it to women in cars. Just stare at them, like at red lights? Sometimes they get so freaked, they just hit the gas and go right through the light."

It was then that the Jaguar's long sleek nose came around the corner. Rita saw Senator Aubrey Denton's real smile then.

They watched the driver let the car glide to the curb behind the Senator's car. The Jaguar made very little sound. Rita thought it looked like a shark, silver, sinister, all snout.

The woman inside the car pretended to fix her hair in the little rearview mirror, but Rita could see that she was waiting for the Senator to open her door. When he did, she slid out in one curl of motion, like a scarf being pulled from a magician's sleeve.

Rita watched the woman as if watching someone on a movie screen. It was like the scene in *Bread and Chocolate* where the poor, low-down guy from the chicken farm gets to see the gorgeous rich kids frolicking in the woods, she thought. Yes. Rita replayed, too, in her mind's eye, the way the woman had eased herself out of the car. *If I had tried that,* she told herself, *I'd have probably caught my heel on something and fallen on my nose.* But this woman, Rita figured, was used to making grand entrances.

Rita was reminded of the Modess ads on the back covers of old magazines in the library, of the elegant models about to sweep up or down a staircase. Yes, this woman could wear those elaborate gowns and hairdos, probably did wear them. To the opera, or wherever women like that went. Rita had an urge to nudge the Senator in the ribs, wink at him, and say, "Some friend." But Margaret would die.

The woman lifted her brows very slightly and smiled at them. "You see, Claire, you have a welcoming committee here," the Senator said. His cheeks had slightly tinged with pink. "Claire Albritten, I'd like you to meet one of my assistants, Margaret Speidel, and Margaret's friend, uh . . ."

He had forgotten already. *Scratch one vote, Senator.* "Rita Puleo," Rita supplied.

"Whatchoo watchin' for, boy?" LeGrande's sister was ready to dig into him again, that much he could tell.

"Nuffin," he said, trying not to look outside, because then Denise would guess.

Except maybe she would think he was looking at that car out there, the silver one, when all along he was looking at the white girl standing next to it. If he were here with anybody but his sister he'd have said, *Mmm-mmm,* the way his daddy used to when his mama would make ribs or something else that was good. *Mmm-mmm,* just as appreciative as he could. The white girl out there, she did look *mmm-mmm* good, she looked like she would taste like icing on a cake, white icing.

"You waiting for the mailman, ain'tchoo?" his sister accused him. They'd seen the Bullworker muscle builder advertised on television together and she'd seen him taking down the address. "You waiting for that muscle-makin' thing, ain'tchoo?" She would have gone on making fun of him like that, except right then she looked outside too, and that was when this gray-haired guy who helped the chick out of the car stuck himself in the way. That girl didn't need no help, neither. It looked like she moved pretty good.

"Hey, LeGrande." Denise waved him over, not taking her eyes away from the street. "Looky here. I think I seen him on television."

LeGrande said, "Oh, me," but he went on and made like he was looking. The only old white dude that LeGrande could remember from the television, though, was the one who talked about his dog being old and how the dog had *got* so old because of Alpo dog food. And who wanted to look at some old dude anyway when he could feast his eyes on that white chick, *mmm-mmm*. Denise, she didn't know nothin'.

He wished he'd have been with Claude, because with Claude he could have rolled his eyes and licked his chops and said it right out loud. But with Denise, shit, he just moved the curtain to the side a little bit and said just as cool as he could say, "Well now. How *about* that."

But they were almost out of sight now, the blonde chick and the old guy. It seemed to LeGrande, though, that they were headed for the house that was covered up with all the boards. Seemed spooky, kind of, a girl as alive as this one was heading in there, where that other one had died.

"Twelve rooms! Twelve glorious, glorious rooms! Oh, Aubrey." Claire hugged him before she spun away again to race through the downstairs and then back up the staircase. From up there he could hear her saying it again: "Twelve *won*derful rooms!"

He had expected to have to convince her, and he had a lengthy speech rehearsed, a very practical speech. But Claire was delirious about the house, and now he found himself trying to think of ways to make her pause and consider, not be swept away. But perhaps that was the way it was with women, the way women made up their minds.

"Aubrey?" Claire rushed downstairs again, pausing at the landing to press against the banister. For a moment he feared it would give way. But she released it. "Did you tell me *ev*erything about this house?"

He was puzzled but sounded quite firm. "Well, yes. Of course."

She laughed and spun like a ballerina. She even bowed. A strand of her long blond hair came undone and tumbled across her shoulder.

She straightened and looked down at him, reaching up to free the rest. She flung the hairpins down the staircase, one by one. They pinged against the floorboards.

Aubrey was mesmerized by it, by the sound of the pins falling and the sight of Claire, so high above him, now tilting her head to one side.

Her flowing tresses, Aubrey thought, and the words did not seem stilted, outdated, or overly poetic when applied to Claire. He had rarely seen her, since she was a child, with her hair undone. Usually she wore it pulled back in a chignon, as if at any moment she might don her hunt cap or her derby and ride off. It took his breath away, seeing her like this.

She came down the stairs and extended her hand. Her fingertips seemed to glitter. "I love these ceilings," she said, letting her eyes sweep up at them. "Come see the upstairs with me."

Aubrey hesitated behind her, afraid again that she was rushing into the purchase, rushing headlong without really thinking. But this was what he wanted, wasn't it? Claire here, in Washington, if only occasionally, to oversee her property. Claire here, with him, and not always stuck away in the Virginia countryside with that hired hand.

"What's the matter?" she teased, when they'd gone part of the way. "Are the stairs too much for you?"

"Non-sense." He huffed between the syllables. He would keep climbing, he wanted to tell her, even if the stairs kept on forever. Even if his heart began to fail.

"There's another flight, Uncle Aubrey," Claire taunted. "A third floor. Oh, can you imagine?" She turned and threw her head back the way a child might, but her throat, so long, so pale, was a woman's throat.

"Perhaps you could have one of those little elevators installed," he joked, for his sake as much as for hers. "One that looks like a birdcage, ornate and gilded. You know the kind."

Claire snapped her head forward. "That sounds oddly familiar," she said. "Now, why would it?"

Aubrey took her hand in both of his, breathing heavily, breathing the scent of her skin and of her perfume and not knowing which was which. *Gently,* he told himself, *mustn't frighten her.* "You were much too young to remember, I would have thought. But we, your parents and I, had friends with a house like this one. Your father and I used to snarl the elevator repeatedly, running it up and down as fast as it would go, jamming the controls. As if it were a toy." He chuckled and looked past Claire, at the memory. "Oh, but your mother gave us the dickens about it. In no uncertain terms." He shook his head from side to side.

"I can't imagine it," Claire said. "Not my father. Why? Why would the two of you do such a thing?"

His gaze seemed to lose its focus. Slowly, with effort, he brought his eyes to Claire's. "Because of you." His hands tightened over hers. "Because of you, Claire."

Claire pulled her hands away. They felt damp. She clenched and unclenched her fingers to dry them.

Aubrey went on. "The elevator was such a great favorite of yours. Your father would hand you in to me and I would hoist you up on my shoulders and take you up and down, up and down, and you'd tell me that it made your tummy feel all funny. . . ." That soft chuckle again.

"Well," Claire cut him off abruptly, and walked away. *Then too,* she thought. And with her parents there!

Aubrey listened to the sound of her heels clacking the length of the hall.

"There's a mirror in this bathroom," she called back to him. "I've got to fix my hair."

He heard the door hinge creak and the catch of the latch. Then her voice again, behind the door. "Aubrey?"

He started toward her. "Yes?"

"I'll need my hairpins. Be a dear and get them for me, won't you?"

Aubrey started down the stairs at once but paused on the landing. He didn't mind groveling on the floor for Claire's hairpins, but he'd be damned if he'd have either of those two girls out there know.

"Come on"—Rita yanked Margaret by the hand—"unless you're

planning to hold a vigil." She yanked harder. "Oh, come on, Margaret, you can pout inside."

They double-locked the vestibule door but left the door to Rita's open wide. "Look," Rita said, "I need some help getting this place in shape, just in case they do come over." She had trouble believing she had actually invited them. It was very much out of character, given that they'd just met. "God, those slacks. I can't have somebody in slacks like that walking through all this filth. And white, yet." She got the vacuum out of the closet and began assembling it. "Do you want to vacuum or do you want to dust? If you dust, you'll have to use that polish stuff, too."

"I don't care," Margaret said. "I'll do whatever you don't want to do."

"Vacuum then. Come on, don't just mope around. Put this thing together."

"I'll bet he marries her," Margaret said, joining two pieces of pipe and attaching them to the hose.

"That's crazy. He's old enough to be her dad."

"Still."

"Well, stranger things have happened," Rita allowed.

"You *do* think he's going to marry her." She lost all interest in the vacuum hose, and Rita reached over and finished putting on the attachment.

What was it with Margaret? First the tizzy about the Senator being here, and now this. "What are you worried about?" Rita reminded her. "You *have* a boyfriend."

"Oh, Rita." Margaret took the hose and switched the vacuum on, ignoring Rita's remark.

"Oh no you don't." Rita switched it off and waited for the noise to die. "Come on, tell me."

"I *like* Jay, Rita, but . . ."

"Yeah, but . . ." Rita waggled her fingers, enjoining her to continue. Did Margaret know about Jay? That would be a relief. Rita was forever afraid she would slip.

"Jay's so . . . oh, I don't know." Margaret looked down at the floor, swaying slightly, like someone who'd been called upon in school.

"So kind of . . . ordinary." She looked up at Rita. "I know I'll probably marry him, but . . ."

"*What?*" Rita didn't know what part to fume about—the part about him being ordinary, which he wasn't, or the part about her marrying him thinking that. Marrying him despite that. Oh, she couldn't wait to see Rosenberg. "Why am I seeing a shrink?" she asked Margaret. "You're the one who needs one."

"See," Margaret said. She reached for the switch on the vacuum again. "I can't tell you."

Rita caught her hand. "Are you saying that—" but it was as far as she got when Jay's special knock sounded. "Oh, brother," Rita said, stalking toward the vestibule door.

Jay gave the cleaning apparatus that was everywhere a wary eye. "What's this?" he asked, stepping over the hose as if it were a python.

Jay's sense of humor was boyish, as was his appearance. He was thirty but continued to look as tousled as he must have growing up. His trousers—khaki usually, but sometimes worn cords—were always an inch too short. He seemed to select socks with holes that showed. Rita suspected he made the holes on purpose, since they were never in places that socks would wear.

"You're an aging I-don't-know-what," Rita once said to his face. "That's what you look like."

"What a wonderful way with words you have, Rita," he had replied. "Perhaps *you* should be the writer."

That was what he went around saying he was, a writer. "Ha-ha," Rita answered, but she didn't dare say more. God knows what he'd retort about her, about being a photographer. But at least she *did* work. At least her pictures appeared, though maybe not in *Vogue.* What had Jay ever done, except talk?

Still, it wasn't a real battle that they had, except occasionally. But what she knew about him! And how his looks belied it. Now *there* would be a way of curling Margaret's hair! And to think that Margaret called him ordinary.

But there was no time for that now. No time to even think about it. "All right," Rita said, clapping her hands at them. "Let's get busy. You"—she pointed at the vacuum cleaner and then at Margaret.

"And Jay"—she pressed a dustrag into his hand. "Wait a sec," she said, "I'll get the Pledge."

"What pledge?" He looked truly befuddled.

Rita laughed at him. "It makes the furniture shine. Don't you ever watch TV?" When she brought the can in, she showed him how it worked.

"What are *you* going to do?" he asked.

"I spilled some wine. I'm going to clean it up."

"Why, may I ask, are we doing all this?" Jay wanted to know.

"Because the Senator—Margaret's Senator—is here. With the most incredible—"

"Here?" Jay interrupted, looking under each of the sofa cushions.

"Funny. Very funny." Rita said it flatly, to imply that it was not. It might have been, but she was in such a hurry.

But Jay persisted. He got down on his knees and looked under the easy chair.

"Ja-ay," Margaret said. She always disapproved when Jay or Rita started kidding around. It seemed so juvenile, like that movie Rita had made her see—*Animal House*. Jay and Rita did it a lot, too, and usually got even sillier when she, Margaret, complained. But this time, fortunately, Rita was being serious.

"Okay, they probably won't stop by," Rita told Jay. "But I told them they could, like if they had any questions?" She measured the look on Jay's face. "Faye Arensberg's place," she explained. "That's where they are. But anyway, if they *do* come, Jesus, I can't have those white wool slacks coming into this place."

"Maybe he could leave his slacks outside," Jay said.

"Ja-ay."

Rita laughed. "No, *she*'s the slacks. I don't know what in the deuce *he* was wearing."

"His Burberry jacket," Margaret declared, "over his beige cavalry twill pants."

"It's gonna be a real mob scene today, hey, Nick?" Zabo was waiting for Nick to sign for the crates he'd just delivered. He had to

29

shout because there was a lot of noise—hammering, squeals, a radio on here, whistling over there—the way it always was when the Market was setting up.

Saturday was special, with everything fresh. Like bread, Polish bread, sweet and yeasty, with big, wet raisins inside. Or French, in long, shiny loaves. There was hydroponic lettuce, real green, and clean, because it never touched dirt. And there was chocolate from all over, even from Mexico, all mixed with sugar and cinnamon, so grainy you could hear yourself eating it. But the kielbasa smell from across the aisle was the best and strongest thing. It made you hungry. It was great for business. On Saturday the guy with the kielbasa strung it up all around the counter, like garden hose.

Saturday was special on the street, too. You'd see people. Not like on weekdays, when it was dash here, dash there, people all dressed up and running for buses or cabs. Not people walking real fast, carrying briefcases and books.

Saturday was slow. Everybody in beat-up clothes, taking their sweet old time. Really shopping, too, not just buy-and-get-it-over-with.

And then, when you took your break, you'd see them out there, working on their yards or their houses or their cars. They'd talk to you sometimes, or at least say more than "Hi."

The Market had been around longer than most of the people who lived near it. They didn't know how it had been back then. Sawdust on the floors, lettuce that was dirty. But in some ways it was just the same: same sounds, same smells, same racket.

"Yeah," Nick told Zabo, handing the pad back across the counter. "That's what I figured from the minute I heard the weather. It's always that way, first warm day. Really brings them in." Nick waited to see if Zabo would pick up on what he was hinting at, but instead Zabo was heading toward the door. Not like the old days, when he and Zabo had time to chew the fat. Now Zabo was married, saving for a house, his wife expecting another kid. Zabo had to hustle these days.

Passing me by, Nick thought. *Yessir, they're always passing me by.* Zabo had been six years behind Nick at St. Adelbert's. Nick was still single, probably always would be. But so what? Working here, didn't he have his pick of girls?

Capitol Hill was loaded with girls; like Zabo once said, "Girls up the old wazoo." And on a day like today, new ones would come in, not just the regulars, but those who had moved into the neighborhood during the winter. Nick thought of them all as *his* girls, even though, to tell the truth, he'd never been out with one, really. Once he had walked Rita home, and maybe he could count that because Rita had been friendly, joked around, even put her hand on his forearm when she came to the punch line.

Jessie was friendly, too, but you couldn't exactly call her a girl, not even years ago, back when she'd come into the Market for the first time. Years ago. They'd all called him Little Nickie then. He'd stand beside his father, making circles in the sawdust with his toe. "Little Nickie has a job," his father would brag. "Keeps my knives sharp." Nick would stand behind the counter every morning, drawing the blades across a big rough gray stone, back and forth, back and forth, this knife, that knife.

Whether Nick counted Jessie or not, he knew that Jessie liked him. About a year ago, maybe right after Faye, she'd started having parties and inviting him, too. He would mix the drinks, make little sandwiches and things, and afterward clear away the trash. Next day he'd tell Zabo about it, even about what they had on. Like how tight their pants were and how low their blouses came down in front. He could tell Zabo the truth about Rita, but the other one, Margaret, dressed so plain that he'd had to make things up.

Before Zabo settled down, he and Zabo used to size the girls up good, deciding which ones would be great to look at naked and which ones were too skinny. "Whadya think of that one?" Nick would say, and Zabo would turn thumbs up or thumbs down.

Except for Jessie, it was new girls all the time. The girls stuck around the neighborhood for about a year and a half, on the average. Then, Nick figured, they got married or something and moved away.

Zabo said that, before it happened, Faye was fixing to get married. She had started coming in with some guy, pretty regular, and early in the morning, too, like maybe he'd been at her place through the night. He was an older guy, so much older that if Zabo hadn't pointed all this out, Nick might never have noticed.

Would Faye have done that? Married some older guy and moved away?

Faye had been their special favorite. Zabo would stop whatever he was doing whenever she came in and butt Nick in the side. But Zabo hadn't needed to butt him, Nick always knew when she was in the place. He could feel her there, feel her come in the door. The feeling was just like the one he got when the priest reached into the tabernacle on the altar and held the blessed sacrament up, the monstrance, bright as the sun, and the little white wafer, safe inside.

Except that Faye hadn't been safe at all. No sir. Nick had walked by her place dozens of times, trying to get up the nerve to take her picture with his Polaroid camera. Dozens of times. It would have been pretty easy, too. Easier than what *did* happen.

A little bell went off, like always. Opening time. Nick looked at the big plain clock that hung against the wall over the pastry counter. On the nose.

Everybody was ready now. Nick flung his arms out and stretched and made a great big noisy yawn. He thumped his chest a couple of times like King Kong, the way his dad used to. He picked up a medium-sized knife. He was ready.

"Oh, hey, Nickie, I almost forgot." It was Zabo again. He must have come through the entrance on the other side.

"What?" Nick asked. The Market had officially opened and customers were streaming in. Jessie for one.

"What I saw," Zabo yelled, "coming over here."

"What?" Nick asked, but now, Zabo should know, was not the time.

"A fox you wouldn't believe," Zabo said. "On the Row. Like what's her name, Faye? Only better."

Nick dropped the knife and bent down to look for it. It must have gone under the counter. He searched along the cutting board for another. When he caught Zabo's eye, Zabo gave him a big stage wink.

Jessie tapped her fingers against the glass of the display case, waiting.

"D'ya hear me, Nickie?" Zabo was louder now, walking away. "Better than Faye."

"Yeah, yeah, I heard you," Nick mumbled. He smiled at Jessie, to apologize for holding her up, but she didn't smile back.

"And I seen her again just now," Zabo shouted. "In a car you wouldn't believe."

Rita stood at the railing of the porch, hands on hips. "All that cleaning up for nothing," she complained, though neither Margaret nor Jay, still inside, could hear.

Both cars—the Jag and the Senator's BMW—were gone.

She saw Jessie coming up the Row and waved, calling, "Hey, Jess," but Jessie ignored her. "Damn," Rita said. "I know she sees me." She considered waiting until Jessie got closer and trying again, but instead she thought she'd get even, turning on her heel and going back into her apartment. She felt snubbed, but good.

She draped herself over the arm of a chair. "I should have known," she said, toeing a stack of magazines until it toppled. "Why should anyone, even Jessie, want to come here? This place is a dump."

It was an overstatement. Rita's quarters were cluttered, but interestingly so. Many of her photographs were in evidence, not merely on the walls, but piled on tables and bookcases.

One had been framed. It was a blowup of LeGrande with his sister, Denise. LeGrande had been teasing the girl, and his face was lit by devilment. Denise, on the other hand, was as pouty and gloomy as can be. It reminded Rita of the two theater masks that you always see side by side.

Mingled with the photographs were odd though not necessarily picturesque artifacts. A Cross and Blackwell jam jar, for instance, filled with sand from a particularly wonderful day Rita had spent at Rehoboth Beach.

"Look at it this way." Jay handed her a glass of her own Ginseng Express. "You got free maid service out of it."

"Yeah, I did." Rita said it glumly. "Thanks."

"I really don't see why you're upset," Jay continued. "Jessie's been here a hundred times. And these other people shouldn't mean a thing to you. You don't know them from Adam."

"Look, I agree. So just drop it, okay?" But why was she bothered? Partly, she figured, it was her whole pretense thing. She wanted to pretend, if only for the duration of the Senator and Claire Albritten's visit, that she was the sort of person they would come to see. She told Jay so. And partly, she had to admit, it was what people like that could do for her career. "They're the kind of people," she said, "who could walk in, just like that, see a picture they liked, buy it, and then tell everyone—like all their rich friends—how terrifically talented you are. They could *make* you, if they wanted to."

"Sure," Jay said. "You could be discovered, right here on the Row. Like in the movies." He always tormented Rita about her movie-mindedness. He had never gotten over her description of a house she had seen. She'd explained that it had a little balcony, just like the one in *The Discreet Charm of the Bourgeoisie*. He teased on. "Maybe I'll invite them, too. I could strew my manuscript around the place so that they could read it."

What manuscript? Rita felt like saying. That would shut him up. Except that he did seem more interested in this murder book than in any of his earlier projects. Real turkeys, those. A biography of some landscape artist was the last thing Rita could remember him working on.

"You should have seen her." Rita tilted the conversation back to Claire. "A little bit like Grace Kelly in *To Catch a Thief*. God, even her name . . ." Claire Albritten. *I really should change my name,* Rita thought. She had planned to call herself Rita Paul, but she'd never gotten around to it, and now she was semiestablished as Rita Puleo, so it was too late. "No kidding," she went on to Jay. "If Faye were a ten, then this girl is—"

"Faye wasn't a ten," Jay insisted. "She just acted like a ten. Believe me, I've been researching her. What she had was assurance, like that ad you like, the Charlie girl. It came from having the right background."

Rita glared at him as if he'd personally insulted her, but before

34

she could say a word about it, Jay went on. "Did you know that Faye went to the Madeira School?"

"Where else?" Rita answered. "Where else would she have learned to talk the way she did? Like she had a pencil stuck between her teeth."

"She was jabbed with something like a pencil," Jay said.

"Stop it," Margaret insisted. "This gives me the creeps."

"Madeira," Rita said. "It figures." She herself had gone to Shaler Township High.

"Right," Jay said, thinking that Rita was, as he had just been, thinking about various other Madeira-connected murders. There was Jean Harris, of course, who'd shot the Scarsdale Diet doctor, but he wondered if Rita knew any of those further in the past. They were sidebars, so to speak, to his research on Faye. "Do you remember ever hearing about a student they found there . . . ?" he began, but Margaret stopped him.

It was as if something had just occurred to her and she had to speak. "I wonder," Margaret mused, "if Claire Albritten knows about Faye. About the way she died. About that house."

"Be serious," Rita told her. "Do you think she'd even look at the place if she did?"

Claire eased the Jaguar to the curb on Pennsylvania Avenue, but a few blocks from the Row. The spot was immediately in front of the drugstore, clearly marked as a loading zone. She left the engine idling.

She arranged a column of dimes, nearly twenty of them, on the little shelf beneath the phone. She tried the house, then the stables. Finally, Steve answered, and she was able to tell him about the house Aubrey had found.

"I don't give a shit," he said. "I don't want to look at any of your investments." He pronounced *investments* with especial distaste.

"Hear me out," she said, starting to tell him about the murder, making more of it than she knew.

"Jesus Christ," he interrupted her, "you really are out of your head."

"Let me finish," she pleaded. But a police cruiser had turned the corner and was coming up the street. It hovered beside the Jag. "I've got to go," Claire said. "I'm driving right back." She swallowed, not wanting to ask. "Will you wait for me?" Her voice thinned on the words.

Silence. Then: "If you're lucky."

She hung up and started driving toward the Southwest Freeway, despite herself, gaining speed.

She'd been so sure that the house would lure Steve. And she had every reason to believe that it would. The last batch of films, for instance, the ones he'd projected while they were making love. Wouldn't those films lead anyone to believe that he would adore the very idea of such a house?

At first the films had been merely pornographic. Once Steve had pulled away from her and stood in front of the wall that served as screen. The images warped along the contours of his body, doubly, marvelously obscene. She had risen to come toward him and he'd lunged at her, hurled her back. She struck her head. Everything blurred for a moment, and when the scene cleared Steve was standing over her, stroking his erection. On the wall, the camera had closed over the genitals of another man. Steve was facing her, not the image, but he seemed to have memorized the film. "Okay, baby." He looked down at her. "Which one will it be? You want this cock, baby?"— kneeling beside her—"or that one, up there?" Her eyes moved toward the projection on the wall, and he slapped her, spun her head back toward him. She tried to focus. "This one, am I right, babe?" His voice was soft, serene. But he slapped her again.

But now he was cruel in other ways, awful, awful ways. Just yesterday, she'd walked into her bathroom and found him dressing to go out. Without her. She'd tried to sound casual, asking, "When will you be home?"

He laughed, but without so much as looking at her. "Home?" he asked. "Just where is that?"

A red light blazed out of nowhere. Claire jabbed at the brake pedal, and the car shimmied to a stop.

Claire shut her eyes and squeezed the wheel. Something growled and then roared alongside her. She abandoned her reverie and turned to see.

It was a motorcycle, the biggest she had ever seen. It was mostly chrome, and it gleamed in the sunlight. It shook with its own power.

The cyclist's face was silver, obscured. A mirror, Claire realized, leaning toward it.

Claire thought of knights in armor atop steeds. She laughed, tossing her head back. When she regained herself, the bike burst forward.

Claire drove behind the black flash of his jacket and up the ramp. On the Southwest Freeway, he drove crazily, weaving from lane to lane. She was more careful, knowing she could overtake him whenever she chose.

Or could she? And anyway, was it what he wanted? Was it the reason he had pulled alongside—to get her to chase him?

She let the Jaguar slow, testing him, his awareness of her movements behind him.

But he didn't seem to notice that she'd fallen behind. He zigged and zagged ahead, and she jammed the gas pedal to the floor in an attempt to come close to him again.

Too late. He took the L'Enfant Plaza exit, swerving onto it at the last possible moment. She saw the bike lean and thought that he'd lost control of it. Then he straightened and was gone.

She hesitated as she neared the ramp, but in the end continued on the freeway. Still, the excitement of the chase was with her.

She'd been thinking about Steve when the bike had appeared beside her, but she'd quite forgotten him in the moments that followed. Forgotten, too, the way he'd disappointed her today, about the house. Forgotten the way he had been treating her. Forgotten all but that mirror mask and the gleaming chrome of that bike. Oh, its *power*.

It was foolish to think that Steve would be the only man ever to please her. He was just the only man so far. Where, since she'd known about herself, had she tried to meet others? *Really* tried. Ah, but here in the city there would be men like Steve, men who would discover her needs.

On the George Washington Parkway now, Claire let the Jaguar straddle the center line. She revved, and for a moment the car's long, lean hood lifted and was all that Claire could see.

She loved it, the car's roar, the whine of speed, the sound of her own laughter. The Potomac glinted to her right, catching at the corner of her eye much as the motorcycle had.

She decided. She would give Steve one last chance, and if he didn't take it, she would come to Washington to stay. She wouldn't rent out the house on the Row, as Aubrey suggested. She would live in it herself.

PART THREE

MID-MARCH

"Hurry up," Rita called to Rosenberg, who was a good twenty feet away. "I'm freezing." She hunched her shoulders and stamped her feet.

Rita had first seen the psychiatrist on a local television talk show. It was several months after an enormous plane had crashed into the river, but Washington just couldn't seem to lay the subject to rest.

The interviewer did a long lead-in, talking about survivor guilt and how survivors frequently found themselves failing in the aftermath of catastrophe. He reeled off statistics about marriages that crumbled, jobs that were lost.

Rita listened attentively. Wasn't she on that kind of downhill slide? And hadn't she just survived Faye Arensberg's gruesome murder?

The interviewer said that those who lived were punishing themselves, and that whatever befell them later was a way of saying "I should have died, too." He turned to Rosenberg with "Don't you agree, Dr. Rosenberg?"

Rita tensed, waiting for his reply. "No," Rosenberg said.

Then there was a long moment of dead air. The interviewer's Adam's apple began to bob. "But the statistics," he said, "the rate of . . ."

"I'm not disputing the numbers," Rosenberg continued. "I'm disputing the notion that it's guilt. Why guilt?" He went on to say that surviving a disaster might lead an otherwise complacent person to reevaluate his marriage, job, or whatever.

That made sense, Rita thought. Before the murder, Rita had been drifting, passively assuming that the circumstances of her life would change, improve. Now she believed that things had to happen fast or it would be too late. Time's winged chariot, now or never, and all that. Rita felt that she'd merely been waiting before Faye and that she just couldn't afford to wait any longer.

And that, in essence, was what Rosenberg was talking about on the screen. How catastrophe led to action. How people who survived were, once and for all, able to risk, take charge.

Later that night Rita called Rosenberg at home. He agreed to see her, but not in the basement office where he'd practiced. "I have to keep reminding myself that I'm retired," he'd explained.

It was Rita who suggested that they meet outside. "In tourist places," she had said. "You know, the ones you never visit once you live here."

Together, she and the doctor had visited the White House, the Lincoln Memorial, and several of the prominent museums. They'd toured the Supreme Court, FBI headquarters, the Tidal Basin at the Jefferson Memorial.

Today they were meeting on the steps of the Library of Congress. The building was flanked by lamps whose standards had greened, whose globes had turned purple with age. It was a transformation that particularly appealed to Rita, because it enabled her to use the longest word that she knew: *chromolithographic.*

"Look," she said to Rosenberg now, making a white puff of breath to demonstrate. "It's too damn cold out here." The warm and sunny day that had fallen several weeks earlier had been a fluke. The temperature had been in the twenties ever since.

"Come on," Rosenberg said. He took her arm to lead her to the staircase and inside.

"I don't know," Rita said about the Library, "won't they shush us in there?"

"Probably." The psychiatrist laughed.

"Hey, wait," Rita said. "I know a great place. A little bakery. Only you can get coffee, even hot chocolate. And they make all kinds of things, napoleons and éclairs and—"

Rosenberg held up a little brown bag to interrupt. "I have a better idea," he said, steering her toward the street.

The wind whipped at them as they walked. "Ooh," Rita complained, cupping her hands over her ears.

"Why don't you wear a hat?" he asked. His broadtail cap was pulled down over his eyebrows.

"Because they look so ridiculous," Rita said. "You should see yourself."

Rosenberg watched the way she walked. "Loosen up," he suggested. "You're cold because you're all scrunched up." His own step was spry, almost jaunty. And he had to be in his sixties.

"Never mind the way I walk," Rita said. "Just hurry."

He took her to the arboretum, a huge glass-capped structure that housed hundreds of exotic plants. The air was moist inside and smelled of earth. "Instant summer," Rita said. "What a great idea." There were even birds chirping somewhere and the splash of water. "Next time I will wear a hat," she told him. "A pith helmet."

They found a wrought-iron bench in one of the alcoves, and Rosenberg presented her with a tangerine. He spread the open bag between them for the peels. "Now congratulate yourself," he said, "for not eating an éclair." He took his hat off, folded it, smoothed his hand along the fur.

"This is real, isn't it?" Rita pinched at the flap. "Bet you didn't need this in Florida." He had just spent nearly a month in the South, visiting his daughter and her family. "So how was it?"

He held his hand out level, then rocked it from side to side. "So-so," he said. He wasn't sorry to be back, even given the weather. "They have their own lives." He finished his own tangerine, eating each segment whole. "I'm not used to talking," he told Rita. "You know that. So you tell me."

Though he'd never met them, he waited to hear about Jessie and Margaret and Jay. He was good at remembering names, and throughout his years of practice had barely had to consult his notes when a patient came for an appointment. He knew thousands of names—brothers, sisters, husbands, wives, friends. But this one Rita kept repeating, Claire, was not familiar. "Back up," he said to halt her. "I'm missing something."

She ran through the story, beginning with Claire's first appearance on the Row. She told him about the work crews that followed, banging and sawing and hammering. "It's a major production," Rita said. "And the last thing I need is to be reminded of how the other half lives. I mean, most people do these things a little at a time, but not her. And the stuff she's doing, God. It's so obvious, so whole hog. Like, she's asking for trouble, advertising that she's really loaded like that. Because she's not just fixing this place up to make it livable, she's doing it up big. Like taking the old windows out and putting bigger ones in—I mean taking the bricks out around them and everything. And putting up this swanky front door. The Row is practically a slum and she comes bopping along with her fancy this and her fancy that. Fancy car, fancy clothes. And this humongous white bed. . . ."

Rita had meant to do a separate riff on the bed, but now continued with the overall effect of Claire on the Row's inhabitants, instead. "And everyone's just sort of watching her. Margaret's watching her because she knows the Senator has the hots for her and Margaret's hoping to pick up pointers or something, I don't know. And Jay's watching her, practically taking notes. It's disgusting. I don't know about Jessie, and—"

"And you're watching her, too?" Rosenberg cut in.

"Yeah, I'm watching her. You can't help watching her. She's rich and she's beautiful and she drives this Jaguar, and you can't help thinking, 'What's she *doing* here? Why doesn't she go live someplace else?' "

Rosenberg chuckled.

"Okay, so I'm jealous," Rita admitted. "But so what? Who wouldn't be? And anyway, it's not really jealousy, not the kind I usually have, anyway." Rita railed, for the most part, at what she deemed inequality: that someone as pretty or as talented—or less pretty and less talented—should have more than she. But with Claire, Rita perceived a huge and unbridgeable gap. "It's more like despair," Rita explained. "No matter what I ever did to myself, I'd never look like her. And no matter how many pictures I sold, I'd never have her kind of bucks. Or style, for that matter." She thought for a moment. "No kidding, she's so perfect, she has everything." Rita's brow furrowed. "You know, if I were Margaret I'd forget all about the Senator, who's ungettable, and worry about hanging on to Jay."

"Jay?" Rosenberg seemed incredulous.

"Oh, come on," Rita said. "I told you what a sleazeball he is."

Rosenberg laughed. "Come on yourself," he chided her. "You went there with him."

"Just to see," Rita squealed. "*He* goes to that place all the time!"

That place was a sex club. After making her pledge that she wouldn't tell Margaret or anyone, Jay had admitted that he was a member.

"So, did he force you to go?" Rosenberg was still laughing.

"Well . . ." Rita let her voice fall back into normal range. "No."

44

When Jay had told her about the place, Rita had thought he was making it up. "I'll believe it when I see it," she'd said.

"Fine," Jay had countered. "Get your coat."

"Wait a minute," Rita said. "Are you serious?"

"Of course I'm serious. Get your coat."

He borrowed Margaret's car—one of the perks of being Margaret's boyfriend—and drove Rita to a section of Maryland just over the district line, a section filled with bungalows and cyclone fences, blue-collar bleak.

"Yuck," Rita said. It was the only word that had come out of her mouth for the whole ride.

"Are you scared?" Jay asked her.

She didn't answer. She wasn't sure.

On the main thoroughfare, surrounding what looked like a truckers' bar, were a hundred cars, at least. Big American cars, little foreign ones. Here and there a van. It took them fifteen minutes, around this block and that block, to find a parking space.

The bar was like every other that Rita had seen, if a little less so. It was strictly BYOB, with bottles numbered and stored on shelves, retrieved by a chip. Setups and soft drinks were free. "They can't charge," a brassy-looking woman kidded Rita, "because later on not everyone will have pockets."

Jay led her from the bar to a doorway through which many of the customers were disappearing. Here, they were given towels.

"What's this for?" Rita asked.

"You'll see," Jay said.

A burly man put his arm around Rita's shoulder.

"Oh, no," she said, shaking him off. "I'm here with *him*." She clutched at Jay.

The man laughed. "Your first time, right?"

"How did he know?" Rita asked Jay.

"I think it's your chastity belt," Jay answered.

She followed him through a series of hallways. *A maze,* she thought. *Probably to confuse the police when they raid the place.* "Jay," she asked, "do you always borrow Margaret's car to come here?"

He ignored her question.

They came to a level that housed a Jacuzzi whirlpool, a sauna, and a steam room. There were patio tables and chairs. A row of lockers. "Big deal," Rita said, tossing her clothing aside and dipping into the hot, bubbly water.

But several hallways later, things took another turn. She and Jay, clad in their towels now, entered a room with several sofas and a huge TV. The color wasn't very good, but a crowd was watching anyway. It was closed-circuit porn. "What do you think?" Jay asked her.

Rita hid behind a joke. "Too much like an Oscar Mayer weiner commercial," she said, moving to the rooms beyond.

The lighting became dramatic past this point, dim and red. "Remember," Jay reminded her, "you can always say no."

They passed several closed doors and just as many open ones. Closed, Jay told her, meant "Keep Out," and entering might mean eviction from the club itself. "Open," he chortled, "means 'Y'all come'—so to speak."

Rita did not laugh. She began to study the other people there. The patrons were ordinary, the sort of people you might expect to find in the subway or on the bus. About the same percentage ugly or overweight. They seemed not to be looking for orgies so much as for a spot to pair off with a single person whom they'd either found or had come with. Couples, the overwhelming majority of them heterosexual, wandered the corridors. "No room at the inn," they would say, peeking in at still another king-sized bed filled to capacity. She heard this line at least twelve times.

"So the dialogue isn't terrific," Jay objected to her complaint, "but what do you expect? People are people."

Then two women came giggling up the corridor. One of them got down on her knees and made a great show of peeking under Jay's towel. "You were right," she told her friend, "It *is* Jay."

The other woman flung her arms around Jay's neck and began licking his cheek with an exaggerated slurping sound.

Jay shrugged them off as though this were an everyday occurrence. Then he led Rita, who was speechless, deeper. "Look," he said, pointing.

Rita was afraid to, but did.

They had come to the Red Room, with its plush red velvet bed, mirrored ceiling, mirrored walls. Rita repressed a crack about touring a pretzel factory. The person behind her didn't repress one about the steam forming on the mirrors.

"Actually," Rita said, "I think the place is just poorly insulated."

"Well," Jay asked her, "want to go in?"

"No," she said. "Take me home."

She reminded Rosenberg of this now. "It isn't as though I *did* anything there," she said. Then she grew pensive. "It made me mad at Jay, for borrowing Margaret's car to cheat on her. And *that* way of all ways. But it made me feel sorry for him, too, because he goes there every week. Why would he?"

Rosenberg shrugged.

"It also," she continued, "made me feel sorry for Margaret. Not to know. Like, suppose he gave her a venereal disease! But now, I don't know, I'm pissed off at Margaret, too. Do you know what she said?" She relayed the business about Margaret "probably" marrying Jay even though she didn't love him. "She's *deeply* shallow," Rita said and was rewarded with the old man's smile.

"So why are you friends with her?" Rosenberg asked.

"I don't know. Why am I friends with anybody? Why am I friends with you?"

The people on the Row hadn't been friends before the murder, but afterward seemed, not just drawn to each other, but bound in some strange way. Not that they talked about Faye. Except for Jay, they made it a point not to.

Rita could remember the night her friendship with the others had begun. She had been afraid to stay inside her apartment. All day long she had contrived errands, ways to keep moving. The other people, she assumed, were not as hysterical as she. When night fell, Rita's fear was even worse. She wrapped a blanket around her shoulders and went out onto the porch. *Stupid,* she told herself. *If there's a murderer out there, you'd be safer inside.*

Except that Faye hadn't been safe inside.

Rita crossed the porch and sat on the top step. She heard a rustling sound behind her, and thought her heart would stop. In fact, it *did* stop; Rita felt it. Stopped, swelled, and then got as cold as an ice cube before it started beating again. But it was only Margaret on the porch behind her, perched on the wooden rail.

"Scared?" Rita asked her.

"Yes."

"Me too," Rita said.

"I'm sorry I moved here," Margaret offered, coming to sit alongside.

"Yeah. Me too." Rita wondered if murder could break a lease. But who could afford to move, anyway? And move where? There was murder everywhere. This was the city.

"My mother used to sing to me when I was afraid," Margaret said.

Rita didn't answer. She didn't know what to say. Then Margaret began to hum. It was "Sentimental Journey," which Rita knew, too. Rita laughed. "God, that's a moldy oldy." Margaret kept on humming.

Rita joined in with the words, and pretty soon Margaret started singing the words as well. They were harmonizing, something Rita hadn't even known she could do.

"Ah, the sirens singing," Jay said. He'd been practically a total stranger then, but he sat at Margaret's feet. Before long, Jessie had also been lured.

"Jessie taught us a lot of songs," Rita told Rosenberg now. "Like 'Beautiful, Beautiful Brown Eyes,' and 'Heart of My Heart.' I think it got us all through the whole awful business, singing like that. We did it almost every night. And a couple of times Nick came, you know, from the Market? And once in a while LeGrande, too."

When the weather turned really nippy, Jessie started having them over to her place for brunch or for drinks. And pretty soon, in between, they were popping in and out of each other's apartments. "I guess it's not unreasonable that we're friends," Rita decided.

"Not unreasonable at all," Rosenberg said. "In fact, if you think about it enough, you might decide that it's *nice*."

Claire had shrouded the furniture in the sitting room of her Virginia home while Steve was still about. She'd hoped to make him feel something. Regret? She wasn't sure. Just something.

But Steve watched her flap the enormous white shrouds and drape and tuck and tie them almost with amusement. Finally Claire couldn't stand it any longer. "Say something," she demanded.

He shrugged. "You know me, babe. Easy come, easy go."

"I can't believe you mean that." She came toward him, hoping, her hands reaching out.

He caught her hands and pushed her away. "Get this through your head," he said. "I lived with a fat lady once. Yeah. A three-hundred-pounder. You know why? I wanted to see what it was like. Well, that's how it was with you, babe. See, you have *weird* written all over you. I thought I could get into that for a while. But a while is over, babe, you got it? I'm fed up."

"But the Row, that girl, I thought you'd—" she began, still hoping that the murder house would intrigue him.

"You can shove that house. I don't care if there's blood dripping off the goddamn walls. Go live in the house with that freak on the motorcycle."

"I didn't mean it about him," she cried. "I just said it to make you jealous. To make you want me."

"Yeah, well, I *don't* want you." He started walking.

She ran to the door to block his path. She waited for him to strike her. She was breathing hard, remembering all the times their love-making had begun this way.

He looked at her coldly, then turned and moved toward another exit.

"You'll see," Claire shouted after him. "I'll be happy in that house. I'll be so happy there that I'll never think about you. You'll never even cross my mind. You'll see."

"Fine," he said, before ducking outside. "Just make sure it makes the newspapers, whatever you do there. So I'll know about it."

"Steve . . ." she tried again.

"I've got your horses to see to." He slammed the door and was gone.

Claire stood in the shrouded room, the very room where their love affair had begun. She tried not to weep. Instead, she told herself, *Once I'm out of here, away from all these memories . . .*

49

The color had been startling, Claire remembered, when she'd first brought Steve here. He had stood with his back turned toward her for a long time, taking in the scene.

Through the glass wall was a meadow, and beyond the meadow a slope, falling. Beyond that, another slope, rising. And then the mountains, their foliage gaudy with autumn. It was as if the room and the meadow that surrounded it defied the season itself.

"Nice place," Steve had said, turning to face her, finally.

"Everyone in the house is off today," Claire told him, kicking off her shoes and padding about in her stockings, first on the slate floor and then across the richly patterned carpet. She lowered herself into a chaise. "I suppose I should offer you something," she said, throwing her arms up over her head. "I will, in a moment."

She watched him pace the room. When he came to the portrait of Claire on her hunter, Dulcimer, he laughed. "Shit," he said. "Is that how you ride? Sidesaddle?"

"Not often," Claire said, bristling. Most of her visitors raved about the painting, and especially about the hand-tailored habit she wore, captured by the artist in every intricate detail.

"Nice horse." He ran his finger over the canvas, along Dulcimer's neck. "I know something about horses," he allowed.

Claire smiled politely, thinking that he probably knew little or nothing at all.

He misread her smile and approached her, swaggering, she thought. "I know something about a lot of things."

"Oh," she said, "I'll bet you do."

She hoped he wouldn't touch her, not just yet. That would spoil everything. She stood before he could come any nearer. "I won't fix us anything elaborate," she said. "Just some toast and tea."

"Toast and tea," he repeated, sinking into the chaise she had vacated.

She *would* sleep with him, of course, but it was this part, the part before they touched, that excited her. She prolonged this period with every man she met. Dozens of men, carefully chosen, men she'd never see again. But then, the inevitable. Their hands would come reaching for her and she would will herself to feel, but always fail. Indeed, it was as if their fingers had some anesthetic property that affected her nerve endings, her skin. Aubrey's fault.

She came in bearing a tray: teapot, sugar cubes in an earless cup, slivers of lemon, pots of jam. "How do you like your toast?" she asked.

"Well done," Steve said, dipping the tiny serving spoon into the rasberry jam and licking it off.

Odd, she thought, or maybe not so odd, that the anticipatory thrill was always greatest with men who seemed the least appropriate. And Steve, she noted, was certainly that. He even had a tattoo, though she could not read it without being obvious.

"Tell me about yourself," she said.

"Where'd you learn that?" he mocked her. "At some fancy girls' school?"

"Learn what?" Claire asked.

"Your little conversation starters. 'Tell me about yourself.' What comes next? 'And what do *you* do?' " He sampled the marmalade.

"I'm sure the toast is ready now." Claire headed toward the kitchen to get it.

"Hey. Your cheeks turn pink when you're pissed. Did you know that?" His words trailed her.

In the kitchen, Claire dropped the toast, dropped the spreading knife, almost dropped the butter dish. She had thought him audacious on the highway, but in a funny, harmless way. Now he was insolent, not nice at all. She regretted picking him up, regretted, especially, bringing him home with her to the farm. He was not like the others, not predictable.

She turned with the toast on a platter and collided with him. "I'm sorry," she said, backing away. "I didn't hear you."

He took the plate away from her. "Took my boots off," he explained. "They hurt like a son of a bitch."

Back in the sitting room, she saw that he had found her scrapbook. He'd been looking through the photographs, taken, for the most part, at horse shows.

"Who's this old guy?" He set the plate down and pointed at Aubrey, who was not really quite so old in the pictures. "Is he your dad?"

"No," she said, "a friend of the family."

51

Steve sniffed, as if he didn't quite believe it. "Christ, he's in every one of them. And look at this one. Here. The way he's staring at your ass."

Claire reached for the book, to snap it shut. "That will do," she said. But he jerked the scrapbook out of range, and several loose photos fell to the floor. Claire waited for him to scramble for them, but he didn't. "Pick those up," she directed, standing as tall as she could.

He sat in the chair beside the fallen pictures but made no move to get them. He laid the scrapbook on his knees and then looked up at her. "Pick them up yourself," he said. "They're your fucking pictures."

"I *won't*," she told him. "And I'll thank you to watch your language."

He laughed, lifted the scrapbook as high as he could, and flung it across the room. A few of the pages fell free in midair, and many, many more came loose when it hit the glass wall and skidded to the floor.

He pulled himself back into his boots, stood up, and hitched his thumbs under his belt. "Guess I'll be going now, babe. You just stay here and clean up real pretty."

Claire raised her hand to strike him, and he grabbed her fingers and bent them backward. Claire tried to pull away, but it hurt no matter how she turned. Finally she stood as still as she could, hoping he'd release her.

He let his grip fall to her wrist and found some awful spot to squeeze. Claire dropped to her knees, but he kept squeezing.

He used his free hand to unzip his jeans.

"No," Claire said, but her mouth moved toward him. The pain was so incredible, unrelenting. She closed her mouth over him, moaning. When he came in her mouth, he twisted her wrist, and the burning and wrenching were somehow a part of it.

Then he stopped, let her arm fall, pushed her mouth away. He did his zipper up, patted his belt buckle. "I'll find my own way back to the highway," he said.

She grabbed at the leg of his jeans, curled her fingers over the toe of his boot. "No, please," she said, "don't go."

Then she heard herself babbling about all the things that she could show him, all the things that she could do for him, were he to stay.

He watched her with amusement, and the more he watched, the more she babbled. She hated herself for it, but she could not stop. It was the first time she had ever felt anything. The first time—in a sexual encounter, anyway—that she'd been thrilled.

"I have a sauna," she said, tugging him back toward her bedroom. "Would you like to see?"

She hardly ever used the little cedar room, though it, like everything else in the house, was kept at the ready.

"It won't take a minute to heat up," she said, fumbling first with the switches that controlled the temperature, and then, less handily, with his clothing.

But he pushed her away. "First thing you got to learn, babe, is when to quit."

"I . . ." She felt so helpless.

"The horses, babe. Let's go see 'em. Then we can come back here and you can lick the sweat off my balls." He watched the expression form on her face and laughed. "You're somethin' else, you know that?"

She led him to the stables, turning often just to look at him.

"Just keep walking," he told her. "I'm still here."

Inside, he eyed each animal knowingly. Finally, he stepped into the box stall that housed a two-year-old Claire had bred.

"This one," he said. "He's your best."

So he did know horses after all. But of course he would, of course he would. He knew lots of things. Hadn't he said so?

"What's his name?" Steve asked, stroking the gelding's shoulder.

Claire hadn't decided on a name for him. She was about to say so, when all at once she knew. She steadied herself and smiled. "Illuminating," she told him.

Well, it had been illuminating, she told herself. And now it was over. She had to think of it that way. Now, she would go down to the stables to oversee the dispersal of the stock. She would sell all of the horses, save the one Steve had admired—and inadvertently named—that first night.

She held her head high and walked the pine-shadowed path to the stables.

She saw Steve entering the tack room, and she followed, watching him open the trunk and take the bandages out.

She wanted to tell him that she'd changed her mind, wouldn't sell the horses after all, but she heard the horse van coming, its big wheels heavy on the gravel. She reached for one of the leather halters, and Steve caught her arm. "I . . . I'll help," she said.

But he held her arm until she was willing to drop it, and then he walked to the tack-room window, the one that faced the courtyard where the van had stopped. "Hey!" He raised the window and shouted at the driver. "You hold 'em, I'll wrap 'em, okay?" And he carried the bandages outside, leaving her behind again.

She watched through the window as he wrapped the first horse, wrapped him in slow motion, motion that underlined his skill. He knew she was there, watching, and he knew, he had to know, that she was thinking of his belt as he bound her wrists. He wound each bandage around and around and around.

The driver must have asked about her, because Steve motioned toward the tack room and the driver glanced that way. Claire ducked back, not knowing whether he had seen her.

"Yeah," she heard Steve say, "you know how sentimental women are about these things." The driver laughed.

She was sorry to be here now, sorry that she hadn't just driven away, to the city, to the Row. She tried to remember the man on the motorcycle, but the image, the memory, wouldn't come.

She leaned against the saddle racks and listened. They were leading the first horse into the van now; she could hear the sound of shod hooves against the wooden ramp.

"How many you got?" the driver asked.

"All of them," Steve said. "This one to Potomac, and the rest of them"—he seemed to raise his voice here, though he didn't need to, she could hear—"to the auction at Marshall."

It wasn't the way he was making it sound, but the driver would know that, the driver would know that good horses went to Marshall, not the ones that the killers would buy for horsemeat, but good horses. They had even bought two of these horses there, gone together to sit in the bleachers and watch the horses as they were led in to be sold. She had suffered the way everyone looked at her, more than surprised to see her there. She didn't care. For the first time in her life, she was wholly alive. If Steve had wanted her right there, at the auction, she'd have let him. He was very careful, though. In public he treated her as though she were in charge.

Oh, would they *hurry* with the horses, hurry taking them away. Then she could be alone with Steve, one last time. Surely he wouldn't refuse her now, not this one last time.

Finally she heard the last horse being loaded, heard the ramp being raised and locked into place.

She heard slam and slam again and then the engine and the sound of wheels on gravel. "No!" she screamed. She ran into the courtyard to see Steve leaning out of the truck, grinning at her from the passenger side. He waved and called to her, "*Adiós,* babe!" And then he pulled himself back into the cab, where she couldn't see him.

"So if you don't want to go, why are you going?" Jay yawned into the receiver as he spoke. He had just dozed off when Rita telephoned.

"I know that sounds like a reasonable question," Rita said, "but I don't have a reasonable answer. I'm going and that's it. If you want to come, fine, and if you don't want to come, that's fine too."

But actually Rita had called hoping he would go. She hated going to parties alone, especially parties like this one, the Corcoran's big spring bash. It would be full of cliquey people and all the men would be gay. And she knew already from reading about the show that was opening that she didn't want to see it. It was straight gimmick, a series of Martin Sinclair photographs called "Funny Faces," a bunch of famous people mugging at the camera and blown up poster size for all the world to see. What kind of talent did that take?

But, oh God, if she didn't go Rosenberg would never let her hear the end of it. He had made it sound so simple: "You want to stop brooding, so stop. Go someplace. Put a pair of shoes on your feet and go." That was what she got for grumbling about her life, about being stuck here all the time, on the Row.

"I can't go with you," Jay remembered. "The coroner's supposed to call and I have to be home."

"The coroner. Well, that's appropriate."

Jay would be seeing him about the murder. About Faye Arensberg. This time out, Rita had to admit, Jay really seemed to be making serious progress on a book.

He had stacks of notes and news clippings on Faye's death, and more on murder in general. He even had those sleazy pulp magazines and was forever quoting from them. "Listen to this one," he'd say, and then he'd be reading out loud from "The Bizarre Case of the Barbecued Family," or some similarly titled tale.

"This is so gruesome," Rita observed, "and it doesn't bother you at all. It's like fun and games for you."

"Of course," Jay said.

"I mean it," Rita persisted.

"I mean it too."

The idea of Margaret sitting around listening to this kind of thing didn't seem very likely to Rita, and she said so.

"Right again," Jay answered. "I save my seamier side for you."

Rita laughed because she knew she was supposed to, but it bothered her that she should be selected to keep his secrets. His sex secrets as well as those about this. Except that this—Jay's interest in Faye Arensberg's death—wasn't exactly a secret. It was just that with Rita he furnished, and so obviously enjoyed, all the gory details.

Still, Rita had found herself unable to stop reading through the clippings. She complained enough, but she savored the most lurid ones—especially about how Faye had been stalked and stabbed even as she stumbled through the upstairs rooms, which had been vacant at the time. It reminded her of all those el cheapo sorority-house movies on late-night TV. "Why didn't Faye run out into the street?" Rita asked. "Why would she go upstairs, where she'd be trapped?"

"Maybe," Jay answered her, "she wanted to die." It was an angle he'd—for a reason he didn't fathom—decided to play.

"Bullshit," Rita told him.

But what had it been like? When had Faye known that someone was in the house? Had she talked to her killer, pleaded, or what? Had the killer been watching her, waiting for the right moment?

"I don't know," Jay said.

"Well, you'd better find out," Rita advised. "That's what people want to know. Why do you think they read this kind of thing?"

"They?" Jay asked. "Shouldn't you include yourself and say 'we'?"

" 'We' nothing," Rita argued. "I don't read this crap."

"Except when you're here," Jay said.

Rita hadn't gone back to his apartment after that. And, while she wanted to see Jay tonight, she certainly didn't want to go over there. Why did he keep the apartment, anyway? Why didn't he just move in with Margaret? "Well, if you won't come with me, then at least come and talk to me while I get ready," she asked him now, on the telephone. "No kidding, I need moral support."

She did, in a way. What she meant by that was that she needed Jay—better Jay than no one—to see her all dressed up and ready for the Corcoran. She wanted Jay to catch his breath and tell her she looked beautiful. She'd never felt so insecure before. Everything that she put on, no matter what she'd paid for it, looked awful, loud, cheap. Claire was the reason, Rita knew.

"Okay, okay," Jay relented. "I'll be there."

Rita had actually begun to go out of her way to look for Claire. Rita would jog up the alley behind the Row to see if she could glimpse the Jag through the slats of Claire's tall fence. Rita had somehow managed to charge a plum-colored running suit to reconnoiter in, so it wouldn't look as though she were spying.

Claire hadn't actually moved in yet, not entirely, but that day, Rita knew, was very near. Nonetheless, Rita saw the Jag a lot but had seen its owner only twice now. Rita would spring to look outside whenever she heard a noise, but never with any luck.

Then one day, while Rita was huffing up the alley, Claire appeared, on foot, like a mirage. In white again. A white loose-fitting jacket over slim white pants. *Christ. Her dry cleaning bill,* Rita thought, *must be more than my rent.*

"Hi," Claire said.

Rita was stunned. She had somehow expected to be snubbed. "Hi," she said in return, but she kept on running.

The next time Rita saw her, Claire was in the house, unaware of Rita, who was coming home after an all-day shoot.

It was dark outside, but the overhead lights in the room where Claire stood were ablaze. The fixture would probably be replaced with crystal, but for the time being it consisted of four bare bright light bulbs, their wattage probably dangerously close to blowing the fuse. The windows facing the street had been elongated during Claire's remodeling blitz, so that, standing curbside, Rita could see the room almost entire.

The walls behind Claire had been plastered, though not painted. Several wide test swashes of various whites had been brushed on the wall, like rays. A tall stepladder stood off to the side.

Somehow—how had Rita missed it?—an immense stone mantelpiece had been brought in there. It reminded Rita of "Beauty and the Beast," of the beast's enchanted castle where the eyes of the carved figures in the mantel followed everyone who entered the room.

It was hard to believe that this was just a house on the Row. It had been, according to Jessie, a Negro funeral parlor before it was made into apartments. Before Faye Arensberg moved in. Faye had lived downstairs. She'd been finished off—as far as Rita knew—in the very room where Claire was standing. Rita shivered at the thought of Claire ever finding out.

The murder was the reason the house had been vacant for so long. Even the winos, who ordinarily staggered into all the empty places as if led by radar, had avoided the house that Claire had bought.

Claire. She was wearing lounging pajamas in a pale, icy satin. She leaned against the window as though looking out, although Rita knew that with the light in the room she could not possibly see anything except her own reflection. *She's on display,* Rita thought.

Rita might have stood there longer had she not become aware of the weight of the cameras she was carrying. *I ought to photograph her,* she realized, then and there. She would ask Claire, she decided, the next time she got within talking range. She hoped it would be soon, before Claire decorated the house. There was something about her in there the way it was now, something about the emptiness of the setting, the scale of that room. If she did it right, the photos would look haunted. There would be echoes that anyone looking at the photographs would hear. *Echoes,* Rita thought. *Faye Arensberg's footsteps.*

The notion frightened her, but Rita knew she would pursue it nonetheless. Back in her apartment, she made sketches, even though she'd never been to the house. She would have to ask Jay if he had a floor plan or something.

When Jay arrived, Rita had one eye on and one eye off. She kept the eye without mascara closed when she answered the door so that the eye that was finished could dry.

"Interesting effect," he said, following her back to the bathroom and sitting on the edge of the tub while she leaned over the sink to get closer to the mirror. "So what's this 'moral support' business?"

"Wait," she said, "I can't talk while I'm doing this." She should have called Jay when she'd finished dressing, not now. Having him watch her this way took away all the mystique. "Why don't you go in the other room," Rita said. "I'll be out."

"I thought you wanted to talk."

"I changed my mind."

"I'm perfectly comfortable here," he said, crossing his legs. "In fact, I like watching you do this. Margaret doesn't wear any makeup."

Rita tried outlining her lips smaller. They seemed too huge. But she slipped with the little sable brush and ended up doing it her usual way. She turned around to face Jay, yanking her kimono off so that he could see her outfit. "So what do you think?" she asked.

"You look fine," he said.

"That's all? Just fine?"

"You look the way you always look. You look fine."

"Hey, tell me something," Rita said. "And I'm not asking you because I want to start something. I'm asking you because I want to know."

"Shoot."

"Okay. Do you think I'm attractive? What I mean is . . ."

But Jay started laughing. "I don't know, Rita. Do you think *I'm* attractive?"

"Aw, come on. You know what I mean. I mean, would you want to sleep with me? If you had the chance?"

Jay stood up and clasped his hand over his heart. He faked as French an accent as he could. "Sex . . . for me . . . ees a matter . . .

of . . . domination. And I know, my dar-leeng, that I could not. Dominate you."

Rita didn't laugh, didn't even smile. "What about Claire?" she asked. "Do you think you could get it up for her?"

"Rita," Jay said, "this is ridiculous."

"You don't even go to the sex club anymore, do you?" Rita accused. "Not since she's been hanging around the Row."

Jay stood up and walked to the door. Then he thought better of it and turned. "You know what?" he said. "I think you're jealous. And I don't mean that the way you think. I think you're jealous about my book. I think you know I'm really going to make it this time and it gets to you."

"That isn't true," Rita retorted. It wasn't, entirely. It was just that she didn't want Jay to make it before she did. "I want us both to make it," she said.

"Like having an orgasm at the same time?"

Rita laughed at last. "You really are a sleaze," she told him.

"But I do want to talk to you about Claire," he said, "because in a way, you're right about that. She haunts me, Rita."

"I'm running late," Rita said, snatching up her things. She tried to sound cool about it, but his admission made her furious.

Claire sat with Aubrey in the restaurant at Dulles as he awaited his plane. It was the safest time to tell him of her decision to live in the house, she'd thought. His protest would be limited by his schedule.

It had rained. Beyond the window glass, the runways glistened. At the edges, blue lights winked. Claire rubbed her fingers on the glass, as if the pane had clouded. "It looks more like a harbor than an airport, don't you think?"

But he was not to be so easily distracted. "Claire," he said, "I simply cannot believe . . ."

"You suggested it yourself." She glanced at him only briefly, then outside again.

"Yes, but, Claire—the neighborhood."

"Oh, pooh." Now she pouted at her drink. "You yourself said—"

"Yes," he interrupted, realizing at once that he had raised his voice. He looked about and caught himself, almost whispering. "But I was thinking of tenants. Not *you*."

"I've made up my mind," Claire told him.

"Another house, perhaps. A few blocks closer to the Capitol."

"*This* house, Aubrey."

He knew she had the winning edge. Every argument he had used to convince her to buy the place could now be turned against him. Still, the thought of it!

"It's really quite nice," trying to cheer him.

He leaned across the table toward her. "One of my *aides* lives there," he said. "And there are *black* people. On that very block."

"Why, Uncle Aubrey!" Claire pretended outrage.

"It is not the right sort of place yet," he went on. "In a year or two. But not *yet*." He looked down at the table. He was trembling.

Claire glanced at her wristwatch. She ought to have waited until he had boarded the shuttle that would take him to the plane. She ought to have called it out to him, "Oh, and by the way . . ."

"I should have telephoned your mother," he was saying. "I should have asked her advice. I simply should not have—"

"Ha!" Claire stopped him. "My mother!" She touched Aubrey's face with her hand, forcing him to look at her. "The last time I saw Mother, she had twelve Jack Russell terriers. Twelve. And once a week she'd have her driver take them off to have their nails done. During my visit, Aubrey, their nails were *vermilion*, I believe." She let her hand fall. "Now," she said, "what sort of advice do you suppose Mother would have given?"

Despite himself, he laughed. "Vermilion," he repeated.

"And, Aubrey, don't forget"—she drew herself back in the chair—"I'm a big girl now."

"Yes, but—"

"It will be *all right*."

Aubrey shook his head. "I promised your father. I said I would be responsible. . . ."

Claire worked to smooth her voice. "And you *have* been. You've done wonderfully." But under the table her hands balled into fists. It was always this way when she thought of her father, who lived abroad. Who never so much as cabled. He had walked away from everything. From her mother. And from what she, Claire, had tried to tell him about Aubrey. She was thirteen when her father had told her that Aubrey would be in charge.

"Father would be proud," she said now, speaking of him as she always did: as though he were dead.

Aubrey beamed. His concession was her reward. "When will you be moving in?" he asked. "In the winter? There's such a great deal to be done."

"All sorts of things have gone on already. Plastering and replacing moldings. Oh, Aubrey"—she brought her hands to the tabletop and dropped them over his—"it's *so* wonderful. And think of it"—she wet her lips—"I owe everything, all of it, even the *idea*, to you."

"When did you . . ." he began, terrified by what she'd said. That work had already been done. That she'd been in the city, ordering it done, and that she hadn't come to him. This wasn't what he'd had in mind when he'd told her about the house.

"I suppose you have to be off now," Claire said, looking at her watch and then patting his hand, as if to send him on his way.

"Yes," he lied. He had already decided, in the course of this conversation, to delay his flight, at least for an hour or so. He needed to think this through, devise a strategy. "Will you go there—to the house—tonight?"

"Aubrey," she assured him, "I've been there lots of nights already, and I'm still in one piece." She presented her cheek.

He kissed it and then watched her walk away before he advanced to the ticket counter to exchange his ticket for a later flight. What was it he felt? Something very like shame.

Looking around the gallery and comparing herself to every other woman in the room, Rita figured that she stacked up nicely.

She had bushed her hair out almost defiantly, though, inasmuch as she'd put twice the normal amount of conditioner on it, it looked pretty good, not wiry at all, but silky, or at least silkier.

Meanwhile, she would give anything to be able to undo the waistband of the pegged silk jeans she was wearing and breathe for a change. But the party had just gotten under way and, she consoled herself, probably the fabric would loosen up if she just moved around a little.

Christ, this outfit had pushed her way over her Saks Fifth Avenue credit line, and just after she'd managed to get that particular charge account down. *But it's worth it,* she thought, looking around the room.

She urged herself to move around, but her shoes had already started to pinch her little toes. She should have known better than to wear them, but they were just the most fantastic shoes she'd ever owned. They'd cost more than a hundred dollars, and she'd bought them in a shoe store with its own security guard. That had been before American Express reclaimed its card. The shoes, all straps and stiletto heels, would have been worth it if only, after five minutes in them, she didn't walk with a limp. She'd sit down as soon as the jeans would let her.

She was glad she had been able to get the Jay episode off her chest, because otherwise it would have spoiled her evening at the Corcoran. But poor Nick, he really hadn't had any idea what she was talking about. She'd collared Nick at the end of the Row and harangued him all the way to the Metro stop and the train that would take her to the opening. "The way I figure it," she'd said, "I must scare the shit out of Jay. And boy, is that a laugh. *Me* scare *him. He's* the one who's up to his neck in that murder. *He's* the one who talks about it day and night. Faye Arensberg this and Faye Arensberg that. God, I can't believe it.

"And that's not all. You know what he has in his apartment? You know what he has in his bookcase, back where he didn't expect anyone to see? I'll tell you what, he has *pictures.* Helmut Newton pictures, all those girls in garter belts and carrying riding crops, all that kinky stuff. Ha! And *I* scare *him.*" She hadn't, of course, told anyone but Rosenberg about the sex club.

Nick had just glommed onto the Faye part, saying, "Yeah, yeah, she was something else, Faye." You'd think Rita would have let it go at that, but she didn't. She kept trying to get through to Nick, telling him, "That's not the point," and then haranguing him some more.

Nick was a sweet guy. He had walked with her the whole way,

and then he'd even thanked her, as if she'd done him some kind of favor. "Hey, Nick," she said, "it's the other way around. *You* helped me, see, by listening." And it was true, even if he didn't have a clue about what he was listening to.

But anyway, yakking at him had put her in a much better mood, so much better, she could look at all the "Funny Faces" and admit that they had something more than gimmick, they had style. Wit, too. She'd find the photographer, she decided, and tell him so. How often was it, after all, that Rita found herself with something nice to say?

She glanced at his bio in the gallery brochure and discovered, oh Lord, that he was younger than she was by three years. Twenty-five years old and opening at the Corcoran!

She spotted him standing under Judge Sirica's mug shot, just past Beverly Sills's and Goldie Hawn's on the far wall. All by himself, too. The way he looked, she couldn't help but wonder why.

He had that heavy-lidded Christopher Walken look, and that same languid, easy way of moving. He was wearing a tux, and Rita figured that he owned it, he was so right at home. Rita liked a man who could slouch around in a tux.

She went over and tapped him on the shoulder, and when he turned she said, just before popping a cracker into her mouth, "So, did the pope turn you down, or what?"

She saw from his face that he didn't take it as a joke, and immediately she pummeled herself: *Why should he? Would you?* "Oh, look," she admitted, "I'm just jealous. I'm three years older than you are, and I'm good, too. And I still can't sell shit. I really like your show, honest. And believe me, I was trying real hard not to."

The look on his face relaxed a little bit, but not entirely.

"I'm Rita Puleo," she said. "You probably never heard of me, but that's okay. Before this show opened, I never heard of you." *Nice going. Rosenberg will kill you when you tell him this.* "I'm sorry, I'm doing it again. But I'm only kidding. I remember the cover you did for the *Washingtonian* two years ago, the June one, with Dan Rather. And then, oh, maybe three months after that, you had a fashion thing in the *Post*, kind of tropical—ferns and guys in white suits. And"—only just discovering how much of his work she really did know—"so, see? I'm an actual Martin Sinclair fan."

She looked over his shoulder at a blowup of Gloria Vanderbilt frowning. "Who would have figured that she had that in her," Rita said.

He turned to view it. "You have to admit," he said, "it's a damn sight better than her smile."

"I would never call what she does a smile," Rita offered. "It's more like 'Here. These are my teeth.' "

He tossed his head back, laughing hard. But someone interrupted, whispering in his ear. He stopped laughing abruptly. "There's someone I have to talk to," he said, "but don't go away." He moved off, already looking past her at whoever it was.

After a decent interval, Rita swiveled to see where he had gone. He was talking to a woman two or maybe three times his age, one of those super-polished party-giver types. And alongside her, some blonde number who looked like she was just out of Bryn Mawr or one of those schools. *They're everywhere,* Rita thought.

Rita decided she'd stay put if he gave some sign that he'd be coming back, like a rueful glance that he was trapped over there against his will. After a couple of minutes, when he hadn't, Rita took herself back over to the table, where there was a tree made of strawberries and big silver bowls of whipped cream to dunk them in. She started to gorge.

He found her. "I thought you weren't going away," he said.

She held a plump strawberry up between them. "Did you really think that you could compete with this?" she asked, then bit into it.

"I know," he said, taking both her hands and making a cup out of them. He filled them with strawberries. Then he took one of the whipped-cream bowls and began steering her back through the gallery, back past Jerry Falwell's picture, and Nancy Reagan's.

"Let me guess," she said. "You *did* get the pope."

"No." He led her into a little office with a high-intensity light over the desk. It was piled high with papers and folders and photographs. He set the bowl atop all of these, and the pile swayed precariously. He took the strawberries from her and put them there, too.

"You're really pushing your luck," she said. "What's the point of this, anyway?"

"I've watched you walking around in those dippy shoes," he told her. "I thought you might like to sit down."

There was a love seat along one wall, but it, too, was piled with junk. He started taking the stacks off the cushions and setting them down on the floor.

Rita ate another strawberry. "If I sit," she said, "I'll have to unbutton my jeans."

"Well, in that case . . ." He set another pile aside and then walked over to the door and locked it.

Now what? She didn't even remember what to do in a situation like this one. She could almost hear Rosenberg, as if he were her conscience: "Well, what do you *want* to do?" Rita blushed. Then knowing she had blushed made her blush even more. "Gee," she said, hoping to sound offhand, "if you had your camera, you could take a picture of *my* funny face." Great. Now she had ranked herself with all of the biggies he had photographed. Great. Rita covered her cheeks with her hands.

He took hold of her hands, pulled them away, rubbed them with his own. "Sticky," he said, kissing her fingertips. Rita looked at them and saw that they were stained with bright red juice. Then she closed her eyes and he pulled her closer, kissed her forehead.

How long since she'd been held or kissed? She couldn't remember. But she'd come into this crummy little office all stiff white peaks, like the bowl of whipped cream he had carried. And just like the whipped cream, she was softening to liquid. If she so much as moved, she thought, he would hear her squish.

But he stopped touching her, let his hands fall completely away.

"Why did you stop?" she asked him, surprised at what she'd said. Surprised, too, to be able to say anything, to breathe, even.

"Because you didn't respond," he told her.

Okay, Puleo, now or never. "I did *too* respond," she said. "I responded in my heart," taking his hands, both of them, and putting them where she, right that minute, felt that they belonged.

"I don't think they ever did solve it," Marvin Jaffe, who'd been chief coroner on the Arensberg case, told Jay. "If they had, I'd have had to testify at the trial. And I found that on the odd side—that they didn't arrest anyone—because it wasn't one of your run-of-the-mill crimes. I see a lot of murders and I feel my opinion is worth something, and I'm telling you, it was somebody who really had it in for this Arensberg girl. Really did." He lifted the top of the roll, sniffed the cheeseburger, and rearranged his sliver of pickle on its surface. "You were right." He winked at Jay, covered the cheeseburger again, and bit into it. "Terrific food."

They were at Gallagher's, an old-fashioned bar with dark wood paneling, bentwood chairs, narrow cloth-covered tables.

Jaffe swallowed. "This girl's face alone," he said, "fourteen wounds. Punctures. Cheeks, eyelids, upper lip. Some of them from the inside out. Think about that. Killer sticks the weapon inside her mouth, see, and jab! Jab! Probably watching her sweat. Jesus." Another bite. "Hunks of this girl's hair, pulled out right by the roots. And the girl is still alive! Oh, sure, the body shuts off, capacity to feel and whatnot. But she's still alive! That's the beauty of forensic science. You can tell this kind of thing." He mopped his lips with the napkin and took a long draw on his beer. "I always thought it would be a dandy book. How long have you been at it?"

Talking about it? Thinking about it? Or actually at it? Jay wanted to ask. Because he'd been thinking about it since it happened, but only recently—because of Claire—was he actually able to get anything down on paper. Images, scenes.

Claire was his muse.

And more than that. Claire was Faye, or at least a model for Faye. He'd fallen into using her this way quite by accident.

He'd walked to the Trover Book Shop one afternoon—it was one of his favorite ways of putting off his work—and he'd stood on the pavement looking at the titles on display in the window. When he glanced up to look inside the shop itself, he saw Claire.

Behind glass that way, it was as if she were a specimen. As if she had been meant to serve that way.

She was browsing, unaware of him and the way he stared. She was unaware, too, of the way the other patrons in the store were regarding her.

Jay watched as she approached the man behind the cash register. Watched the way she looked at him, straight on. She wasn't like the others, the beautiful women who shortened their gaze to avoid real contact. These women didn't actually look away. They just didn't *see*. Faye had looked straight at people too. For this reason, more than any other, the two women, Faye and Claire, merged in Jay's mind.

Later, at his desk, Jay was able to write the sort of scene that had always stumped him. He was able to re-create a section of Faye's daily life. After that, he watched for Claire, following, observing, whenever he could. He had put together quite a number of pages as a result. Now, in fact, he could conjure her at will. Now, too, he could place her in a variety of settings and situations. But, try as he might, Jay could not imagine Claire—and therefore Faye—in bed. That seemed an enormous omission. Though the police found no evidence of rape or even recent intercourse, Faye's murder had seemed so sexual. Like those Florida murders, the ones in the sorority house. Hadn't that killer bitten his victims almost to the bone while murdering them?

Sexual, yes.

Jay had tried to think of Claire while he was in bed with Margaret, but that was ludicrous. And Margaret kept asking him, was something wrong?

He broke from these thoughts and looked across the table at Jaffe, then down at the tape recorder. Jaffe was filling the entire cassette.

"You handle a thousand cases," Jaffe said, "and then one comes along that really sticks in your gut."

Jaffe had photocopied the official Arensberg file. "It will probably read like Greek to you, but what the hell. I'm not supposed to, but it's my personal file now, more or less." He said he'd give Jay his address, too, in case Jay had questions later on. "I could probably set you up with the detective who was in charge of the case, too. Used to be a pal of mine. He's working the counties now, out near the Eastern Shore. It got to him, D.C. Gets to a lot of the good ones."

When the check came, Jaffe took it and said, "No, my treat. I've heard about you starving writers."

"Thanks," he told Jaffe, thinking now that maybe the interview hadn't gone as badly as he feared. Jaffe believed him, believed he was the real thing.

"Oh, me." Jaffe stood outside on the pavement and stretched before he shook Jay's hand. "Talking about this sure does take something out of you."

It didn't take from Jay at all. It fired him up.

He ought to have borrowed Margaret's car. He pulled out his wallet, checked his funds. She'd just cashed her paycheck, so he had plenty. Jay hailed a cab and headed for Maryland.

He called her using the telephone behind the club bar. There was a window there, through which Jay could see the pool. A couple sat on the concrete edge, their feet dipping into the water. The woman had a fist around the man's penis. The man had his hand between the woman's legs. They kissed as they touched each other.

"Margaret?" he said. "I finished up a little early." He caught the eye of a woman at the bar he had never seen before. He crooked his finger at her, and she slid off the barstool. "No, no, it went very well," he said. The woman stood beside him now. He held the phone against his shoulder with his chin and unbuttoned the woman's blouse. He pulled the lapels back. She wore no bra. "No, don't wait up for me. I'll stay at my place. Right, right, I just thought I'd get in a little game." He placed a palm under each of the woman's breasts and bounced them. He listened. "Uh-huh. Uh-huh. Right. I love you, too." He hung up and buried his face in the woman's flesh. He thought of Claire. He thought of Faye.

"Hey," the woman said, pulling away. "Take it easy, okay? I don't want to criticize, but come on now. That hurts."

Margaret went over to Jessie's because she just knew that if she didn't, she would wind up doing something stupid. Maybe even call him on some pretext he would see right through. She never had any real reason to call him, not even when he was in town. Everything she did was checked by Bob Sandusky, his administrative assistant.

She dreamed about calling him, though. "Sorry to bother you, Senator, but . . ." And then, when they'd finished the business part, he would say, "Margaret, my dear, I hope this doesn't seem terribly forward, but I was wondering . . ."

He always complained about traveling and about hotels. Not to her, of course. This time, she'd written down the number of the place where he'd be staying. It was a harmless thing to do. With Jay there, she would never use it.

But Jay never got back from the racket club early, and Rita was out, too. Margaret kept watching the clock, calculating: Dulles. Then on the plane. At the airport. In the taxi. To his room. Then the number, which she'd memorized by now, would pop into her mind.

Did *she* call him? Margaret could imagine the way he'd sound, picking up the phone. "Why, Claire . . ." His voice tightening with pleasure.

Margaret had to admit that Claire matched him in a way. The way she looked and the way she walked, graceful and assured, like a dancer. Maybe Claire was a dancer.

But Margaret knew, even while she was thinking it, that it wouldn't be true. She had seen women like that before, and they were never dancers, though they took dancing growing up. They were the women important men married, women who knew what to say and when to laugh. Women who knew how to fool men into listening to their stupid talk. They were the women who would make fun of Margaret behind her back.

Still, he might notice her if she just kept doing her work as well as Bob Sandusky said that she was doing it. And once he noticed, he wouldn't even think about Claire.

"Jessie?" Margaret was surprised to find the door ajar, but she didn't go inside, she just stood there and called.

"Yes?" Jessie answered her from the kitchen, and Margaret heard some papers rustle.

"I came to visit," Margaret said.

"Come in," Jessie shouted, "but don't shut the door. Come up and have a drink."

Margaret started up the narrow stairs, wondering why it was that no one ever remembered that she didn't drink. She always had to remind everyone. As she neared the kitchen, she smelled paint.

Jessie was wearing a dark denim jump suit, almost like the kind mechanics wear. The jump suit had paint all over it, not just the blue that Jessie was using on the sill, but every color under the sun.

"Oh, it looks so pretty," Margaret said, speaking of the sill.

Jessie misunderstood. "This?" she asked, gesturing at herself. "It's just some old thing that I wear for messy work. I picked it up long before the damn things got to be fashionable." She looked at Margaret and realized her error. "Oh, but you weren't talking about this cover-up of mine, were you?" She laughed.

Margaret shook her head, no.

Jessie had a little island of newspapers all over the floor under the window. She seemed reluctant to step off. "You came just in time," Jessie said, kneeling at the edge of the newsprint. "Because I'm dying for some Scotch, but my hands have paint all over them. So get me one, won't you? And use one of the old glasses up there over the sink. Not the good ones, but one of those awful striped things."

Margaret took a glass down and then stood holding it. Jessie went on painting and finally glanced at her. "What's the matter?" she asked Margaret.

"I'm not sure how much you want."

"Oh, for God's sake." Jessie dropped the brush and wiped her hands against the denim and then came over and snatched the glass away, making little blue smears against the stripes.

Margaret was afraid that she was angry. "I want one too," Margaret said, all of a sudden. Jessie raised her eyebrows and then shrugged and motioned for Margaret to take another glass down, which she did.

"I'll make you a weak one," Jessie said, and Margaret noted that Jessie's drink was much darker than her own. "Now what's on your mind?" Jessie asked.

Margaret began telling her; but in a tangle of false starts and qualifications.

"Get to the point," Jessie said.

"The point is," Margaret said, looking down into her glass, "I think I'm in love with the Senator. And as long as *she's* around"— Margaret gestured at the window, toward Claire's—"there's nothing I can do. He can't even *see* anybody but Claire. It's as though the rest of us don't exist. And what will happen is, I'll end up with Jay and the Senator will end up with her, and I can't stand thinking about it. About him ending up with her. If he *knew* me," Margaret went on, "if he'd give me a chance . . ." She held out her empty glass, expecting Jessie to take it away. Instead, Jessie filled it again.

"Help me," Margaret pleaded. "Tell me what to do."

Jessie drained her own glass and resumed her spot by the sill. She picked up the brush and started painting again. She cleared her throat, and Margaret waited, but Jessie didn't say anything.

"Jessie?"

Jessie's strokes were faster. She slapped at the sill with the brush. The paint splattered onto the wall, way over the masking-tape border. She tore a piece of the newspaper off and began to wipe at the spots, but they only smeared. Worse, the newsprint mixed with the paint, blackening it. Jessie tossed the wadded paper to the floor and stood. She looked at the marred wall and then at Margaret with the same expression. "Did it ever occur to you," she said, "that I'm sick to death of hearing this kind of thing? That I just don't care? That I just might want to spend an evening without hearing one of you talk about love's sweet dream?" She said the last three words as if they were soiled. And she didn't stop. "It's all you ever think about, all of you. Pairing off, living in some happily ever after. What ever happened to the women's movement? What ever happened to careers? What ever happened to serious conversations about things that matter?"

Jessie might have gone on, but Margaret had begun to cry. "I don't always talk about this," Margaret said. "And I *am* serious. I've never talked about this except maybe once, to Rita, but never to you. Never to you."

"Oh, Margaret." Jessie would have patted Margaret's shoulder, but for the paint and newsprint on her hands. "Here." She stepped across the room and fetched Margaret's drinking glass off the counter. "Have some more." She grabbed the Scotch decanter and poured Margaret another drink. She watched as Margaret gulped the drink, saying, "Oh, forgive me, Margaret. I've just been in a terrible mood. Nothing's going right at the store, and I've let this place get dowdy. Really, it doesn't have anything to do with you."

Nick lit the sanctuary candles, each in its own little blue cup. He watched the blue lights shimmer on the wall and on the statue of the

Virgin. Sometimes the dance of light and shadow made it look as though the Virgin's mouth had moved. Nick would wait to hear her speak, but she never did.

He kept the place just as his folks had, though now he needed just one floor. He'd let the third floor go in favor of this one, directly over the Laundromat. The smells from down there—bleach and ammonia, suds and steam—reminded him of his mother.

Nick lit the candles just the way his mother used to, the ones in the red cups in the morning before he went to the Market, and the ones in the blue cups at night. He thanked the Virgin, too. He thanked her especially tonight, for letting him know that he wasn't the only one still thinking about Faye. Before he made the sign of the cross, he asked the Virgin for forgiveness.

Still on his knees, he moved the throw rug aside and looked down into the hole. The hole had always been there, at first just a knot in the wood. Nick had only enlarged it, taking the penknife and cutting away one night after the Laundromat had closed.

It was directly over the folding table, so that when someone carried a load from the dryer, Nick could see exactly what it was.

Once Nick had seen a colored girl with the tiniest pants. They were pink, and like he'd told Zabo and the other guys, "just this little triangle to cover up the you-know-what and the rest all elastic."

But Nick hardly ever got to see that kind of underwear. Mostly it was plain old pants—what his mother called "step-ins"—and slips and brassieres.

But sometimes the *way* they folded their stuff was worth watching. There was one girl—Nick didn't know who she was, she wasn't from the Row and she never came into the Market—who had a whole routine.

"First she shakes everything real good." He'd demonstrated for the guys. "Then she holds it up to her nose. Sniffs it, yeah. Then, if she likes what she smells, she folds it up, real loving like, and puts it in the pile."

"And what if she don't like it, huh, Nick?" someone in the produce section yelled. Everybody laughed.

"I don't know," Nick said. "So far she likes everything."

At first the guys would razz him after that. When he'd leave to go home, someone would always ask if he had a date. "With the sniffer, huh?" the next person would say. It didn't bother Nick, and when they saw that, they dropped it.

He was glad he hadn't told any of the guys about how he'd hoped that Faye would come into the Laundromat, the way she used to come into the Market. Half the time, when he was looking down that little hole, he was looking for Faye.

He'd go to the Row to see her, too. See her windows, anyway, back before they boarded them all up.

He hoped the new girl—the one Zabo said was better than Faye—would take his mind off things. That was why Nick had gone to the Row tonight, to take his mind off things.

That was when Rita caught him, but it helped, and he would have to thank the Virgin for that. It helped to know that he wasn't the only one thinking about Faye all the time. Rita was thinking about her, "Faye Arensberg this and Faye Arensberg that," using her name like that, over and over, and loud, too.

Rita kept using both their names—Faye, Claire, Faye, Claire—and real loud, too. Rita talked so fast, Nick had trouble keeping up with what she was saying, but one thing he was sure about, it had something to do with that guy on the Row, the altar boy, Zabo called him. Jay.

But at least he wasn't the only one thinking about Faye.

Rita walked home through the icy drizzle transported by what had taken place. It beats riding the Metro, she thought. She felt terrific, warm in the cold night air. Even her shoes didn't pinch anymore, though it was probably because they were soaked clean through. She and Sin—his all-too-appropriate nickname—had only messed around. Rita wouldn't have stopped there, had it been up to her. But sure enough, someone came pounding at the office door. Sin thought it meant that they should make their way back into the gallery.

Instead of hanging around, hoping he would offer to take her home, Rita told him that she had to get up early the next day. She would do it, too. She was inspired.

"I'll call you," he said, putting his arm around her and kissing her ear.

She walked home the long way, up lighted avenues rather than through side streets, which were quicker. She felt good, but not invincible. No sense taking chances.

Pennsylvania was deserted, probably because of the rain. Even in front of the all-night drugstore, there wasn't a single car.

Rita wanted to take a long, dreamy bath and thought she'd go inside for something scented. Something that smelled of lilac or lavender, something delicate. And maybe a magazine. Something with a lot of ads for sexy lingerie.

She pushed her way toward the back of the store and was surprised—maybe even dazzled—to find Claire there. She was at the magazine rack, one foot on the bottom shelf, reading. A circle of raindrops had dripped off Claire's white silk coat, cut like a chemise. The hem was midcalf. Claire was wearing short white leather boots.

In her Corcoran outfit, post-Sin, Rita felt equal to an approach.

Claire looked up. "Oh, hello," she said, closing the magazine. "Rita, isn't it?"

"That's right," Rita answered, pleased that Claire remembered. Even more pleased not to have to wonder whether it was all right to use Claire's first name. "I've been wanting to talk to you," Rita said, "about some pictures."

"Pictures?"

Rita laughed. "Oh, I'm sorry. See, I'm a photographer. I take pictures. I want to take some of you, in your house." They'd be dynamite, too, Rita knew. The fluorescent light in the drugstore didn't blue Claire's skin, the way it did nearly everyone else's. And that look of Claire's—so pure, so total, so direct. *Here we have your basic knockout,* Rita thought. She tapped the magazine in Claire's hand, the *Washingtonian.* "I could probably sell them right here. I've done some work for them."

The skin between Claire's brows furrowed. She was puzzled.

"Here." Rita took the magazine away and flipped through it. "Oh shit," she said. "They *usually* run the kind of thing I'm talking about."

Claire looked over at the rack, reaching for *Architectural Digest.*

"No," Rita told her, "I don't mean those finished-interior kinds of things. What I mean is, I don't know, just stuff of you, walking around that empty house, you know, kind of, um . . ." She waved her hands about, cursing herself inwardly.

"You mean before and after pictures," Claire suggested.

It wasn't what Rita meant at all. But it was one way of getting the stuff she wanted. "Right," Rita said. Hell, she could probably sell the after shots all by themselves. That reminded her, "Don't think I'm going to charge you or anything. See, I'll sell them, and that's how I get paid. So. When could I?"

Claire put the *Architectural Digest* back in the rack. She stared at the cover for a while. Then she turned back to Rita. "Anytime, I suppose," she said.

"Monday?" Rita pressed. "How about noon on Monday?"

Claire took a slender leather-bound notebook from her purse and scanned it. "Monday, noon," she repeated, writing with a stubby gold pen. "Done." She looked up and smiled.

"Come on," Rita said, "I'll walk back with you."

"Oh, I'm not going back . . ." She stopped. "But I could drop you. I have my car."

"Sure," Rita said, following. A ride in that Jag was worth several baths, she figured.

But outside, Claire turned in the direction away from the Row. Again, Rita followed. They'd gone several blocks when Rita finally asked, "Hey, where'd you park it, anyway?"

Claire smiled. "It's not too far. And at least it's stopped raining."

Both women paused, momentarily, to look at the sky.

Indeed, it had stopped raining. The air had a wonderful misty quality. The streets gleamed, the streetlamps wore halos. Still, Claire was leading Rita toward the Capitol, and though the huge dome glowed bright against the sky, the area surrounding it was dark and practically deserted at night. "Why'd you park here, anyway?" Rita asked. Had she and Claire gone toward the Row, even on foot, they'd have been home by now.

"Oh, I don't know," Claire said. "I've been driving all day. I came up from Virginia, and that took about three hours. Then I took

Aubrey out to Dulles. When I came back to the Row, I got restless. I decided to drive out to Potomac, but I never got there. There must have been something going on. There was just so much traffic that I couldn't stand it, not even for another block. So I pulled over and more or less abandoned my car." She looked at Rita, measuring her.

"I'm all ears," Rita said. "Go on."

"Well, I'm sure you're used to it, but for me it was exciting. Just being in the city, just walking around, with no specific place to go. I don't know what all I did. I walked up and down a lot of little streets. I sat at the fountain at the railroad station. I walked around the Market. I did it for hours. And finally I ended up right where you found me. In that drugstore. I'm going to love Washington, I think." She turned to cross the street. "It's right over here," she told Rita, indicating a street flanked by a block-long construction site.

From where they stood, the Jaguar was barely visible. There was the mist, and also the street was much darker than the others they'd been on.

"Someone must have knocked the streetlight out," Rita said. "Kids, I guess." She was relieved when they reached the car, and then startled to find that Claire hadn't locked it.

Rita climbed in as gracefully as she could, and almost immediately felt moisture seeping through her clothes. "What is this?" she asked, slipping out of the car again.

Claire was back on the pavement, too, feeling at the seat of her raincoat. "I don't know," she said. "The seats must be wet. But that's impossible. The windows were rolled shut."

"Yeah, well, look at this," Rita said, lifting a strip of the Jaguar's roof. "It's in ribbons."

The edges felt fairly ragged, as if the wounds had been made with a dull knife. Rita said so. Claire didn't speak at all, but, like Rita, ran her fingers along the narrow strips. "Come on," Rita said. "We'll drive to the police station. We'll get a little wet, but what the hell, it's only rain." She started to get back into the car.

But by this time Rita's eyes had adjusted to the lack of light. "Oh, wait a minute," she said. "Look. They got the seats, too!"

Claire was squatting beside the Jaguar, feeling at the upholstery. Rita wondered what was going through her mind. What a shitty introduction to city life, Rita thought. "I'm really sorry," she told Claire. The car's roof was canvas, but the seats were leather and would cost a fortune to replace.

"It doesn't matter," Claire answered, her voice very breathy. She climbed in and stared straight ahead and waited for Rita to do the same. But she didn't drive to the police station, as Rita had expected. She drove to the Row.

"Aren't you going to report this?" Rita asked.

"I don't know."

"What about insurance?" Rita reminded.

"Oh, yes," Claire said, sounding vague.

"Look, why don't you come in for a minute," Rita offered, "and have some wine."

"No," Claire said, "I just want to get a few things . . ."

"And what? Drive back to Virginia?" She was afraid this had scared Claire that thoroughly.

"No," Claire said, "not there."

Rita thought about asking where, but decided not to. "Well," she asked, "do you want me to come in with you? To your place?"

"No," Claire said, "really. I'll be fine."

Rita might have prodded more, but the instant she was out of the car she heard her telephone ringing. Sin! she thought. And—a wonderful sign—on the very same night they'd met. "Okay," she said, fumbling with her keys and quite forgetting Claire and the Jaguar.

But it wasn't Sin at all. Far from it. It was Margaret on the telephone, weeping.

Please, not tonight, Rita wanted to say, though she didn't. She had had the weeps herself too many times to do that. Even if Rita didn't go in for wee-hours phone calls, she had certainly felt like it often enough.

But the call from Margaret was exasperating. Margaret didn't say a word, only cried and cried and cried. Finally Rita told her just to hang up, she'd come right upstairs.

Why me? Rita wondered. And why now? A little more than an hour ago her whole life seemed to have been tumbling into place. Then she'd run into Claire and that car business. And now, to spoil everything even more, she had Margaret to contend with.

She went to the refrigerator for a bottle of wine to take up with her, but then remembered that Margaret wouldn't drink it. She took the wine for herself, but snatched a couple of tea bags, too.

Rita smelled the liquor, though. It seemed that she could smell it right through Margaret's door. "Oh, for Christ's sake," she said, wondering why she was so pissed about Margaret drinking. "I brought tea for you," she said, holding up the bags. "But what the hell? Have wine." She went into Margaret's kitchen, couldn't find any glasses, and came back with cups.

Margaret shook her head; she didn't want any.

"What happened?" Rita asked.

Margaret started to sit in one of those secondhand-store chairs of hers. Rita yanked a box of tissues out from under her just before she squashed it. There were a lot of used tissues, all balled up, on the floor, especially near the telephone. "I never thought you'd get home," Margaret sniffled.

"Well," Rita said, "I did," handing her the box and, when she didn't take it, stuffing it into her lap.

That started Margaret crying all over again.

"Come on," Rita said. "I'll make you some tea." She went into the kitchen and put the kettle on. "You're just drunk," she called out, and then she started laughing.

"It's not funny!" Margaret shouted. Shouting made her cough. Coughing made her jump up and run to the bathroom. She did manage, though, to shut the door.

Eventually Rita knocked on it. "You finished?" No answer. "Hey, did you throw up?" Rita opened the door and crouched down beside her, stroking her shoulders, her hair. "Hey," she said, "it had to happen sooner or later, you know?" Margaret tried to holler again, but she couldn't get a single word out. *Oh boy,* Rita thought, but she went on patting until she was pretty sure that nothing more would come up.

"It's so embarrassing," Margaret gasped.

It's no picnic for me either, Rita thought. But what she said was "No, it's okay. Come on. You're sobering up or you wouldn't have said that. It's fine." The kettle was whistling in the other room, and Rita didn't know whether to leave Margaret there and take it off or what. Take it off. "I'll be right back," she said, running in to make the tea.

Margaret was in the living room by the time it was ready. "I don't want any," she said. "It will make me sick again."

Rita sipped and wondered what would happen now. *Puking I can take,* she thought, *but please, no more crying.* "So, who got you drunk?" Jay, Rita guessed.

"Jessie," Margaret said. "But she didn't get me drunk. I got drunk. And oooh." She was off again.

Jessie? And oooh? What could it be with Jessie that rated an oooh? For a very fleeting moment, Rita was afraid. "What's this 'oooh' part?" she asked, picking up the tissue box again and tossing it back into Margaret's lap.

"It's what I did. What I did after."

Rita felt like Perry Mason. "And what *did* you do?" she asked.

"I . . . I . . ."

Rita leaned forward, nodding the way Rosenberg always did, encouraging her to speak.

"I . . . I . . . oooh . . ." More crying.

Rita leaned back and waited. Margaret got up and paced around the room. She was barefoot but still wearing one of her A-lines with a matching sweater. "Margaret, goddammit," Rita said, having run through all her techniques for extracting information.

"All right," Margaret said, as if afraid that if she didn't, Rita would leave. "I called him. I called him and I told him everything. I told him . . . oh my God!" She was screaming again, this time like someone out of *Marat-Sade.* She clapped her hands against her temples and squeezed. Her eyes bugged out, red-rimmed.

"Hey." Rita got up and hugged Margaret, swaying with her, shushing her, letting Margaret drip tears all over her new silk blouse. She eased her back into the chair again. "You told him what? Come on. You'll feel better." Could she have found out about Jay? Ha! That would fix him!

"I told him I loved him," Margaret said. "I told him I would make him a home. A better home than *she* ever could. I told him how I'd always pictured that, not just working in his office, but making him a home."

Oh shit! Was Margaret talking about the Senator?

80

"And," she continued, "I told him that I daydreamed about the way it would be. How everytime he went to some reception, I would go down the guest list and read the names, 'General and Mrs.' and 'Ambassador and Mrs.,' and I would make sure it just said Senator Aubrey Denton. Make sure he went there by himself. And how sometimes I'd picture my name there. 'Senator Aubrey Denton and Miss Margaret Speidel,' and how sometimes I'd imagine more than that. 'Senator and Mrs. Aubrey Denton,' and . . ." Her eyes shut and she caught her breath, as if she'd remembered something even worse, although what could be worse, Rita couldn't imagine.

Rita was thinking, *Maybe she didn't call him. Maybe she's just so drunk she thinks she did. Maybe she got a wrong number.* Hadn't Claire said something about taking him to the airport?

"And I told him how I always dreamed about taking him home. Driving up my street with him, with my parents and all the neighbors watching. And how they'd all say they knew it would happen, they knew it all along." She looked at Rita then.

"Where did you call him?" Rita asked.

"At his hotel in Philadelphia."

Rita thought, *Oh crap.* She wished she could pull it off, tell Margaret, Hey, no sweat. Happens every day of the week. But she couldn't. She settled for "Well, what did he say?"

"Oooh." Margaret was crying again.

"That bastard! What did he say?"

"Oh, Rita, he was wonderful. He asked me if I'd been drinking, and I said yes. And he said—he even called me his little darling—he said, 'Just go to bed, little darling, and in the morning it'll be all right.' And he said I wasn't even to think about it again, and he wouldn't either." She sniffled and tried to smile.

"Did he say anything about your job?" Rita asked. Margaret nodded yes. "Well, what did he say?"

"He said—oh, it was like a little pep talk—he said, 'Now you just forget that all this foolishness took place, do you hear? When I get back to the office, it'll be business as usual.' " Margaret made a staunch face, unconsciously, when relaying his words. She deepened her voice, too. It made the whole thing sadder in Rita's eyes. Margaret went on. "I made him promise not to tell, and he did. He promised."

Not bad, Senator, Rita thought. Not bad at all. "There," she told

Margaret, "you see?"

"He's coming back next week. When he looks at me, I'll die."

"Okay. So you'll look for another job. And meanwhile, you'll take your vacation and your sick leave or something and you won't be there when he gets back. You'll do something, Margaret, you'll be all right. It isn't the end of the world."

"I had to call him," Margaret said. "I had to."

"Maybe you could even move to another city," Rita said. "Some place glamorous, like Waikiki."

Margaret wasn't listening. "I knew it when I copied down that number," Margaret said.

Rita carried the cups back into the kitchen and rinsed them. When she came out, Margaret had her head on the arm of the chair, nearly asleep. "Good," Rita said, picking up an afghan and draping it over Margaret's shoulders. She let herself out, and tiptoed back to her own place.

I'm sane, she thought. *But if I don't get off the Row soon, who knows what I'll be?*

Jessie took her clothes off and put her nightgown on quickly, revolted by the idea of her own body. Her flesh felt slacker than it usually did, as though her skin were making some special effort to pull free of the bone.

It was Margaret who had made her feel this way, Margaret with her pathetic yearnings and confessions. She would never have suspected Margaret. Faye, yes. Claire, yes. But never Margaret!

What man the Senator's age, or the age of the man Faye had chosen, what man Edward's age would not be flattered and succumb? The men were not to blame. It was the women, the young, firm-bodied women who led them, tempted them.

What was Jessie, at fifty, to do?

No one on the Row had ever asked her age, but if they had, she'd have told them. They didn't ask at the store, either, but there they at least speculated about it.

She had overheard them once—Megan, who was Jessie's assistant, and a trainee sent in from one of the branches.

Megan had outlined two camps: those who thought Jessie closer to forty, but with much exposure to wind and sun, and those who thought her nearer sixty, but with eye lifts and face lifts and wrinkle tucks and perhaps a chemical peel.

Jessie always imagined what it would have been like had she stepped from behind the display materials and told them. She decided not to. Decided that they, and Megan particularly, would be mortified. Or had she decided to stay back there and hear the rest of what they had to say?

"You have to admit," Megan said, "she is rather striking." Striking. It was a word Jessie had often heard before.

Her hair was gray and cropped close, like a man's. Her face was slender, but not drawn. The wrinkles were there, but not visible from a distance—across an aisle, say. Nor were the wrinkles deep, not even those that ran straight up from her upper lip. Jessie's eyes were gray, too, and she made the most of them, lining them carefully each morning with kohl and sometimes with a deep mauve shadow. She was the sort of woman who could have worn a turban well, though Jessie was never seen in a hat of any sort.

"Striking, yes," the trainee said, "but I think a little . . . severe?"

"In appearance only," Megan said. "She's a real lamb to work with. You'll see."

"That's not what *I* heard," the trainee said, and Megan laughed.

"Oh, the Johnston story. He was a total moron, you see. She was right to get rid of him. His idea of a spring display was hyacinths in little foil-wrapped pots."

Jessie was relieved to hear the trainee laugh with Megan. You could never tell about trainees. Some, like Megan, had the knack, spark, gift, whatever. Others, like Johnston, were better off gone.

"You should have seen Jessie's face, too, when he presented his ideas." Megan must have done a fair imitation of it, because the trainee squealed with glee. "After that, she just ignored him. We all did, all of us pretending that he wasn't even there. Jessie would sketch on her pad, and we'd all lean forward to see, everyone except Johnston, who knew he'd had it. And, in fact, he didn't even get through the day! Jessie went right out after the meeting and called upstairs and it was good-bye Johnston, just like that."

"Suppose she does that to me?" the trainee said.

"Are you kidding? After Johnston, they're really careful who they send, believe you me."

"I know, but I'm always . . . well, it's one thing to come up with a few good ideas, but to keep coming up with them, the way she does, year after year after year."

". . . After year after year after year," Megan continued, though, strangely, it was not unkind. And then they left the area, went back onto the floor.

Year after year after year.

That was what it had become.

Writing a check or a memo, Jessie would suddenly wonder, *What year is it?* Would have to think hard about it, sometimes would come to the brink of asking someone and then remember, with a start, that it was 1982. Such a little while ago it had been 1972. Or 1962. She would be stunned, too, by the birth dates of some of the people around her. Megan, for instance, had been born in 1959.

And everyone looked so young. The trainee whom Jessie had overheard with Megan. She had seemed a child. Yet later Jessie learned that the girl was married, had children!

That hadn't been possible in Jessie's day. Then a woman chose. It was either a husband *or* a career. Then, too, they'd still used the term *old maid.* Jessie was content with it.

At thirty-six, it had seemed worth it to Jessie. At thirty-six, she was offered a job at The Tailored Woman. The whole store, eight floors in all, with six calling for displays. Twelve exterior windows. She'd walked around the building and counted them before going inside. And she'd have—they didn't call it a staff in those days—a crew.

Edward Moring headed the Pittsburgh branch. Jessie could still remember his office, the size and sweep of it, the leather-and-wood smell of it, the way the sunlight fell behind his desk in the morning and across the room at day's end. She could remember the deep wine color of the rug, and the way her heels sounded *click-click-click* until she gained it and then didn't sound at all.

She remembered especially the way Edward had looked up at her from his papers the day she'd arrived. The way he stood and came around the desk and toward her.

He was forty-eight, divorced. The whole store buzzed about it, especially the girls who worked behind the counters, girls right out of high school, not cheap-looking, exactly, but girls he'd never have been seen with, whatever their fevered imaginings.

They all seemed to know so much about him, talked about it endlessly, about how he had lived in Sewickley, where his wife and children had stayed on—the younger children, anyway. About his apartment in town, the meals that he took at the Duquesne Club, and so on.

They'd talk about him in the ladies' room, over the row of sinks where they all stood, primping, combing their hair.

"I don't think he ever goes out." Pause to place a bobby pin.

"No, well, whenever would he? It seems like he's always here."

"The divorce must have been her idea. I guess he's taking it pretty hard."

"I'll bet he is. She's the one with the money, from what I hear."

"Well, he doesn't seem about to look in my direction, and don't think I haven't given it the old college try."

They talked as though Jessie were invisible. Perhaps, at thirty-six, she had been. She would sometimes look in the mirror just to assure herself that she was not.

Then one day Jessie was on the telephone trying to locate a rolltop desk for one of the displays. "I don't want to buy it," she kept telling dealer after dealer. "I want to use it, just *use* it. Well, never mind, and thank you," hanging up and thinking about tossing her pencil like a dart, but holding on to it instead, bashing out the point against the pad and then having to sharpen it anew.

Edward walked in just as she was readying for another call. "What *is* it?" he asked.

Jessie didn't even stop to think that it was Edward Moring, she just let loose about how stupid it was, how stupid everyone was, and how if she wanted to buy a damn rolltop she'd buy one, but she couldn't spend hours on end having it sanded and fixed up and an already fixed-up one would put her way over budget, and why couldn't some antiques dealer simply lend the store one? It was a small enough thing to ask, and what sort of harm could come to a rolltop desk anyway, behind glass in a store window?

"If you'll just calm down," he said, "I can get you a desk. . . ."

"I've seen your desk," Jessie said, "and it won't do. What I need is—"

He stopped her. "I heard you. And I know where there is one. In this very store. Trust me."

"Here?"

He nodded. "In Shipping. I've been trying to decide how to get it out of there and into my apartment, and actually, you've solved the problem, because it will go from Shipping to your display, and then . . ."

"Ah," Jessie said.

"I know what you're thinking. That I'm stealing it. In a way, I guess I am, but can you imagine if I try to find some legal way of doing it? Seven board meetings and five independent appraisals and then a deadlock when they try to amend the bylaws to cover the situation."

They laughed together at the thought of it. "Why did you come here?" she asked him. "To my office, I mean." He'd never been there before.

"I overheard my secretary talking to your secretary about the nervous breakdown you were having over a rolltop desk. And I thought, 'The bugger has discovered it! She's stealing my desk!' " He shook his fist, but clearly in jest. "Now. Should we have a drink? To celebrate my solving your problem and your solving my mine?"

"Is it time for a drink?" Jessie hadn't any idea. When working, she often lost track of time.

"I'd say so. We closed more than an hour ago."

"Oh," Jessie said. "Well, there's something I still have to check. If you don't mind waiting. Or . . . if you'd like to come along."

"Fine. And after that we'll go out by way of *our* desk."

They took the metal fire stairs, and Jessie still remembered the counterpoint of their footsteps, hers and his. "Where are you taking me?" he asked when they'd gone three flights.

"Oh, you'll make it." Jessie was surprised to hear herself tease him. "It's much harder going up."

"Do you always take the stairs?" he asked.

"Yes, always."

They walked through the darkened aisles until they came to the display Jessie wanted to see.

"What's this?" Edward asked.

"A yard," she told him. "Not finished, but getting there."

A portion of the carpeted floor had been raised, and bricks had been set down in a herringbone pattern. Two sides were fenced with thick wood slats, slats painted over and over again so that a multiplicity of colors showed through where the paint had peeled. "The crew really moaned about this. About getting it to peel this way," Jessie said.

"Wicker!" He sat in one of the chairs.

"Wicker and chintz," Jessie told him. "And there'll be flowers, real ones, pots and pots of them. And, naturally, mannequins in Tailored Woman clothing."

"Say," he said, "forget the desk, for now. Let's have our drink here. I'll go up to my office and I'll be back down in a flash."

"All right. I'll wait for you," Jessie said, settling deep into the plump chintz cushions. "But hurry. Take the elevator."

And while he was gone, everything changed for Jessie, everything that she wanted changed. While he was gone, she imagined herself married, imagined waiting for Edward, married.

When he came back, he pulled his chair closer to hers before sitting in it. He gestured at the yard. "What inspired this?" he asked.

"I don't know," Jessie said, looking at him steadily over the glass he had handed her. "What inspires anything? Something you remember, or something you see, or dream."

That was the beginning. Jessie wouldn't think about the end.

PART
FOUR

LATE MARCH

Claire stood near the glass-encased booth at the parking garage of the Madison Hotel, aware that her riding garb was drawing the attention of every downtown passerby. She'd spent much of the night at the Madison, and now would drive to the stable in Potomac where Illuminating had been boarded.

That, and all else that had happened, conspired to make her think of Steve.

Naturally she thought of Steve this morning when she was getting dressed to ride, stretching the thin white breeches along her legs and hips and pulling her tall black boots on with metal boot hooks. She always wore breeches when she rode, and at first Steve had laughed at her for not wearing jeans.

But he liked her in breeches, she knew—knew from the way he eyed the outline of her panties beneath them and from the way he would swat her behind. In the beginning he liked to watch her put her breeches on, would sit on the bed and watch, sometimes pretending to roll a cigarette, but watching even then.

She had bought him breeches and boots, too, and he wore them, though never with a proper shirt. He preferred either a T-shirt with the flimsy sleeves rolled up so that it was almost sleeveless, or no shirt at all. He'd even gone to the Foxcroft show dressed that way— no, worse: in a T-shirt with its bottom half ripped away, his whole midsection revealed. Except for that, he had acted just fine, and Foxcroft had worried her, because there she'd see everyone she knew. But he was deferential, almost, the towel that he used to rub the horses draped over his shoulder and the crop that he used tucked straight up in his boot. *Let them talk.* He had the horses gleaming, and the saddlery, too. He held the horses while she mounted and was waiting for her outside the ring when she finished each ride.

"You get us a little trophy here, babe, and then you'll get the real trophy when we get home," he told her under his breath. She was so excited, she barely heard the little bell that called her to enter the ring, but Steve heard it and stepped away from the horse so that she would gather up the reins and trot into the clipped green rectangular arena to give her salute. "You put your cunt down on that horse and you ride it," he said with that grin of his, and she didn't even look around to see if anyone was listening. She got the trophy, of course.

He was good with the horses, good with her, good with the car.

The car. Finally she heard it spiraling up the hotel ramp and toward her. The roar of its engine was heightened by the concrete walls. The attendant made its tires scream. He didn't seem to notice that the leather on the seats was slashed, and, of course, the tattered roof was down and therefore out of sight. Claire tipped him and slid behind the wheel.

The Jaguar threatened to stall whenever Claire had to come to a stop, so she was glad to leave the traffic behind and gain the Capital Beltway. She would have to have the timing readjusted, she thought. Steve had tuned it to be driven fast on winding, cambered blacktop roads, not in the city, not stop and go. She had let him take the car whenever he pleased, and she'd supplied the gas, too, letting him fill up from the pump down by the stables. *Let him drive it God-knows-where and with God-knows-who beside him.* She had found prophylactics in the glove box, but she suspected he had put them there on purpose, knowing that she'd find them, knowing what she'd think. She left them there as if she'd never seen them at all.

The man last night had used a prophylactic. He had carried it in his wallet as a teenaged boy might. He had been rough, but not purposefully. Only through lack of finesse.

She'd gone with him to a cheap hotel where the air was thick with the smell of artificial blossoms. She imagined those nasty cardboard room deodorizers, the sort that Harnette had hung in the bathrooms once, to Mother's dismay. She could still remember her mother cutting each of the cardboard blossoms down, Harnette's palms upturned to catch them. "I didn't spend none of your money on them," Harnette had pleaded. "I bought 'em myself."

The man had offered Claire money, and she'd laughed at him. He misunderstood, offered even more. "Here, take it, you're worth it, worth plenty. Here. I can see you've got class."

Her breasts felt like cardboard beneath his hands. Claire had closed her eyes to try to think of Steve or the cyclist, but couldn't, not with the man's hands upon her.

It was Aubrey who came to mind.

Aubrey, huge in the wicker pony cart, a present for her thirteenth birthday. Aubrey saying, "Here, little darling, let me show you how to steer this thing," and then hunching over behind her while she held the reins and the pony trotted smartly, pulling the cart back toward the pond and down through the orchards.

"I can do it," she said, squirming and trying to shrug Aubrey away because his hands were way too high, higher than they'd been when he was steering all by himself. So high they brushed against her breasts. Her breasts hadn't felt like cardboard then, they had ached even before Aubrey touched them.

"Don't," she said. She had learned many birthdays ago to make her bottom half go dead at Aubrey's touch. Now she'd have to do that to the top half, too.

"Don't what?" Aubrey asked her.

She concentrated on her breasts, and before long they didn't ache. They didn't feel like anything anymore. *Cardboard blossoms.*

During the entire drive, Claire's thoughts ricocheted this way, from last night's stranger, to Aubrey, to the cyclist, to Steve.

Illuminating.

She pulled into the parking area at the stables. She would, she reminded herself, find another *like* Steve. The point was to keep searching, everywhere, here. She leaned against the fender of the Jaguar to strap spurs on her long leather boots.

"Hello?" she called when she entered the stables, and a young woman emerged and looked at her quizzically. "I'm Claire Albritten. . . ."

"Oh yes!" the woman said. "We've talked on the telephone." She had an accent, British, the way so many horse people did. She ushered Claire to the aisle where Illuminating stood, the rich bay of his coat clipped and dappled and clean. "A shame you haven't been out to ride," the woman said, "but we've kept him very, very fit." She patted the horse's shoulder.

"He looks just fine," Claire said, walking from shoulder to haunch and examining him, waiting while another girl blacked the horse's hooves with a brush that she dipped into a little tin can.

Still another brought Claire's saddle and bridle. The leather, Claire noted, was dark and oiled, and all of the buckles and the bit had been polished to a deep shine. "Very nice," Claire said. "Thank you."

"We have a lot of help here, you see." The British woman smiled at her. "Our working-student program. We have girls from all over."

Claire nodded, taking the gloves she had tucked beneath her belt and pulling them on with some ceremony while the trio fussed with the girth and then the latches on the bridle.

"Will you be able to get out very often? From now on, I mean," the British woman asked.

Claire swung up into the saddle, adjusting the stirrup leathers. *Girls from all over.* It was not what Claire had in mind. "Unfortunately, I don't think so," she said.

"You needn't worry about him, then." The woman looked up at Claire only briefly before turning her attention to the horse again. She lapsed into something like baby talk. "You're one of our favorites around here, aren't you, big fellow? Aren't you, Illuminating."

Claire glanced at the mirrors along the long side of the arena. She could see the glass-walled gallery reflected in it, the gallery where five or six more girls had gathered to watch her ride.

The woman noticed this and seemed embarrassed. "I hope you don't mind, but so many of them have heard of you. Know that you've had very good instruction and whatnot."

Portugal, Germany, France, but all of it now seemed interim time, years spent waiting for Steve. "I don't mind," Claire said, and then she laughed. "My best instruction"—she leaned down toward the woman, as if to share a confidence—"came from an American cowboy. Of sorts."

Claire picked up the reins and backed the horse before pressing him forward, to remind him that her will would be enforced. She entered the long mirrored riding hall establishing the horse's rhythm. *You put your cunt down on that horse and ride.* She pushed Illuminating to brilliance.

Rita approached Claire's at the stroke of noon, having first walked through the alley to make certain that the Jag was there. Now she stood and noted the door, which was flush and made of a grayish wood. Centered at eye level was a large black knocker, a fox head. Rita lifted it and was impressed by its weight.

Eventually Claire appeared. "It was open," she said, standing aside so that Rita could pass. Her hair hung down behind, but she had swept the sides up, Alice in Wonderland fashion. She was wearing a leotard, its pink so pale it might have been white, white tights, pink slip-on ballet slippers. "I was doing my yoga," she said.

There was a second door, a tall, sheer panel of glass framed with the same wood as the outer door. "What is this?" Rita ran her hand along the grain. "God, it's beautiful."

"Weathered cypress," Claire told her.

Rita walked down the long bare hall and entered the room where she had seen Claire standing that night. It was just as it had been: the ladder, the rays of paint, the splendid mantelpiece. "Jesus," Rita said. "It's almost a shame to put anything else in here. Furniture and shit."

Claire agreed. "I know just what you mean. Come on, I'll show you the rest." She noticed Rita's camera. "I thought you weren't going to snap anything today," she reminded Rita.

"Actually, I'm not," Rita told her. "But I always carry this around when I'm looking. It sort of helps me see."

Claire nodded her head as if to say she understood, but her expression said she didn't.

"You kind of isolate what you want to get," Rita explained. "I know it sounds goofy, but it works. The whole business is goofy when you think about it. I mean, I see what's there. It's just there, for everybody. But it's like, I don't know, people would miss it if I didn't point it out. That's all I do. I just separate things out." Hey, Rita thought, there's my philosophical statement! She'd get Jay to make it sound a little fancier, and she'd try it on the next art director she came across.

Claire was wriggling into a pair of white cotton trousers. "Let me start by showing you my bathroom," she said. "That's pretty much finished." She led the way upstairs.

Rooms and more rooms, enormous, empty. In the one next to the bath, that spectacular bed! It was not set against a wall, but stood dead center in the room. Rita looked at it and whistled. She had seen it from a distance when it had been delivered.

"I had it sent from Spain," Claire said. "It's made of some sort of driftwood."

The wood had been bleached a milky white by the ocean and the sun. It seemed made of a thousand gnarls and twists, all of them reaching skyward. The tallest pieces were in the center of the headboard. Rita walked behind it and measured. "God, it's taller than I am! What do you call this kind of thing?

Claire shrugged. "Rustic, I suppose."

"Rustic." Probably a thousand dollars' worth of rustic, Rita thought, eyeing the bed through her viewfinder and backing toward Claire's voice.

The bathroom had an anteroom, where Claire apparently dressed. Drawers and closets were built right into the walls. There was a long stainless-steel vanity with a huge mirror above it and a row of incandescent bulbs.

Draped across a bench was a fur coat, a long-haired many-pelted full-length something that trailed to the floor. Rita picked it up, holding the fluffy white fur against her face and tilting her head to the side to see if it became her.

"Lynx," Claire said. "I've got to get it into storage, but you know how it is. It'll be winter again before I get around to it." She took it from Rita and held it up so that Rita could slide her arms into the sleeves.

Rita did so, fluffing the silky hairs around her face and swirling once or twice. She took it off and put it back on the bench, very carefully. She patted it and then followed Claire into the bathroom.

There, the floor was made of glass block. There were lights beneath the block, Claire said, but now the room was daylit. A huge free-form window, rather like a comma, had been cut into the wall and filled with sparkling clear glass. The floor led to a tub of stainless steel, with steps leading down into it. There were whirlpool jets built into the side and a row of gadgets in lieu of faucets above.

There was a toilet and a bidet. And a magazine on the floor, the same *Washingtonian* Rita had seen Claire looking at in the drugstore. As soon as Claire saw Rita looking toward it, she picked the magazine up and carried it away.

Rita just walked along, into this room, then that one, up the staircase, down again, one door, another door. She was figuring light and angles through the eye of the camera. She heard Claire somewhere, and she turned, just a little turn, and—well, it was partly the lens, but it was partly Claire, too, smaller than small at the end of the tubular hallway, the light falling in bars across her slight body. And that look in her eyes, whew! Rita knew for sure it would disappear the minute she knew Rita was looking. She snapped it, hoping Claire wouldn't hear the shutter, hoping the camera was loaded. *Better be the right film, too,* she thought. The minute she'd done it, Rita looked up.

But Claire hadn't heard the sound. She was in a world that seemed impenetrable.

"Something interesting out there?" Rita asked, trying to sound casual.

"Just my car," Claire said.

Rita went to the window and peered down at the Jag. Claire had raised the roof so that, from this angle, each ugly gash was evident. The gashes were wider in some places than in others, and some looked, now, to have been made in a frenzy.

The whole thing about the car gave Rita the creeps to start with, but now seeing the way Claire was looking at it made matters worse. Did Claire get off on the notion of being victimized? Or had Rita misread Claire's expression? *I've got to get out of here,* Rita thought. *I've got to see this film. See if any of this exists.*

But Rita couldn't just leave. She had to force herself to stay for a little while longer at least.

"I'll pour the champagne," Claire said. "You just come down when you're ready."

Rita entered the kitchen just seconds after Claire had popped the cork. She saw froth all over the bottle, all over Claire's hands. Claire was giggling, as if she'd already had some of it.

"I'm so bad at this," Claire said. She reached for the glasses and got the stems all bubbly. "I have some things to show you," Claire said as she poured. "The sort of thing I'd like to do eventually." She gestured at a box of pages torn from magazines. "You can help me decide," she told Rita.

Rita reached into the box and began to go through it. There was an Allmilmo kitchen where even the faucets were white. Another ad showed a shimmery Miramar table. Some icy marble things. An article on Alessandro. "What's this thing of yours with white?" she asked.

"Oh, I don't know. Everyone's going back to colors, but white seemed right somehow. Fresh and newborn."

The wooden floor where the bed was, Rita remembered, had been painted white. "Yeah," Rita said, "you're right. Fresh and newborn." She'd have to remember that when she tried to peddle her pictures. She guzzled her champagne and was instantly dizzy. "Oh no," she said. "I can't afford to get high. Not in the middle of the day."

Claire laughed at that.

"I think I've seen everything I need to see," Rita said, turning down a second glass. "Just make sure you don't do any fixing up before I come back, okay?"

"Won't touch a thing," Claire promised.

LeGrande turned his regular walk into a strut, a strut he'd seen on one of those television programs, but he couldn't remember which one. He really had Claude going now, but he had held out just as long as he could.

"So come on, niggah"—Claude was starting to get pissed now—"you gonna tell me or what?"

They were almost at LeGrande's house anyway, and LeGrande felt as though he just might burst with it. "Well, first off," he said, "it's that Albritten lady, the one with the blonde hair and the fancy car and all? That Albritten lady, she like me."

"Oh yeah, I can believe that, boy," Claude answered, so elaborately that LeGrande couldn't possibly miss the fact that Claude didn't believe it one tiny bit.

Claude was a good ten years older than LeGrande. It seemed to LeGrande that Claude had always been on the street. Claude hung around. Hung around the pool hall over in Northeast, hung around the Market, hung around the Row. He always had money. Never a lot, but enough. No one knew where it came from, but then, no one ever asked, either.

Claude talked about Vietnam all the time, trying to make it seem as though he'd been there, but LeGrande knew better. Claude had never been—and wasn't going—anywhere.

"No shit, I'm telling you, she stop me on the street, and she's wearing these here boots come up to her knees, and these white pants that fit her like *skin*. No shit, Claude, and she gives me one of those great big smiles . . ." He was smiling pretty wide himself, just remembering it.

"You crazy, LeGrande? White ladies always smile like that. It don't mean nothing. You crazy if you think she got the hots for you just 'cause she smiled."

"Nobody said nothing about no hots," LeGrande said. "I say she *like* me. And she do, you wait and see. She ask me to work for her. She didn't ask *you* to work for her, she ask *me*."

"If she ask you, she prob'ly gonna ask me," Claude said.

"Sure. She gonna have every nigger in the world in there working on her house, is that what you think?"

They passed an empty beer can and kicked it, from habit. First Claude, then LeGrande, then Claude again. Finally, Claude said, "So what she ask you to do?"

"She didn't say, exactly. She said 'odd jobs.' She need someone for 'odd jobs.' So I figure, maybe a little plumbing, and I told her, like, how I helped put the bathroom in for Mama and all, and she say, 'That's real wonderful, LeGrande,' she used my name and all. And she say the plumbers she had, they didn't do such a great job, and how there was this leak already coming out of her bathroom and how maybe I could fix it."

"I can see you fixin' it," Claude said. "I can see you fixin' it good."

He was sorry he had told Claude. "Look, motherfucker. If I do a good job for her, no telling. She can recommend me to some other people. I could get lots of jobs that way, one right after the other."

"Yeah, *if* you do a good job."

LeGrande kicked the can so hard, it sailed way out of Claude's range. He was sorry he hung around with Claude, because Claude pulled him down this way, every chance he got. Whenever he had plans of any kind, Claude pulled them right down. "Hey, look, my man, maybe she *will* ask you. Or maybe, if she don't, I can *ask* her to ask you."

"I don't do no 'odd jobs,' " Claude said. "Not for rich white ladies. No matter how tight what they wearin' is."

That really riled LeGrande. "Oh, that's right, brother," he said. "I forgot. I forgot that you gonna jiveass your fucking life away."

"Least I don't get all excited and think some white chick got a *thing* for me just 'cause she smile and ask me to fix her baf'room."

"I didn't say she had a *thing,* Claude. I didn't say she had a *thing.* I say she like me. But if you think she has a *thing,* then maybe you know somethin' I don't. Maybe she does have a thing for me. Damn!" He strutted real good, strutted like a fucking parade, strutted to get even with Claude. "Damn, I bet she does have a thing for me. Like, maybe when I said plumbing she thought I meant something else. Like, maybe what she thought I meant was her. Maybe what she really wants is for me to work on her. What you think about that, Claude? What you think about that, baby?" But LeGrande started laughing at himself because the whole idea was pretty damn stupid, and pretty soon Claude was laughing right along.

"Probably wants you to do it to her with a monkey wrench," Claude said. "Or a *screw*driver."

"Yeah, man, a *tool,*" LeGrande said, but he didn't really like this kind of talk too much. Talking about her the other way, like about how tight her pants were, that was one thing. But the kind of talk Claude did, that was something else. And also, LeGrande kept having to look up at the upstairs window all the time to make sure his mama wasn't up there listening. If she was and if she heard what he and Claude were saying, *whooo-wheee!* "Hey, come on, come on," he said. "Keep it down, all right? I got enough trouble."

"Yeah, you got trouble all right," Claude said. "This honky chick got a thing for you, then you know you got trouble."

"Claude, I didn't say— Hey, look, I got to go inside."

"Yeah, you goin' inside all right," Claude howled. "I can see you goin' *inside*."

"You got some kind of filthy mind, Claude," LeGrande said. "If you see me talking to her, don't you say nothin', you hear me?" Claude just might, just to mess everything up. He was like that, always going too far. There was no stopping him sometimes.

Claire sat on the chaise in her dressing room and waited for the telephone to ring. She glanced at her watch at least three times in the space of a minute. Any time now, *any time now*, he would call.

She had answered four of the ads in the *Washingtonian*. Four of the hundred or so that she'd read. Each of her replies had been addressed to a box number at the magazine, and to each she'd sent only her phone number.

One hadn't responded at all, one had been boring—in fact, if his voice hadn't been so different from Aubrey's, it might have *been* Aubrey she was talking to. The third had called only once, but ah, the fourth!

He tried to tell her his name, but she halted him. "No, don't," she said. "I want to think of you as my mystery man." He had understood. He had never brought up the business of names again.

He had asked, of course, to meet her. Claire made a game of it. She told him he would have to stalk her, find her. She would supply the clues.

Her first clue had been a nursery rhyme. "Mary, Mary, quite contrary," she singsonged into the phone.

He interrupted her. "I already know that about you, doll."

And Claire had laughed with him, though, in truth, she couldn't wait to give out the last line—such a good clue—about the "pretty maids all in a row."

The waiting was intolerable. She would have to occupy herself.

She spread her lynx coat on the floor and used it as a mat while she did her yoga, bending, stretching, trying to calm herself with long, deep breaths.

She had just arched into a fully extended cobra when the phone call came.

She forced herself to rise slowly, as if she hadn't been waiting at all. She balanced on the edge of the driftwood bed and answered the phone on the third ring. "Hello," she said, giving her voice an extra, breathy edge.

He asked what she had been doing when he called. She tried to think of a sexy answer, but couldn't. "The cobra," she said. She was about to add that it was a yoga posture, but decided not to.

"Cobra, huh?" He sucked his breath in; Claire could hear him. "I've got a cobra," he told her. "Guess where."

Clare couldn't answer. She could only lean back, close her eyes, and imagine it.

He went on, the cadence of his voice suggesting chant. He told her where the cobra was and how it had risen up to find her. "This is a long, black cobra, doll. Long, black cobra, looking for you."

"Oooh," Claire said. "Will it get me?"

"When you least expect it. This cobra will rise right up and strike you dead."

"Maybe I'll escape," Claire said.

"Uh-uh. Uh-uh, doll. See, this cobra will come in while you sleep and wind around your legs and your arms. Wind around your wrists. Ankles. Around your neck. You won't be able to escape."

His words made her shiver, as though, indeed, she'd felt the cool, dry scales of a serpent sliding across her body. Claire moved the telephone cord back and forth across her thigh. Then she spread her legs and let it snake between them.

Neither she nor her mystery man spoke. The connection hissed. Claire was dizzy with it, coiling her body, pulling on the thin, white cord.

Then, stupidly, he asked what she was wearing.

Claire sat upright, snapped the cord against the floor as if it were a whip. Then she spun the cord, listening to the swoop of it in the air. "Silver bells and cockle shells," she said. She flexed her wrist to crack the cord again.

"I'd like to come over and see for myself," he said.

"I've just given you another clue," she told him. "It's up to you to find me. I don't want to make it too easy for you."

"Yeah, doll. I bet you don't."

Aubrey Denton walked down the long, dimly lit corridor toward the sound of a lone typewriter rat-tat-tatting at an impressive rate of speed. In his hand was a letter-sized manila envelope. It was addressed to Claire, care of his office.

He had found the envelope, unopened, in a pile that had been stacked for his perusal. It was the annual spring housecleaning that his staff made, during which time even he was expected to wade through accumulated folders and letters and things in order to throw away anything that wasn't absolutely necessary.

When he first came upon the envelope, he'd run his finger across Claire's name and felt his heart quicken. He hadn't spoken to her since that day at Dulles when she'd told him that she planned to move into the house on the Row.

When he reviewed the conversation they'd had that night, there was nothing he could recall to justify the feeling that he had—that she was somehow warning him away. And yet, the feeling was sufficiently strong to have kept him from contacting her.

He knew she had a phone. He'd called Information and recorded her new listing. He simply hadn't used it, knowing—not just suspecting, but *knowing*—that if he called, she would reject him.

Now, though, he'd found a piece of mail to deliver. He'd sat at his desk with his hand on the telephone. But instead of calling, he'd yielded to a premonition and opened the envelope. He could always tell her he'd found it that way.

But whatever fear he'd felt when Claire announced her intention of living on the Row paled when the Senator read the photostats of the newspaper articles that were inside. They told of a murder, right there, in the very house he had all but forced Claire to buy. His eyes raced over the details. Words, some quite alarming, jutted from the page: *Faye Arensberg . . . puncture wounds . . . blood . . . prior to death . . . cigarette burns . . . hands tied . . .*

He read the dates and realized he'd been out of the country when the girl's death occurred and so hadn't known. He forced the papers back inside the envelope just to get them out of sight, but his hands felt clammy and his collar seemed suddenly much too tight.

Then he'd started down the hall toward the sound of the typewriter. Toward Margaret Speidel's office.

He tried to imagine how he would confront Margaret. What would he do, for instance, if she denied having sent for these? But who else could it be? Wasn't it Margaret who had cause to be jealous of Claire? Hadn't she said so the night she'd called him at his hotel in Philadelphia? *I'd be better for you,* she'd said, crying so pathetically, *better for you than Claire Albritten*—and she'd said Claire's name with such venom, too—*would ever ever be.* And wasn't Margaret also, by virtue of living on the Row, the only one in the office who would know about an event such as the Arensberg murder?

Ah, but wait. Why would Margaret have used Claire's name? Why wouldn't she simply have ordered these materials from the library using her own name? It couldn't be Margaret, and at any rate, the girl had quite gone back to normal after that call. But alas, he was knocking on Margaret's office door when this realization came to him. But who, then? If not Margaret, who?

"Yes?" Margaret said it pleasantly, but covered her mouth as if she'd said something awful when she saw who it was. Her face reddened. Her office seemed a great deal smaller, too small. Margaret stood as if to flee.

The Senator shook his head at her, and waved his hand, too, to stay her. "It's all right," he said, realizing that he'd never come into her office before, nor had the two of them ever been alone.

"Really, Margaret, relax," he told her.

Margaret sat. He pulled a chair up to her desk and sat as well. "I have a slight problem," he said, "and I think you might be able to help me get to the bottom of it." He handed Margaret the envelope and watched her as she read Claire's name on its face.

104

She colored again, but her voice was calm. She handed the envelope back to him. "Does she often have her mail sent here?"

He could barely reply. He felt the same terror he'd felt when Claire had spoken to him in the airport. The same terror, in a highly exaggerated form, that he'd often felt with Claire. And complicating all of this was the icy realization that he'd never before admitted what he'd felt. Never before named it.

Yes, terror.

Oh, at first it seemed a harmless sort of thing, a tomboyishness and daring that set Claire apart from other women. When Claire was young, for instance, it was a matter of her always having to ride faster, jump bigger fences. Then, when she was driving, choosing cars made for speed—like her Jaguar, for instance. Now, however, it was *this,* and he was in large part responsible. He had found the house for her.

He looked at Margaret and was momentarily reassured by the matter-of-fact way she flipped through the stories about the Arensberg girl's death. "Why would she want these?" Margaret asked. "And why"—she flipped the envelope over and gestured at the date that the postage meter had imprinted—"would she have bought the house knowing all this?"

Aubrey took the envelope from her and read the date, automatically defending Claire as he did so. He would have to check the dates, but he was certain that Margaret was right. Claire had bought the house knowing.

Margaret sensed the Senator's need to vindicate Claire, however. She tried to appease him. "I could be wrong," she offered. "After all, Claire never *got* these articles, now did she?"

He looked at her blankly.

"What I mean is," she went on, "the articles are still here. Claire never picked them up. She might have asked for any and all information about the property and then forgotten the whole thing. She might have been expecting historical articles of some sort. . . ."

Margaret broke off, rather pleased with herself for coming up with such a reasonable explanation. The Senator, she could see, was struggling to believe it. But he was still not certain. He was still so—what? Pained. Margaret's heart went out to him. "I can see that you're still worried," she said, even going so far as to pat his sleeve. "And I have an idea. Someone who could keep an eye on Claire for you."

Jessie's office remained, at her request, separate from the others, in the old part of the store. Cobbled glass served to partition it off from the warehouse of display materials. Bolts of cloth were heaped on tables, as were sketches, rolls of graph paper, huge bound books of full-page newspaper ads. There was a dressmaker's dummy and a sewing machine, cans of paint and boxes of tools.

Senator Aubrey Denton was not quite comfortable here. It seemed everywhere he tried to lean he threatened something. Finally, he suggested that he and Jessie go to a coffee shop down the street.

Jessie might have taken him through the warehouse and down the seldom-used back stairs. Instead, she led him through the corridor connecting the old building with the new. On the way to the elevator they passed Megan's office and scores of others before she led him through the bustle of shoppers on the main retail floor.

Jessie could not help but think of Edward Moring, of the stir he'd caused among The Tailored Woman employees whenever he came to her office to solicit her opinion or to take her to lunch or just to talk.

But the Senator made her think of Edward in other ways, too. Oh, not specifically of Edward, but of the yearning that Edward had aroused in her.

Jessie had met Aubrey Denton more than a year before Claire Albritten had come to the Row. She remembered it all too clearly.

She'd been dining at Chinoiserie, a restaurant on M Street in Georgetown, alone, as usual. She'd looked up when a rather large party came in, drawn by their laughter, their jovial conversation. The Senator, apparently, had invited his entire staff to dinner, and Margaret was among the group.

Margaret spotted Jessie at once and stood on tiptoe to whisper something to her employer. Jessie flushed when she saw him looking at her. He was far more attractive than his television appearances had led her to believe.

Before Jessie could adequately protest, Aubrey Denton had taken

106

her arm, saying, "Well, of course you'll join us. I insist." Jessie could still feel the thrill in yielding to his looming presence, to his confidence, his maleness. It was all against her better judgment, certainly, but judgment receded entirely, and yield she did.

They sat at a long, white-clothed table. Jessie was directly to the Senator's right. The staff talked, naturally, about things that Jessie had no knowledge of, but each time a new subject was raised Aubrey Denton would lean toward her to give an encapsulated account that enabled her to follow and even once or twice to join their conversation.

What Jessie recalled more than anything, however, was the rosy feeling that had washed over her whenever the Senator bent her way.

Toward the end of the meal, Jessie had feigned interest in some upcoming legislation, and Aubrey Denton had assured her, in what she had thought a particularly meaningful way, that he would be glad to provide further information on the matter.

For days afterward, Jessie waited for his call, or better yet, his visit.

And then the information came—via Margaret: several typed reports, a reprinted speech, and some newspaper articles.

Nonetheless, when he'd phoned today, Jessie's expectations began to balloon as though no disappointment had ever intervened.

"Miss, uh, Margaret Speidel," Aubrey Denton said, "my assistant . . ."

"Well, yes, of course, Senator," Jessie interrupted, largely to ease his obvious awkwardness. "It was she who suggested that I join you. At Chinoiserie. That night." *That night.* She felt so stupid, to have marked its importance that way.

A long silence preceded his reply. "Oh, yes. *Yes,*" he said, laughing with relief.

Then they chatted, briefly, about that restaurant and other, similar places. He wondered if she'd been to Lalibela. "Oh, but you must," he told her. "Ethiopian cuisine. It's marvelous."

Jessie did not even hope that he would ask to take her there. She was proud of herself for that. "Yes, I will. Now, then, if you'll just tell me what it was that you wanted. . . ."

His uneasiness returned. "It's rather personal," he said. "I think that we should talk. It's quite important."

"Now?" Jessie asked.

"If it's convenient."

"Certainly," Jessie had answered. "Just come up to Reception on the fourteenth floor. I'll tell them I'm expecting you."

Then Jessie had slipped down to cosmetics to buy a few things. She had spent a great deal of time applying them. She had just walked back to her office when Reception called to say that he had arrived.

Now, outside the store in the bright spring sunshine, she wondered if she'd applied the cosmetics too ambitiously. But the lighting was better, more flattering, in the coffee shop.

He toyed with the ear of the cream pitcher, and Jessie watched him. "This is," he said, "more complicated than I would have thought."

On the phone, he had begun by mentioning Margaret's name. Perhaps, Jessie speculated, remembering the night that Margaret had consumed all that Scotch, perhaps he'd unearthed the girl's romantic interest in him. It would, of course, mortify him. And so he would come to her. Because she knew Margaret. And because she, Jessie Wood Trotter, was not a girl but a woman, mature, and wise. She imagined herself soothing him. *Really,* she would say, *these silly young girls.*

Impulsively, Jessie reached across the table and touched his hand. It was, for her, an uncharacteristic gesture. But it served to end his reluctance.

He started by telling her that he had known Claire Albritten since she was a child. "A lovely child," he said, "as you might well imagine." He was thus more protective of her than he might otherwise be. "Particularly since Claire's mother was . . . is . . . a rather frivolous woman." He smiled in a way that let Jessie know he had understated the case. "Claire's father left, you see. Left them both when Claire was thirteen." That, he reasoned, was why Claire had always been aloof. "She's never been married," he added, as if that proved it.

Jessie waited patiently, sipping from her cup.

"I'm afraid . . . that house. I'm afraid that house is part of some . . . *impulse* that she has." He looked at Jessie and saw that she didn't understand. "I haven't explained myself very well at all. Let me ask you this: Were you aware . . . ? How long have you . . . ?

Jessie placed her cup back in its saucer. "Are you asking me about

108

the murder?" she said evenly. "About Faye Arensberg?"

He looked away. Yes, he nodded.

"What of it?" Jessie asked. "A lot of people live on the Row. Rita, your own assistant, Jay. . . ."

"In *that* house?" the Senator demanded.

"Well, no. That house was always a bit of a white elephant. It was bigger than the others. Even after they managed to rent the first floor to Faye, there was some question about whether or not the other floors would be rentable because there weren't separate entrances or even doors up there. None of that sort of thing had been done. The owners at that time had merely . . ."

He held up his hand to interrupt her. "Perhaps I should tell you the rest."

He looked so sorrowful, telling Jessie about the clippings he had found, about his speculations, about Margaret's.

"Ask Claire," Jessie suggested. "Ask her point-blank if she knew and what she's up to."

He smiled. "I could never simply ask her. You just don't know Claire."

"No, obviously, I don't. But in any case"—Jessie crumpled her napkin, reached for her handbag—"she's hardly a little girl anymore. Hardly in need of your . . . protection."

"Wait," he said. "I think she is, or might be. Oh, not in any formal way, but if you'd only watch her for me, tell me if she seems in any sort of . . ."

Jessie waited. When it seemed that he would never think of the word, she supplied it. "Danger?" she asked.

PART
FIVE

MID-MAY

"I can't believe that you don't know this," Rita told Rosenberg, who was groaning up what seemed the thousandth flight of the steep stone steps that led to the top of the Washington Monument.

"Don't know what?" he gasped, grabbing for the handrail and sinking so fast that for a minute Rita thought he was having a heart attack instead of just sitting down. Usually she was the one who had trouble keeping up.

"Don't you read?" Rita asked. "Exercise is what psychiatrists are supposed to prescribe for patients with depression."

"I can just see the practice I would have had. Better for me to give out drugs."

"Yaaaaaa-aaaaaah." A voice came toward them, a kid's voice rising around and past them and up and up and up. A second later the kid himself appeared, arms spread out like a plane's wings. He just about knocked Rita over when he whizzed by.

"Wise-ass!" Rita shouted after him.

"Overachiever!" Rosenberg added.

Rita sat down on the steps beside the old man.

"We're blocking traffic," Rosenberg told her.

"If traffic comes, I'll move, okay?"

But before they could talk, someone—the kid, probably—began rolling a pop bottle back and forth on the stone landing overhead. The sound was magnified by the setting, part ring and part rasp.

"Oh Christ," Rita said. "That noise goes right through me."

"Come on." Rosenberg got up and offered his hand. "We'll take the elevator down."

"With the tourists," Rita grumbled. The weather had warmed and the onslaught of visitors had begun.

He opened the thick metal door that led to the elevator. "What's wrong with that?" he asked her.

"Nothing. But their cameras depress me. Half of them have better cameras than I do."

"I see." Rosenberg pushed the button, and they both looked up to track the elevator's progress on the dial above.

"So what is this about depression?" Rosenberg asked her.

The elevator doors opened. The car was so full that Rita and Rosenberg couldn't even turn around to face front. They had to squish in, chests again a sea of Hawaiian shirts and sun visors.

"I can't believe your timing, Doctor," Rita muttered.

They didn't speak again until they were outside. Rosenberg went up to a vendor's stand and bought two orange drinks, handing Rita one.

"Thanks," she said. "Look, can we sit down on the grass or something? I really do want to talk."

"How about a bench?" he suggested. "The grass isn't so thick." He kicked at it. "Probably it has ants and bees."

"Maybe snakes too," Rita teased him. "Better yet, how about someplace air-conditioned?"

"My office is air-conditioned," he said. "My whole house is air-conditioned."

"I remember," Rita said. "But if I went there, then I *would* feel like a mental case. And anyway, you're retired, remember?"

They sat on the grass.

"So," Rita said. "Everything is falling apart. All around me, my whole life. I'm doing stuff, I'm trying to live like a normal, undepressed person," she went on, not noticing that he'd smiled, "but I'm telling you, it isn't working. Everything is not only falling apart, but everything, if you really want to know, is shit."

"For instance . . ."

"For instance last night." Rita's television set was in the repair shop and she'd called Jessie, just like old times, and asked if she could come over to watch a rerun of *The Starmaker*. "It's this thing with Rock Hudson and Suzanne Pleshette and Brenda Vaccaro, right? I missed it the first few times it was on. They were running both parts last night, too. Anyway, Jessie stayed out in the kitchen doing God knows what. Didn't come into the room the whole time."

"So is that part of the deal?" Rosenberg asked. "If *you* watch television, *she* has to watch television?"

"No," Rita said. "But the movie really pissed me off in a major way, and after it was over I wanted to talk about it. So I went in there and Jessie was sitting at the table slicing mushrooms on a cutting board. I started telling her about the film. There's Brenda Vaccaro, and she has this young daughter, this starlet in Rock Hudson's picture. He's the director. He's in Brenda Vaccaro's age group, right? So naturally, she's hot for him. Brenda Vaccaro's not married, she's been living alone, raising this starlet. And Rock Hudson falls for her—not Brenda Vaccaro; but the starlet.

"So I'm telling Jessie this, and she's slicing away, slicing faster, faster, faster. 'Does this surprise you?' she says. 'No,' I told her, 'let me finish.' The thing is, Brenda Vaccaro doesn't do anything so awful. She says, like 'Hey, Rock, let me fix you a drink,' or 'Here, you had a hard day, let me rub your back,' stuff like that. But the way the movie is put together, it's making fun of Brenda Vaccaro. It's like the audience is supposed to say, 'Oh God, here she comes again.' They even play this dippy little music whenever she appears. That's what pissed me off. That they would do *that*. Anyway, I'm telling Jessie this, and wham. She slams the knife down on the cutting board and she says she's very tired and she's done her bit, she's let me watch the movie, but now why don't I just go back to my own apartment and go to bed. Nice, huh?"

"Maybe not nice," Rosenberg said, "but at least honest. At least direct."

"You're taking her side?" Rita asked. She felt as though she might cry.

"Rita," he said, "the mood you're in, you were probably yelling your head off at her."

"I don't think I was," Rita protested.

"Maybe not. But Jessie is not the problem. And you know it. It's this man you met, this Sin. Now, Rita, I don't know why he hasn't called you, but give him the benefit of a doubt. Call him. Just call him up and get rid.of all this gloom."

"I can't," Rita said, and tears spilled down her cheeks. She didn't wipe at them, either.

Rosenberg took a handkerchief out of his pocket and shook it. He thought of simply handing it to her, but instead dabbed at her cheeks. It only made Rita cry harder.

"Go home," Rosenberg said. "Fix yourself up. And call him."

"I can't," Rita sobbed. "I'd feel so stupid. Really. I feel so stupid now." It had been nearly two months since that night at the Corcoran Gallery. He'd *said* he would call.

"Your exhibit," Rosenberg reminded her. "Is there anything stupid about that?"

"Yes," Rita sniffled.

That night with Sin had left Rita zinging, despite what had happened in its wake—Claire's car, Margaret's phone call. And on the strength of that feeling, she'd not only photographed Claire but had called up the manager of the bank on Pennsylvania Avenue, all but forcing him to look at her portfolio.

And the strangest thing was, it had worked! More than forty of Rita's photographs, all blown up and matted just as Sin's had been, were going to be shown in the bank's community room, and the bank would advertise the opening of the show, too.

"So that's stupid, is it?" Rosenberg said.

"In a way, yes," Rita said. It seemed so because she'd pulled it off while still high on Sin. Still thinking that he *would* call, that this relationship with him would, as women were wont to put it, "go someplace." She'd sold herself to the bank manager and now she felt guilty of fraud. She looked at Rosenberg and managed a wan smile. "Do you know, I actually went out and bought underwear? The sexiest stuff I could get without going mail order. Now tell me that wasn't stupid."

"This underwear, does it have an expiration date?" Rosenberg asked.

Rita laughed.

"There, see? Now you look good again. Drink your drink and then go home, frizz up your hair, and call."

"And say what?"

"Rita . . ." Rosenberg drained his cup, tossed the ice on the grass, then crumpled the cup in his fist. "What did you tell me about Margaret?"

"What has Margaret got to do with anything?" Actually, Margaret, now that she'd really cemented things with Jay, was making Rita feel much worse, always saying *we* this and *we* that: *We've decided not to use sugar in our tea.*

"Her phone call," Rosenberg said, "to the Senator."

"Oh Christ, that."

"Yes, that. But even *that* wasn't the end of the world, was it?" He watched Rita glower at the Monument, the tourists, the grass, the circle of American flags. He chuckled. Rita always glowered before she gave in.

"Hey," Nick shouted, "what's with you, Jess? You're not coming in like you was," and it was true. Not only did she used to be the first one in on Saturdays, but she liked to stop in after work, buy things fresh, carry them home in a grocery bag made of string. She was the first one Nick had ever seen do that, but now a lot of customers did. Nick called them "dinky bags."

Jessie was the first one in a lot of ways. With the cheeses, for instance. "Hey, come on over here, Jess." Nick held up a pockmarked pale yellow slab. "Come on. I got a special going on. I got that— how do you say it?—that Danish stuff." Of course, Nick did know how to say it. He'd been ordering all sorts of special cheeses since Jessie moved to the Row and started asking for them. But somehow, Nick always lapsed into his dumb act.

Jessie was the first person Nick had ever waited on all by himself. He'd been frightened, too, because of the way his father had treated her. With extra politeness, extra care, extra effort. He remembered going around with his dad to the warehouses, sometimes a couple of them, looking for the cheeses with the fancy names; Jarlsberg, Stilton, there was no telling what she'd ask for next. Everybody else wanted American, pimento, Swiss. But not Jessie.

Once she'd asked for Baby Swiss. Nick thought she was joking. He had cut a small corner off a big block of Swiss and said, "Okay, here you go, Baby Swiss." His father had given him the dickens about that, but Jessie had only laughed.

"So where you been keeping yourself?" he asked her.

"Oh, around," Jessie said.

"Around how?" Nick pressed her, but Jessie only smiled. He looked at her carefully. *She must have been okay, maybe even a looker, in her day.* He had never thought of Jessie in that regard before.

"Haven't had any parties lately, huh? What's the matter? You mad at everybody or is everybody mad at you?"

"Everyone's busy," Jessie said.

"You're gonna have to get us all together, like the old days. Singing on the steps that time, that sure was fun."

"It was Rita who got us together," Jessie said, pointing at the cheese she wanted. Nick wrapped it, wrote the price on the paper with his felt-tip marker, and asked if he should put it on her bill.

She nodded.

"I heard you was buying flowers," he said, but he hadn't really heard. He had seen her a couple of Saturdays ago walking through the bedding plants on the pavement outside, picking up a basket here and there. They were half price now, most of them wilting. The best ones were the first to go.

"Who told you that?" she asked.

"Well," he corrected himself, "I seen you, I guess."

"Flowers," she said, smiling as if in some kind of dream.

Everybody's different these days, Nick thought. *Everybody.* Rita would come in and bite your head off if you looked at her the wrong way. Margaret was the opposite, friendly, at least compared to the way she had been. He used to jack up his prices for Margaret, but the last few times he hadn't been tempted to. The new girl, Claire, never came in, though sometimes she sent that black kid to buy something for her. That was one thing he had to say for Faye, she hadn't messed with lowlifes.

"Okay, Nick," Jessie said, "I am making plans. I've been fixing up the yard."

"What yard?" Nick asked her. Far as he could remember, there was just this little dirt place out back. "You mean where the landlady used to hang her wash? Out there?"

"She hasn't hung her wash in years," Jessie said, her old self, kidding Nick again. "She hasn't even *lived* on the Row in years."

"Oh, yeah. So, how are you fixing it up?" Jessie was fixing, Claire had spent all that time fixing; it seemed to Nick as though all women ever did was fix things up.

Jessie reached for the marker and held her hand out toward the paper. Nick gave her some, tearing a big piece off the roll. Jessie drew little zigzags on it. "I had them lay bricks, like this. Herringbone."

"Oh, yeah. I seen the truck come. I figured it was Claire, though."
He felt a little hot squeeze inside, to have said her first name like
that, out loud. *Claire.*

Jessie paid no attention, just kept on drawing. "And I'm having a
fence put up," she said, "like this," drawing wide slats. "And I'm
having a gate made." She drew it as well, with some little squiggles
to mark the latch and a round hole above the little squiggles, for
reaching in and opening up the latch, Nick thought.

"You spending your own money doing this, or what?" Nick couldn't
imagine that landlady of hers springing for it, and it sounded dumb
to him anyway, putting up a wood fence when you could have cyclone, putting in bricks when there was concrete. If you were going
to spend your money, you might as well spend your money right.

"Yes," Jessie said, "and when it's all done I'm going to have everyone in. Like the old days."

"Oh, I get it," Nick said, finally seeing why Jessie had gone into
all of this. "And that's where you've been keeping yourself. Working
on this here yard. And hey"—he gave her a little razz—"here all this
time I thought you had a boyfriend or something."

Claire was thrilled by the latest clue that she would give her Mystery Man. She would say, "Pretty little maids, all in a row," and
hope that he would know the city well enough to find her.

She envisioned herself lying upstairs on her bed, waiting. She would
listen intently, but hear nothing. All the same, she would know. The
minute he entered the house, she would know.

The house would be dark, and he would wait until his eyes had
adjusted to the lack of light. And then, softly, he would mount the
stairs.

She would breathe deeply, breathe her yoga breath—a long draw
in, a hold, a long expulsion. And then, suddenly, she would quicken
to the sound of *his* breath in the room.

Her breath would still be long, smooth, controlled. His would be
swift and thick. She wouldn't look at him, but would only listen.

Mystery Man. Cobra.

But of course she would be tempted to look at him. If only the room were darker. . . . Then Claire remembered a sleep mask she had bought. She had never worn it and wasn't even sure why she'd purchased it. Now she was glad she had.

She went to the closet and took it from its box. It was satin, white, plain, rather like a Halloween mask. It was perfect. She placed it beneath her pillow.

When the phone rang, her hand quivered as she reached for it. "Yes," she said, but with no lift of the voice to indicate that it was a question. Finally she'd be able to provide the last clue.

"I don't get it," he said. " 'Pretty little maids all in a row.' That's a fairy tale. That's kid stuff." Gruff. Unappreciative. "Once and for all," he demanded, "let's stop playing games. When am I going to get to meet you? Where do you live?"

She might have pouted, but instead grew angry. She abandoned all the subtlety she'd so long planned. "Where Faye Arensberg died," she said evenly, dropping the phone in its cradle.

Then she waited, expecting him to call again. But the phone did not ring.

But she'd told him, hadn't she? She'd told him where to come, where to find her? He *would* come now. Yes, of course he would.

Claire went downstairs and opened the doors to the night. Then she sat in one of the chairs and waited.

"Door was open, Miz Albritten," LeGrande explained, crouching down beside Claire's chair. It was morning. "It seemed like you wasn't here, but I poked my head inside, jes' to make sure. When I saw you there, oh, man! I was afraid for a minute you weren't just sleepin'." He stood up, mad at himself for having said that, the wrong thing. "What I mean is, I thought maybe you sick or somethin'." He tapped his fingers nervously against a marble-topped table. "You said you had something you wanted me to do today? Last time, remember? Today was what you said."

She rubbed her eyes and finally came to. "Yes, today," she said, standing up, "that's right." She took him into the kitchen and showed him what she wanted done.

LeGrande hadn't expected her to stay there in the house. He thought she'd tell him what to do and then, as usual, go out, leaving him behind to do it. But she went upstairs and stayed there for the longest time.

LeGrande crept to the bottom of the staircase and listened. He thought he'd go crazy. She was running the water in the bathtub. He could hear her splashing around. He had to force himself to resume his work.

The phone rang, and he almost picked it up, knowing that she was in the tub. But then she'd know he knew. And anyway—he'd almost forgotten—she'd had telephones put in everywhere, even in the bathroom.

A telephone in the bathroom! And a tub big enough for two people, maybe three if the third one was someone little, like Denise. The tub had holes all around the side so that hot water could squirt all over you. It had a name, but LeGrande couldn't remember it.

He went back to the staircase to hear her and he could, not whole words, but just her voice, her laugh. Her laugh, he thought, was like a pocketful of thin silver dimes.

Maybe he could fix her something—cocoa, maybe—and carry it up to her. It wasn't as though he would get to see her naked, because he was sure she'd have bubbles all over her body. He'd just carry the cocoa up, and then she'd reach out over the bubbles and she'd say, "Why thank you, LeGrande. How nice." And some of the bubbles would break loose when she talked, and they'd float on up to the big glass window and break.

"LeGrande." She was behind him, scared him.

"Yes, ma'am." He turned so fast he almost fell.

Her hair was wet and flat against her head and down her back. Her skin was wet, too, and pink. She was wearing a shiny white robe that tied. "Could you put some water on?"

"Yes, ma'am." He rushed the kettle to the faucet and filled it.

She took a square tin can with a dragon on the side and then she took a teapot from one of the shelves. She opened the can and took a spoon and put a little batch of what was in the can inside the teapot. Then she looked at him. "You're laughing," she said.

"No, ma'am. It's just . . . it looks like chew tobacco."

"Well, it isn't chewing tobacco, silly, it's tea." She smiled at him.

"When the water boils, pour it in here, all right? And then, after about five minutes, pour me a cup, and yourself a cup, if you like. And bring my cup up to me."

"Which cup . . . ?" He waved back to where the dishes were. It seemed to him that she had several sets of them.

"Any cup at all," she told him, going away again.

It made him think about his mama, back when she was working in white folks' homes. They fed her and gave her stuff to drink, Mama told him, but off separate plates. Separate for her. He would have to brag about this to Claude: *"Have a cup of tea, LeGrande. And take yourself jes' any cup at all."*

He found a cup that was all by itself, nothing around it that matched. It was white, fine white, the way she was, white that you could see the light through. And it looked as if spiders had woven their webs down inside the glass, silvery line things. He took it and poured the tea from the pot, hoping none of those tobacco leaves would fall into it. They didn't and he thought they must have dissolved, but when he looked down into the teapot they were still there, wavy on the bottom.

He set the cup on a big silver tray with handles. Then it occurred to him she might want milk, so he took the carton out of the refrigerator and set that down on the tray, too.

Up where the tea tin had been, there was a box of sugar. He put that on the tray, too. And a spoon, the same spoon she used when she put the tea down inside the pot. He blew at the spoon to make sure it was clean, and wiped it along his sleeve.

He wished he had a flower or something, but he didn't, so he carried the tray up like that, thinking about how he was going to hold it in one hand while he knocked on the door and then hold it even better when he turned the knob to open the door. Sucker was heavy, too.

But the door was wide open when he got up there, and she was sitting on the bed, rubbing her hair dry with a great big towel. All the light in the world seemed to be in that room, and there she was, in the center of it. She still had the robe on, but it had spread apart at her legs. The robe was starting to spread at the neckline, too, not so much so that he could see anything, but enough to make him want to see.

She smiled at him and at the tray and thanked him, showing him where to set it down. "Where's yours?" she asked.

"I had mine," he lied.

"Well, sit down anyway," she said.

He went over to a long couch kind of thing and sat all stiff, the way he used to do in the principal's office. A magazine was there, and open, with things circled. LeGrande looked down at it and almost started picking at the edge of it, but he stopped himself. "Seem like you in a much better mood," he said finally.

And she laughed, got up, and reached for her cup of tea. "Yes, much better," she said.

He was trying to think of something to say next.

"Do you ever feel," she asked him, "as though you won't be in a better mood ever? And then something happens, some little thing, and like magic"—she swept her hand up, and it did seem to him like magic; he half expected a white bird to appear in her hand, spread its wings, and fly away—"like magic, the bad mood goes away?"

"Yes, ma'am," he said. But he was still confused. Then he remembered the telephone call that had come in. "Yes, ma'am," he said with more vigor. "Like somebody calls you, somebody you been hoping would."

"Or maybe someone new," she said. "Someone you didn't even know about before."

"Yes, ma'am," LeGrande agreed. "Somebody you never heard about before."

"Exactly," she said, getting up again to put the cup down on the tray. "Well," and the way she said it told LeGrande that it was time to take that tray and head back downstairs. "Thank you, LeGrande. That was very nice."

She came down in those skin-licking pants and high black boots of hers, with her hair pulled back tight as if it weren't even there.

She was going to ride her horse, she said, and LeGrande kind of shook his head.

"You're laughing again," she said, with another one of her sideways looks. She laughed back and asked him, "What is it this time?"

"Seems like you get awful dressed up," he said, "just to go out and get on some horse." And she did, too. Everything was clean as could be, even her boots. Also, she was wearing earrings, little pearls.

"I guess I do," she said. "You aren't the first man who's ever told me that."

And then, before he had to come up with an answer, she was out the door and he was listening to that car of hers start up.

He went back upstairs as soon as she was gone, just to remember having been there. He sat on the couch thing again, only this time he leaned back and put his feet up as though he belonged.

Claire tried to sort out the sudden turns and twists her emotions had made since last night. First, exhilaration at the thought of her Mystery Man's impending call. Then disappointment when he'd responded in such a dull and stupid way. Finally, after she'd hung up and while she'd waited for him, despair.

The sleep she'd fallen into had been dreamless.

The upswing had begun with LeGrande's appearance. He was so young, so concerned. She liked toying with LeGrande, though in a wholly harmless way. She'd already begun to revive when she'd gone upstairs for her bath.

But then, on the heels of LeGrande, that call! She'd lifted the phone warily, saying nothing, thinking that it might be her Mystery Man calling to explain his failure. But it had been a new voice.

"Bitch," the voice said, "I've been watching you." Then, when she hadn't replied: "Say something, you common bitch." She'd burst out laughing. She hadn't thought she'd laugh again so soon.

Still, chances were great that he'd turn out all wrong. So many men did. They were rather like the Potomac countryside she was driving through, all too tame. New-mown fields and white board fences, bounded, measured, a polite suggestion of the real thing. The real thing—tangled, unkempt, overgrown. The places Steve had taken her.

She would drive in search of Steve, if only she knew where to look. If only Steve had been the voice on the telephone: *Common bitch. I've been watching you.* Still, it was terribly exciting, someone new.

Claire pulled at the pins in her hair until it was free, whipping about her shoulders. She pulled into the stable yard so abruptly that the Jaguar bucked and stalled. She left it there, not quite out of the driveway, and walked into the narrow office to ask to have Illuminating readied.

Common bitch. She was so excited, she just had to ride.

Rita, still gloomy over Sin, headed for her apartment like a vampire going back to his box of earth. She wanted nothing more than to tuck herself away inside. Close the lid of the coffin, she thought, shifting the jug of wine that she'd bought from her left arm to her right.

She had big plans for the night. She would drink. And listen to sad songs. Cry a little. Maybe overeat. She wished now that she'd bought a pack of cigarettes, too. She wasn't really what you'd call a smoker, so it wouldn't take terribly long until her throat got raw. Big plans.

She thought of Margaret, who would probably spend the night curled up with Jay. She thought of Claire, who could doubtless have her pick of men. And then she saw Jessie up ahead.

Rita slowed her pace. The last thing in the world she wanted was conversation. But, for some reason, Jessie turned and saw her. Worse, she waited for Rita to catch up.

"Hi," Rita said, but not happily.

Jessie didn't seem to notice. She was more animated, Rita thought, than she'd been in a long time. While Jessie talked, Rita eyed the creases in Jessie's face, so apparent in the light. Why had Rita barely noticed them before? Rita half heard as Jessie talked on and on about the yard out back and how she was fixing it up.

For Rita, it was the last straw. Rita got away as soon as she could and locked herself inside and wept. She was crying for herself, certainly, but now it was all bound up with Jessie. Rita was bitterly sorry for Jessie. Sorry that a yard was all the woman had to get excited about. What had gone wrong for Jessie?

And worse, was it a prediction of how Rita's own life might unfold? Rita had, since she first got to know Jessie, gone around saying that she'd like to *be* like her. She admired Jessie's independence, Jessie's flair. And now she, Rita, was a younger version of Jessie. Alone.

And why? Jessie looked terrific, had a great job, was intelligent, witty. Jessie could even cook, and not just ordinary food, but fancy Oriental dishes or Oysters Rockefeller or omelets for a bunch of people. So why didn't Jessie have a man by her side?

Rita put the wine in the fridge and looked Sin up in the phone book. She'd already underlined the number in red. Then she walked around, hugging the phone book, thinking about Jessie, and about Sin, and about all the men she'd ever been interested in from grade school on up. And then she called Rosenberg.

"Look, Rita," he said, "you're tossing a coin, okay? You want heads and a hundred times it comes up tails, okay? You stop tossing it and you won't get heads ever. You keep tossing and there's always a chance."

"Do you think Jessie's stopped tossing?" Rita sniffled.

"Jessie. I don't care about Jessie. I care about you."

Still, it was well into the night when Rita finally managed to dial all of the digits of Sin's phone number. After two rings, a recording intervened. "The new number, in area code 301 . . ." Rita scribbled it on the cover of the directory. Another hour passed before she managed to dial again.

Sin answered on the first ring.

"Is this Martin Sinclair?" she heard her voice cracking.

"Rita!" he said.

Now she wasn't even sure what she'd said to him. Whatever it was, it must have been okay. He was coming over—no, down, he'd said. From Baltimore. He would be there in an hour.

An hour. Get busy, she told herself. Get that ironing board out and move! And don't dare say a word about why he never called. Not a word. Not even a hint.

But what was he doing in Baltimore? Why had he moved? What had he been doing all this time?

On the other hand, hadn't he known her voice? Hadn't he sounded pleased? Wasn't he coming? God, you are an asshole, she told herself, spitting on her finger to test the iron.

She ironed the pillowcases and the sheets. She ironed her T-shirt and her jeans. She ironed the nightie and slung it, by its wispy straps, over the crook of an extension lamp.

She was gargling when he rang the bell. She rinsed with plain water, not wanting to smell mediciny. She ran to the door and stared at it, thinking, *Jesus Christ, he's out there.*

"Rita?" he called.

"Right here," she said, opening the door and then practically hiding behind it.

It was awkward, and it wasn't just her. It was everything, him, the room, the situation. It took a century for the telling moment—when she might have hugged him or taken his hand, or smiled, at least—to pass.

But maybe it was just Rita, because Sin just shrugged and walked across the room to bat at the nightie that was dangling there. It looked so obvious and so stupid. "I hope I'm not the one who's expected to wear this," he said.

And, poof, like that, Rita felt herself relaxing. "Why should you be any different? Everybody else has been willing, so far."

He reached out and ruffled her hair. "Let's sit down," he said. "Okay?"

She picked the *TV Guide* up off the sofa.

"Is television what you had in mind?" he asked.

It wasn't. She just hadn't wanted him sitting on her magazine. But she kidded him. "Right. Channel Five's all-night movies. Right now they have *The Woman in White*." It was what she'd planned to watch before she'd screwed up the courage to call him.

"Funny thing," he said, "guess what I just saw?"

"*The Woman in White*," she said, "isn't that too bad?"

He didn't kiss her. He just moved closer and pulled her body up against his own, and it seemed right, just right. She could have stayed there forever, just like that.

"Don't let go," she said.

"I won't," he told her.

"Well, all right, let go. But just for a minute. Just long enough for us to get in there." She felt him looking past her and was glad she'd done all that ironing. "But don't let go," she said, "just yet."

"All right." He held her tighter. "We'll count to three. One," he said, and he stood up. "Two," he said, and he pulled her to her feet. She put her arms around his neck just as he reached three, when he lifted her, shifting slightly so that he could hold her threshold fashion.

"Is this your caveman routine?" she asked, as he carried her toward the bedroom. She said it softly, though, with her lips brushing the side of his neck.

"Part of it," he told her.

Jay sat by lamplight scrawling on a legal pad and occasionally sifting through his notes and clippings. He would like to have used the typewriter, but Margaret couldn't sleep when he typed, even when he tried to muffle the sound by folding a bath towel under the machine. And she wouldn't consider their staying at her place, where she could have slept in the bedroom with the door closed, because she was convinced that Rita would hear them in bed.

Precious little to hear, he wanted to say, and might have, in the beginning, when they had what he thought of as an arm's-length relationship: considered a pair, though they were more often apart than together.

The Row had helped to distance them. Jay's basement apartment was too small for comfortable cohabitation and Margaret's had those paper-thin walls, and Rita below.

But something had happened. Jay wasn't quite sure what. Margaret's need to be with him increased. It had nothing to do with sex.

It had to do with time. She even talked of their moving away from the Row, to a house somewhere.

That was fine with Jay. Even marriage was fine.

He smiled at Margaret, asleep in her cotton panties and one of his sleeveless undershirts. Margaret suited him.

Jay felt as if he'd been an actor all his life. His clothing, for instance, carefully chosen to portray innocence. His relationship with Margaret served the same function, at least at the start. And certainly he'd been playing at being a writer, never really doing it, until recently.

Was he offstage when he walked into the club? When he removed his clothing and made love to strangers? Or was he offstage now, smiling at a woman he had come to care about, working on a project that did seem to be taking shape? Since Faye, he wondered, or since Claire?

He sorted through the file of newspaper clippings. One word was common to them all. *Murder. Murder* was a word people feared, but in this case it was murder that had enabled him, for the first time, to reach some . . . well, maybe normalcy. Jay had never felt quite normal. Oddly, he felt more normal when Rita called him what he'd long feared he was: a sleaze.

Was the way he was approaching this book normal? He had thought that if he ever did write one it would be an act of imagination. Instead, all Jay did was record. Follow Claire-Faye and record. Claire, not he, breathed life into the dead girl. Claire gave motion to Faye's days. It was wonderfully simple, only to record.

But it was time to forget Faye Arensberg's day-to-day life and proceed to her death. It was time to record her terror, her fear. That was why he had telephoned Claire. To frighten her.

But Claire had laughed, and not cruelly, but as if in invitation. Claire had been drawn—attracted—to the threat he'd meant to convey. Claire was courting her own death.

It would give the tale of Faye Arensberg exactly the twist he'd suspected. And perhaps it had happened just that way. Jay scribbled, partly noting what he knew and partly in projection:

Faye had opened her door. Either expecting someone else or killer was familiar to her. If former, disguise? Killer attacked immediately (blood gush in vestibule), slashing Faye's cheek. Faye stumbled backward, feeling the sudden warmth across her cheek. Faye raises hand, sees it covered red. Tries to push past her killer, run into the street. She fails, runs upstairs and into the empty unrented rooms. Her footsteps ring against the bare floors. The killer is calm, closes both doors. The windows are already sealed. No one on the Row will hear her screams.

But Faye doesn't scream. She hides upstairs. The killer's footsteps are steady on the stairs, then down the hallway, then into the room where Faye cowers.

There is nowhere to hide up there, and even if she had hidden, the killer would have found her. Smell of terror easy to trail, a mixture of urine, salt, sweat. So. The killer stands before Faye. Faye looks up, knows, accepts, raises herself. The killer leads Faye downstairs, ties her to her own bed. Faye waits, watches. The wound on her cheek still weeps. It has begun to ache. Faye sees the killer sort through the various devices and choose one, then another. Stab. Slash. Burn.

Jay's hand was trembling. He lowered his pen. He stared at the tip of it, expecting to find blood right there. Something like the pen had been used. *Killer stabs this girl from the inside of her mouth. Puts the pick inside. Killer really had it in for this girl.*

Jay tossed the pen aside, then jammed all of his papers together inside his top desk drawer. He was frightening himself, approaching Faye's murder this way. And anyway, what had happened to the notion that Faye had known, had maybe even wanted to die? Where had that come from? Nothing he had just written reflected it. Better only to record.

He satisfied himself that Margaret was truly asleep and walked outside. He needed some air. He leaned against a telephone pole, looking up the Row to the house. Faye's house. Claire's house.

And then he didn't so much see Claire as feel her there. He turned to confirm what he felt. He had just decided to speak to her when she walked past him as if he were the one who did not exist.

He followed her. It was almost a habit now. And, perhaps because he was always there, she didn't seem to notice. She never looked back at—or for—him.

Why was she out walking at this hour? Was she looking for her caller? Wouldn't she be surprised to learn that he was the one? *Common bitch.* Jay trailed her with a sense that the whole thing was happening in some other form of time. Delayed, like slow motion, or walking underwater. Or through a dream.

LeGrande bought the whole album on tape just so he could get that one song. It wasn't the music that he liked, it was the words, *She came from Planet Claire,* over and over and over. He had to be careful not to play it around Claude, though, because Claude would laugh at him for playing honky sounds.

LeGrande had first heard the song coming out of one of those VW bugs that double-parked in front of the 7-Eleven late at night. He pretended he was reading the sticker in the back window, George Washington University, but he was really grooving to the words.

Planet Claire. It made it sound as though there were a planet full of them, a planet full of chicks like Claire.

LeGrande had gone into the record store way down on Fourteenth Street to buy it. He'd had to sing it and hope they'd know what album it was off.

LeGrande had thought a lot about what if Claude were right and Claire did have the hots for him. It seemed to him that if she did she wouldn't do much different from what she did do: flaunting herself around the house at him, smiling, being real nice. *Anything you need, LeGrande, you just let me know.* Using his name all the time the way she did.

But like Claude said, "Don't forget, blood, the chick is *white.*"

How was he going to forget? Being around her was having white shoved down your throat. There were so many different kinds of white, he would look around and be amazed. White like milk, white like dishes, like eggs, white like wedding dresses, like smoke, like

131

bones. Thick white for fur coats and see-through white for those lacy things she had in her drawers.

In her drawers, the kind of stuff he'd only seen pictures of before. LeGrande hadn't meant to go into any of her drawers, but he had such a hard-on one time after she stood there talking to him that when she went out it was like he couldn't help himself, he just pulled the drawers open, one drawer after another, and looked at all of her lacy stuff. It wasn't as though he touched any of it, he just looked.

Then he went into the bathroom and he pumped himself dry, thinking about how he was pumping her, and how she'd look with that practically white hair of hers all falling down and hanging over the edge of that big white bed.

Shit. He could actually *be* fucking her and Claude would never believe it. Claude, he didn't believe nothing. First time LeGrande saw that bathroom, he tried to tell Claude about it, but Claude said LeGrande was making it up.

"Sure," Claude said, "she got this thing squirt up her pussy."

"I ain't jivin' you," LeGrande said. "She does. It's called a bee-day, only you don't spell it like it sounds. I'm telling you, she told me what it was and even wrote it down for me on a piece of paper."

"Lemme see the paper."

"Shit, she took it with her or something. I ain't got the paper."

"Oh, right," Claude said.

"Just forget it," he told Claude. "I ain't tellin' you nothin' else from now on."

Still, he'd have liked to have Claude believe him, have liked for Claude to see how Claire was. The way she always stood up on the staircase to talk to him, for instance, so that he could look right up her dress if he had the nerve. The way she teased him, always asking him about himself. If Claude could only see, then LeGrande would say, *Well, my man, were you right about this chick having the hots for me, or were you right?*

It wasn't as if no white girl in the world had never been nice to him, either. Lots of them had, even acted familiar. But not like this one.

She came from Planet Claire.

LeGrande was grooving down the street this way when all of a sudden someone grabbed him from behind. He would have heard whoever it was coming if he hadn't been so deep into the song. Sucker grabbed him and pulled the earplug right out of his ear.

It was the dude from the Market, Nick or something. Good thing LeGrande was in a fine mood. Good thing, too, that LeGrande was by himself and not with Claude. "Wha's your problem, man?" LeGrande asked. The earplug dangled from the sound box rigged at his waist. LeGrande could still hear the words of the song, only far away. "What? You drunk or somethin'?" LeGrande asked.

Nick was breathing like he'd just run a long way, chest all puffed up, cheeks, even under the stubble, bright red. "Why are you walking around like that?" Nick wanted to know. "Why are you singing her name like that?"

"You crazy, man." LeGrande turned to walk away. He started to put his earplug back on.

"I heard you," Nick said, grabbing him again. "Singing up the street and all."

"S'a free country," LeGrande said. "If I want to sing up the street, that's what I do." LeGrande moved closer to Nick when he said it, and just like he expected, the dude's chest caved in and he kind of hunched himself over.

LeGrande felt bad for him, coming on strong like that and then having to back down. "Hey," LeGrande said, "it's just a song. You know? Tha's all. Just a song." He hit the rewind button and then held the plug to test what the tape was playing. He rewound a bit more, checked, and then offered the plug to Nick. "Here, listen."

Nick held it against his ear until he'd heard the whole song through. *She came from Planet Claire.*

Jay had walked all the way around the block behind her, down the Row and up the alley behind it and then down the Row again. She had slipped inside her house a few moments ago. He waited for her to turn on the lights. She did not. He was ready to return to his place, when he noticed that she'd left the front door ajar.

He approached it, entered, shut and locked it behind him. The second door, the glass one, was open, too. Once inside, he locked it, too, then stood in the downstairs hall and listened.

The air was cool and silent and still. Despite that, Jay's shirt stained with sweat that burned, but at the same time was cold as ice. He tugged at the cloth where it stuck against his skin, tugged at the back and then the front.

He was on the staircase now.

He thought of Faye in the upstairs rooms. His heart began to race. He thought of Claire, too, leading him, goading him.

Jay had reached the second-floor landing. He looked down a row of doors. One—just one—was open. He tried to tiptoe, but the floorboard just outside the room creaked. He expected her to flutter at the sound, but she didn't. For a moment he thought that she, like Faye, was dead.

The bed seemed a catafalque, positioned in the center of the room with a blue-white light falling around it from above. It was a strange bed, at once lavish and crude. Irregular tongues of white wood licked up, from the headboard, the corners, the base.

Jay looked down at his hands, as if he expected them to know what to do. His hands were trembling as they had earlier, when he'd written about the murder, but with what emotion now? What need?

Claire lay diagonally across the bed, her eyes shut, her lids silvery, her bare breasts heaving. Her skin seemed to shimmer. Her hair had been arrayed against the bed sheet, each pale strand drawn outward from her face. She wore panties. A white satin triangle of panties.

Her left arm was flung over her head, her wrist bound to one of the headboard tongues with a long pale strand of pearls. Pearls wrapped around and around her thin wrist, then straight along the length of her arm, the end of the strand trailing, as if accidentally, across her swan-white neck.

She squirmed slightly, her lips pursing and unpursing, her body twisting so that the pearls shifted ever so little, tapping against each other with a soft clicking pearl-on-pearl sound.

She sighed. She was, he guessed, pretending to be asleep.

He removed his shoes and then his trousers. He stood beside the bed in his shirt, socks, and shorts. He did not have an erection.

What was being asked of him? Something operatic in its urgency, its excess. Something planned, or more than that. Foreordained. Faye. Claire. Faye.

Margaret knew, even before she opened her eyes, that Jay was gone. She jumped from the bed and looked inside the bathroom anyway. She then looked around the rest of the apartment for a note, but knew, too, that he'd left none. She went to the door, opened it, and listened to the night. She poked her head outside and glanced up the Row.

The Row had always seemed spooky after Faye. At night, though, it was positively sinister. No one had any lights on, not even Rita. And the only sounds seemed far, far away. Traffic, in the distance.

She went back inside, dressed, and wondered what to do. She was afraid, of course. She tried to tell herself to stay inside the apartment, but couldn't, knew she wouldn't. She went into the night, closing Jay's door behind her. She sat in the little alcove by his door. That way, if she saw him coming she could always duck back in. Pretend that she was just awake and doing something, not worried about him at all.

But why would he have gone out? Could it have something to do with his book? Or—this was what she continually feared—had she said something in her sleep about the Senator? Had Jay heard and left her?

She often thought that she ought to confess to Jay. Not the whole thing, not about the phone call, but about the crush she'd had on Aubrey Denton. That way, if she ever slipped or if Rita ever said anything, Jay would already know. Or think that he knew. It seemed so devious to be thinking that way, but she couldn't help it. She couldn't imagine anything worse than Jay finding out before she'd more or less prepared him. And he'd forgive her. Anyone would forgive a silly little crush.

Claire sat up so abruptly that the strand of pearls encircling her wrist broke. Most of the beads dropped onto the bed, but a few skipped onto the white wooden floor. She waited for the pearls to settle. Waited for the silence. When the silence came, she laughed at Jay. Laughed as if he were the funniest thing she'd ever seen. "You!" she said, when she could manage a word. "You!"

Jay groped blindly for his trousers and his shoes, unable to look away from her. It seemed to him that she had become a lamia, her body coiling in upon itself as she laughed and taunted him, her beautiful face reshaping itself into one that was ugly. He meant to back away but stepped forward, into the circle of blue-white light.

Laughing. Laughing. "You don't even have an erection," she said, grazing him with her nails. Still laughing. "Of all people. Of all the men in the world, it's *you*. . . ."

Jay managed to get into his clothes, but she was out of the bed and upon him. "I've seen you," she said, but she wasn't laughing now. "Wait," she told him. "Don't go. The thing is . . . don't you see, you're supposed to . . ." She stopped talking. Jay looked down at her with an urge to strike her. But would she laugh again? If she laughed again, he would do more than strike her, he would—

His thoughts frightened him almost as much as she did. He backed toward the door.

"What is wrong with you?" she accused him. "Are you impotent? Are you queer? Are you always a failure?"

What was she trying to get him to do? Jay's fingers seemed to stretch out toward her throat. He curled them into fists to keep from strangling her and then had to fight to keep his fists at his sides.

And Claire railed on at him, chanting her insults.

He was downstairs now, but her voice followed him. He was insanely afraid that she would reappear and come at him again. That she would come downstairs before he could open the doors, which he himself had closed and locked.

But she stayed up there, deriding him. "Idiot. Queer. Impotent little fool."

Margaret saw Jay run from Claire's house. She reached out her hand to him, but she knew that even if she had been in the light instead of in the shadows, he would not have seen.

The first thing she felt frightened her: She thought that she was seeing Faye's murderer flee. The next thing she felt was the knowledge that he had been there, inside that house, with Claire.

Margaret sank to her knees on the brick stairs in the alcove and wailed. But Jay couldn't hear, he was gone. He'd run, his clothing disheveled, down the Row and around the corner.

Margaret forced herself to stop crying out that way. She took several deep breaths and then stood up, her knees quaking. The next thing she felt was anger.

It didn't seem fair, that Claire should have everyone. The Senator, and now even Jay. She wished Claire were dead, she wished Jay had gone in there to murder her. But she knew, even while she was thinking it, that it wasn't what he'd gone inside that house to do.

How could she ever hope to compete with someone like Claire? Why had Claire come to the Row? And why would she want Jay?

It was more than unfair, it was criminal. Everything had been all right before Claire moved in. Claire had spoiled everything for everyone. Why didn't somebody just go inside that house and—just the way they did with Faye—kill Claire?

Margaret was so deep in her thoughts that she hadn't paid attention to the streets she was taking, nor to the sounds around her. She was smack in the center of what Rita called "a very bad street" when she heard the motorcycle.

It was directly behind her and going very slowly. She could feel the beam of its headlight on her back. It came closer, closer, making a low, grumbling sound. It was like an animal's growl, deep and low. She turned, saw the mirror face just a few feet behind her. She began to run.

He toyed with her, knowing that she couldn't outdistance him. For the most part, he kept to her rear. Occasionally he'd swoop to the right or left, if she seemed to be veering that way.

Margaret was so panicky, she didn't think to run to the sidewalk, nor to reverse her direction. She ran straight ahead, with the cycle in slow pursuit.

She was wailing again, but she made no effort to stop herself from crying out. But the houses that flanked the street stayed dark. As if no one could hear.

It occurred to Margaret that she was being punished for what she'd just thought about Claire. She wailed on, but in her mind she said a sort of prayer. *I didn't mean it, didn't mean it.*

She thought the prayer had worked when she saw someone at the end of the block. On the corner, in the lamplight. Someone. She couldn't make out who it was, and she didn't really care. She ran toward him, wailing, but the person didn't look up.

When she came nearer she saw why. He was listening to one of those Walkman cassette things and couldn't hear. She knew him, too. It was LeGrande, the black boy from the Row.

She heard the cycle rev behind her and thought that the cyclist, seeing that LeGrande couldn't hear, would murder her right there. Run her down, or pick her up and carry her off to murder her elsewhere.

But she was wrong. The cyclist wheeled away from her, roaring off in the opposite direction. She stumbled toward LeGrande, panting, exhausted, tugging at him.

LeGrande pulled the plug from his ear. He reached to touch her, comfort her, reflexively. Then, just as reflexively, stopped himself, pulled away. "What's the matter?" he asked. "Something happen or what?" He looked back up the street, the way Margaret had come, but it was empty, quiet, dead. "Come on, stop crying," he said.

He got her to sit beside him on the curb, and eventually she told him about the biker. But after she had told him that, she started crying even harder. "Hey, now," he said, "it's over, you hear? The dude is gone and you gonna be okay now."

But Margaret cried that it wasn't over, wasn't over by a long shot, and LeGrande pried it out of her and then was sorry that he had. Because it turned out that she had a boyfriend and this boyfriend had just paid a middle-of-the-night visit to the Planet Claire.

They'd messed around so long that Rita had to summon all her courage to face herself in the morning mirror. When she did, she was astounded. "My God!" she said. Sin hugged her from behind. "I

138

expected to look totally dissipated," she said, "but I don't. I look fantastic. I look better than I've ever looked in my life." And it was true.

Her hair was tangled and every trace of makeup had been worn from her face, but her face was flushed, too, probably from scraping against his face, his shoulder, his chest, his everywhere. And her lips were dark and full, probably from all the kisses she'd been giving him, his eyes, his lips, wherever she could reach.

They'd been like puppies, kissing and cuddling and nudging and fucking and then stopping after just a bit to tickle or laugh or talk. She'd sucked at the tip of his nose and then, while she was laughing at herself for doing it, he did the same to her. It was the silliest, sexiest lovemaking she'd ever had, and it went on so long, so long, so long.

"I don't think I can come anymore," she'd said at some point, and he shrugged at her.

"Suit yourself," he said, rolling onto his back like a pasha, hands clasped behind his head.

"Of course," she said, lowering herself over his erection, over just the tip, and then pulling away, "that doesn't mean I won't help you out."

So easy, all of it, as if they'd been together forever.

He shuddered when he came, the way he'd shuddered when he reached for her earlier, before either of them had undressed. "Oh, I missed you," he said. "I missed you so much."

And afterward, even though it must have been dawn, he put a record on, saying, "I don't believe it. Tell me this is not a Frank Sinatra record."

"This is not a Frank Sinatra record," she said.

He pulled her up off the bed and started dancing with her, just two steps this way and two steps that way, and he hummed along with the song. They were both naked.

"Well," she said, "no one can accuse you of rolling over afterward and going to sleep." She didn't feel like sleeping either, but didn't men, always? Didn't they eventually? This man would kill her. She pulled away.

"Where are you going?" he asked her.

"I want to find another record," she said. "I want the one where he says at the end"—she tried to sing it—" 'Come to papa, come to papa dooo . . .' "

"Find it later," he said, pulling her back and even closer this time, making the steps so tiny they were barely steps at all.

"Did we get *any* sleep?" Rita asked him.

"Who knows?" he asked back. "Who cares?"

She saw her nightie, still hanging where she'd slung it, on the elbow of the lamp. The lamp was still on. "Oh shit," Rita said, "I never did get to wear that thing."

"Next time." He hadn't brought any clothes. He was finding his clothes from last night everywhere and putting them back on.

"Do I have to make you something to eat?" she asked.

"No," he said, "I have to get back."

"Back? You mean now, this morning?"

At least he didn't look glad about it. He had to work at a smile. "Come on," he said. "We'll find someplace that's open and I'll buy you breakfast."

Rita grinned her way up the various streets that led from Le Patisserie back to the Row. It was a general grin. Occasionally she remembered some specific thing that Sin had said or done and she grinned more widely—more specifically. What was it about being with a man that got you feeling just the way she felt? And why was it that thinking about it later on was almost as good as actually doing whatever had got you feeling that way in the first place? And why was it that that was exactly what you wanted to do afterward—go away somewhere by yourself and think about it?

While Rita had been in her glum period, waiting for Sin to call, she'd scowled at couples who were even so much as holding hands. But minutes ago, just minutes ago, she had been involved in a wonderfully sticky farewell right in the middle of Pennsylvania Avenue. Well, on the sidewalk, but still. *Zabriskie Point,* the scene on the beach where the lovers became lovers and lovers and a whole beach full of lovers.

She had let Sinnie kiss her and kiss her and she had run her hands—

they felt like a swarm of hands—all over him, his face, his back, through his hair, along his ass. Right there in the street! If she had let him drive her home, she probably would have created an even stickier scenario right there on the Row. *Dressed to Kill,* the taxicab scene.

She turned onto the Row and smiled at all of the houses. She hoped that everyone she knew was playing out a similar scene inside. She felt—what?—*generous.* But when her eyes hit Claire's house, her smile and all her sweeter thoughts ground to a halt, the way a film does when the projector goes kaflooey.

The outside door, the one made of cypress, swung open wide. That was scary enough, for Rita. But the glass door within was plainly visible, and it was smeared with a god-awful bloody mess.

Rita swallowed, then approached it. It looked like somebody's insides. The glob was still wet in places, glistening a deep purply red. Rita thought of a placenta, though she'd never seen one.

The clotted part had dripped, and the trickles were close to hardening. Before they had solidified, however, someone had smeared through them, making a wide, translucent streak.

The whole thing was fascinating, though, in a way. Rita couldn't turn from it. She came closer, closer, holding her breath because she was afraid of how the thing might smell. She came up the steps, closer still. She gasped when suddenly, through the smeared portion, she was able to see Claire's startled face.

Rita thought about running away, but it was too late.

"What *is* that?" Claire asked, wrenching the glass door open and frowning at the mess there.

"I don't know," Rita said. She took a whiff now and was relieved to notice that no hideous odor assailed her.

Claire had her face very near the spot. "My goodness," she said, dipping her finger into the clotted part and sniffing at it. "I thought for a minute there that it was blood."

'You mean it isn't blood?" Rita asked.

"Uh-uh," Claire said. "It's cherries, I think." Then she actually tasted from the tip of her finger.

"Cherries!" Rita made a face.

"Canned," Claire pronounced. "That's why there's all that syrup.

It's somebody's notion of a joke, I guess."

But it didn't look like a joke to Rita. At least, not like any joke any of the other people on the Row had ever had to endure. How could Claire be so calm about this? "You're sure it's cherries?" she asked, thinking, *This is weird, all of it. It happening in the first place, and Claire's attitude, in the second.*

Claire laughed. "I can even tell you what kind," she said. "Bing. Harnette used to use them all the time. On my birthday. To make Cherries Jubilee." She glanced past Rita and into the street. "Look," she said. "They've even left the can." She walked down the steps and picked it up. The lid had been opened with one of those hand openers. It had a wicked, jagged edge.

"It could have fingerprints on it," Rita said, thinking that this, coupled with what had happened to Claire's car, ought definitely to be reported to the police. "It might even—" She stopped herself. She was about to say, *might even have something to do with Faye.*

"It's a prank," Claire insisted. It seemed almost as if the situation called for her to console Rita, rather than the other way around. "It's just somebody being silly."

"I hope so," Rita said. She almost asked, *But why?*

Aubrey Denton's BMW emerged from the underground garage just minutes after Jessie had gained her station near the ramp. She managed to look surprised. She smiled, waved, and waited with satisfaction as he pulled to a stop and leaned across the seat to unlock the door on the passenger side.

"Going home?" he asked. "If so, I'll drop you."

"Why, yes." Jessie slid in and shut the door behind her.

The car was air-conditioned and the glass all around was tinted a soft blue-green. The engine hummed reassuringly.

"Too muggy out there to be walking," he said.

"I'm glad I ran into you," Jessie said, reaching into her handbag and pulling out a small white envelope. "I was about to mail this. It's an invitation." She laid it on the dashboard. "Brunch," she said. She watched his forehead furrow, probably because of the dozens of invitations he received every day, and added that she had invited Claire. "I've kept an eye on her," she told him, "since our talk."

He glanced at her approvingly. "That was just what I had in mind when I called you." He chuckled. "But at any rate, so have I."

Jessie knew that. She had seen his car drive past the Row often. Only twice, to her knowledge, had it stopped and he gone inside. Both times she had waited for Claire to emerge on his arm, but he had exited alone. He had not stayed at Claire's for very long, either.

"She's kept herself busy with the house," he said. "Decorating and whatnot. She doesn't seem to have time for anything else."

He waited and was grateful when Jessie did not dispute that. He turned onto the Row and pulled to the curb in front of one of the houses. "Is it this one?" he asked.

"Yes," she said. "I have the upstairs. Why don't you come inside?"

He followed her up the stairs and down the narrow hallway into her kitchen.

"Look," Jessie said, pointing through the window to indicate the yard she had just completed. It replicated the one she had designed for The Tailored Women so many years ago. She had even potted the bedding plants, though she might have, in this instance, placed them right into the earth. "The brunch will be its inauguration." She turned to smile at him, and saw that he was looking, not at her yard, but at Claire's.

"Her car is gone," he said.

Jessie could not resist. "It often is," she told him, moving to the sink and filling a kettle from the faucet. "Coffee?" she asked. "Or would you prefer tea?"

"Either one," he said.

Jessie wondered if he knew about the damage to Claire's car, but his next statement indicated that he did. "She hasn't had it repaired," he reported absentmindedly.

"No," Jessie answered. He was still looking out through the window. Jessie came up behind him to see what he could see.

Jessie's yard was small and square, Claire's long and rectangular. Claire's had been enclosed with a high cedar fence. There was a free-form concrete slab where she parked her Jaguar. The concrete wasn't of the usual sort, but was nubby, filled with large pebbles. Surrounding it was fine gravel that had been raked into swirls. But a long section beside the fence hadn't been graveled. It was marked with pegs, a string boundary stretched between them. Jessie had wondered what it would be. Now she asked.

"A swimming lane," he told her. "The yard's too small for an entire pool, so she'll have just one lane. Enough to take a dip in, or swim laps. She saw one someplace and wanted to copy it right away, · even before she'd moved here."

"How unusual," Jessie said.

"I actually prefer what you've done," he said, settling into one of the kitchen chairs. "Colorful. Old-fashioned."

Jessie smiled and chose tea so that he would not have to endure the whir of the coffee grinder. It was Richmond Blend, and its dark, cinnamon scent filled the air the moment she took the lid off the canister. She had expected him to comment on it, but he didn't.

"What did she say," he asked, "when you invited her?"

Jessie hadn't, yet. She'd never spoken to Claire, nor even so much as met her. She had lied on the spur of the moment, without intending to, only afraid that he would not come without Claire. "She said she'd love to come."

"That's our Claire," he answered, sipping. "Brimming with enthusiasm. She is something."

He left pledging that he would attend the brunch, and later Jessie walked along the Row, distributing the invitations. Jay's mail slot, Rita's, and Margaret's. She saved Claire's for last, sliding it beneath the glass-and-cypress vestibule door.

Jessie thought the Market would not take up much of her time, but she was wrong.

"Wait a minute, Jess," Nick insisted. He had other customers, but he didn't seem to care. "Let's go over this one more time. To be on the safe side, what do you say?"

"Nick, it's all written right there on that slip of paper. And you've done this before."

Nick ignored her protest. "Bloody Marys, right?"

"Right."

"Aw, Jessie, you don't know how happy this makes me. Like old times. Hey, thanks."

"You're welcome, Nick." To hear him, you'd think he'd been invited, when in fact the arrangement was as always. Nick would make the canapés, serve, tend bar. And here he was, thanking her.

"Five people besides you, right?"

"That's what it says on the paper, Nick."

"Rita and Margaret and Jay and who else?" He was hoping, but he was almost afraid to. It was something like not telling someone what you had wished before you wished it.

"And Claire Albritten," Jessie said. She did not mention the Senator.

"And? That's four."

"And Rita said something about bringing someone. Look, Nick, just make lots. Pretend there are ten people, all right?"

"I'll make those little sausage things, you know, the pinwheel kind, like strudel? I made them once before, remember? You liked them."

They were on Jessie's list. "Fine," she said.

"Maybe, I dunno, some stuffed mushrooms or something. I could get the big ones, stuff 'em full of—"

"The sausage wheels are enough. No mushrooms."

"But that won't fill everybody up, them little sausage things."

"I'm going to make omelets, Nick. Now, really, you've got customers, and I've got a million things to do. . . ."

Jessie wondered, walking home, if, indeed, Claire would accept. It would certainly be embarrassing if she didn't. But jutting from Jessie's mailbox, on elegant ivory vellum, was Claire's note.

Jessie smiled as she read it. It was almost as if, when she'd lied to the Senator, she'd known Claire's mind. Claire's exact words were that she'd love to come.

"What do you mean, you can't go?" Rita whined into the telephone. "How can you tell me that?"

"Can-not go," Sin overenunciated. "Go by yourself. What's the big deal? You came to the Corcoran by yourself."

"Yeah," Rita said. "Funny about that, isn't it?"

"Personally, Rita, I was delighted."

"Oh, I'll bet you were. You. You meet me at the Corcoran and you make out with me and then, *months* later, *I* call *you*. And what do you do? You come rushing over to screw me. And then, couple of days later, you do it again. You screwed me yesterday. But you can't go to Jessie's brunch. No. That's too much to ask. All you do is show up to screw me."

Silence.

"Say something," Rita ordered. "Say *some*thing."

"If I were overhearing this conversation," Sin said, "I'd probably be laughing, but as it is . . ."

"Why didn't you call me?" Rita demanded. "Why did you let all that time go by? All that time!"

"I thought we were arguing about the brunch," he said.

"The brunch is only part of it," Rita said. "The brunch is a symptom."

"And," he asked, "the disease?"

"I don't know. Falling in love with you is the disease."

More silence. Then: "Rita, I would like to go. I would *like* to meet your friends. And I will. Someday. Right now, though . . ." He let it hang there.

"Right now what?" She sucked in all the breath that she could hold. "Sin, you have to tell me. Are you married?"

"No."

"Are you living with somebody else?"

"Somebody . . ."

"Somebody," she said angrily. "Another woman. Younger, prettier, a better fuck. Somebody with bigger tits and a Ph.D." She couldn't tell whether she was laughing or crying.

"Okay," he said. "Who squealed. Who told you?"

Laughing, she thought. Except that there were tears running all over her face and she had to wipe her nose with her knuckles.

"Come on," Sin said. "Think about the time we had yesterday, okay? Be happy."

"Yesterday you watched baseball," she said.

He had, too. "Can I talk while this is on," she remembered asking.
"Mmm-hmmm," he said.
"Is that 'yes'?"
"Mmm-hmmm."
"So where was I?" She poked at him with her index finger just as he leaned forward, the better to see something on the television screen.

Then he leaned back. "What? I don't . . . wait!" He sat bolt upright, almost knocking her right off the bed.

"Fuck baseball," she said, looking over at the television just as the camera panned the stands, full of fans who were on their feet and screaming their heads off.

"Triple play!" he shouted, turning the sound way up. "Watch! They'll run it again!"

And so they did, both in slow motion and at regular speed.

Rita couldn't believe the excitement in the announcer's voice, nor that which she heard in Sin's. Ecstasy, pure and simple. "You know what Jane O'Reilly says about sports?" she asked, not waiting for his answer. "Jane O'Reilly says that sports exist to prove that men do have emotions and that they're not afraid to show them."

"Sssh," he said, listening to the announcer recite some statistics. When the commercial came on, he turned to her and said, "I'm sorry. What were you saying?"

"Stop being difficult," Sin said now. "Think about before the game. The pregame warm-up."

"Well . . ."

That *was* better. The air conditioner turned up full blast. She and Sin snuggled under the satin comforter. The sound turned down so low that Rita couldn't make out a word that anybody on the warm-up show was saying. She had her head against Sin's chest, which smelled faintly of gardenia because earlier he'd showered using her soap.

"Okay, okay, okay," Rita said. "You win and I'm going to hang up because this is long distance and I'm sorry I bitched at you and I'm sorry that I sound like I'm keeping score. And I really don't give a shit about the brunch, okay? Forget the brunch, and I mean it. But, Sinnie, listen—"

He cut her short. "Hey, I'll see you soon. How about the day after the brunch, all right? Monday. I'll see you on Monday."

She didn't know why, but it made her mad all over again. She didn't let on, though, just said, "Monday, right."

PART
SIX

EARLY JUNE

Jessie was thankful for the sunlight on the morning of her brunch. Though it was far too early, she went down into the yard to lay the chintz-covered cushions on the chairs. She stood back and surveyed.

It was better than the store display had been.

A tall tree in the alley filtered the light. Its new leaves rustled like taffeta. Even the air seemed to sway. The flowers nodded in their pots, their scents drifting in currents.

When Jessie went back into her apartment, it seemed gloomy, musty, closed. She would have flowers there too, she decided. She went into the cupboard and took down every vase. Then she telephoned Margaret and asked if she would mind driving her to the flower mart in Georgetown.

Jessie walked up and down the long aisles of flowers, choosing. She was at the cash register with her purchases when the sky turned gray. By the time she and Margaret finished loading the car, it had rained.

When they reached the Row, there was sunlight again. "Maybe it didn't rain here," Margaret said. "That happens sometimes."

But Jessie ran to the yard and felt the cushions and knew that it had. "Damn!" she shouted.

Margaret looked up at the sun. "Leave them out here," she advised. "They'll probably dry."

But the branches of the tree, which earlier seemed to add so much to the setting, guaranteed that they wouldn't.

"Let's take them out there then," Margaret tried. "Over there." She pointed to a patch of sun beyond the fence.

"And have someone steal them?" Jessie asked.

"Steal what?" Rita was jogging by. She stopped and leaned on the slatted board fence and wiped her forehead with her sleeve.

"Oh, Rita, Jessie's pretty pillows got all wet," Margaret explained.

"What about the Laundromat?" Rita asked. "They've got those jumbo dryers."

"There isn't time," Jessie protested.

"Sure there's time. I'll take them. Margaret can drop me off."

"While you're over there," Jessie said, "could you check on Nick? He should have been here by now."

"There, see," Rita said. "It all works out. Margaret can bring Nick back with her."

But Nick didn't answer Rita's knock, so Margaret went back to Jessie's alone. "Take down the number of this pay phone," Rita said. "And call me if he still isn't there. If he's not, I'll go down to the Market while these pillows are knocking around and bring him back here. You can pick us both up in forty-five minutes, okay?"

There were three jumbo dryers. Rita stuffed cushions into each of them. They had just started tumbling when Margaret called to say there was no sign of Nick.

Sunday. The Market was closed, of course. Rita should have thought of that, but hadn't. She went around from door to door, banging on them all. When she got back to the Laundromat, she tried Nick's own door again.

But wait a minute. This was a vestibule door. And if Nick was way up on the second floor, he might not have heard. Rita tried the knob and it opened, revealing a long, dirty hallway and a rickety flight of stairs. She could smell the sausage. Even here, it smelled appetizing. She followed her nose.

"Hey!" Nick opened the door, glad to see her. "You're just in time. You can help me lug this thing down the stairs." He stood back to show her a child's wagon filled with cookie sheets, each foil-wrapped. The wagon had rusted everywhere, bed, handle, wheels. "Comes in handy," Nick said.

"Will this thing fit in Margaret's car?" When he answered that it would, she pulled the handle, tugging it out onto the landing.

"Hey, I can't go yet, Rita," Nick said. "There's something I gotta do."

"What?" Rita asked.

"Just somethin'."

She assumed that he had to go to the bathroom. "Fine," she said. "Go do it."

Rita watched from the doorway as Nick began to light the sanc-

tuary candles in front of the plaster statue of the Virgin. There seemed
to be a hundred of them. Rita figured this would take the rest of the
day. She walked inside and sat on the sofa. It had been velvet once,
but now was worn almost through. A little of the velvet remained
in the corners and along the top.

There was a Polaroid camera on the battered coffee table in front
of the sofa. "Gee," Rita said, reaching for it, "I didn't know you
took pictures."

Nick turned suddenly, knocking two of the candles in their glass
cups to the floor. They rolled but they did not break. He stepped
over them and grabbed for some snapshots that Rita hadn't even
noticed. He laughed nervously. "I don't want you seeing none of
these. Being as you're a professional." He tilted the statue back and
tucked the photos under its base. Then he relit the long match and
went back to his candles.

"Jess was worried," Rita said. "She thought you'd be there by
now."

"Yeah, well, I had to get ready." He lit the last of the candles,
waved out the match, and turned.

Rita was suddenly aware that Nick was far more dressed up than
usual. He wore a plaid jacket and even a string bow tie. His hair
was slick with pomade. "You look snazzy," Rita said. "You really
do."

"Well, natch," Nick said. "It ain't every day that a guy gets to pal
around with, you know, a United States senator and his girlfriend."

Rita halted. Jessie had invited them? Did Margaret know? On the
other hand, Margaret did manage to pull off going into work and
seeing him every day, so it would probably work out okay. On the
other hand, Jay wasn't there when Margaret saw him, so it might
not.

But what had possessed Jessie to invite them? Wasn't that a lot of
nerve? How well did Jessie know them, anyway? Well, maybe they
wouldn't come.

"Okay, let's mush," she said to Nick, pulling the wagon forward.
She braced herself so the whole thing didn't come careening down
the stairs. Nick grabbed the rear and balanced it.

"Did they dry?" Jessie pressed her cheek against one of the pillows. "Great. Just put them anywhere for now." Then she turned to Nick, picking up a corner of the foil. "Wonderful. You've already cooked everything."

"I'll stick 'em in the oven," Nick said. "Two hundred degrees. Gotta keep 'em warm."

"And I'll go change," Rita said, indicating her jogging outfit.

"I don't have to change," Margaret announced, "but I'll go see how Jaybird is coming along."

"Come back in about an hour," Jessie told them.

"God," Rita said, watching Claire and Aubrey make their approach. "Who's going to notice my Anne Klein socks when she comes in here dressed like that?"

"Let me see." Jessie joined Rita at the window. Together. She might have known.

"That's real linen she's got on," Rita said. "If our local muggers knew what that kind of outfit was worth, they'd make her strip on the street."

"Let me let her in," Jessie said, descending to the outside door, "before the muggers discover."

Rita looked Jessie's apartment over, trying to determine what Claire and the Senator might think of it. She had always loved the look of this room, but it seemed tacky now. The worn Oriental carpet, the oversized furniture that Rita had once imagined Jessie's ancestors carting across the Appalachians. Everything seemed wrong for the room—the things in it, and possibly the people, too. For the first time, Rita sensed that everything was out of scale here, the ceiling too low, the windows too small for the furnishings. The rug was turned under at the far end of the room, way too large for Jessie's quarters. What had brought Jessie to the Row?

Rita watched Claire and Aubrey walk into the room. Watched

them take it all in. If they thought anything bad, it wasn't obvious. Claire was cool, beautiful. Rita wondered how Sin might have reacted to her.

"Oh." Claire went immediately to a vitrine in which Jessie displayed a wonderful collection of glassware. "This is Biedermeier, isn't it?", running her hand along the veneer. "Oh, Aubrey, look," and Aubrey did so at elaborate length, obviously admiring it.

"My mother has been looking for a Biedermeier sofa," Claire said, looking up to speak to Jessie, but discovering that Jessie had gone.

"She's getting the door," Rita explained. "More people."

"Biedermeier is one of my mother's current . . ." Claire paused, and Jay appeared in the doorway. "Passions." She tilted her head, as if that took care of hello.

"I thought dogs were your mother's passion," Aubrey said, taking two drinks from the tray that Nick proffered and handing one to Claire.

It seemed to Rita that this was a little conversational shtick they had planned—a party opener.

"The dogs are nothing new," Claire said, "but Biedermeier is a passion Mother's only recently acquired." She didn't seem to notice that she had to step completely around Nick's body to sit down.

"Where's Margaret?" Rita asked.

"Right beside me," Jay answered, but without looking to see. "Or she was, anyway, a minute ago."

Rita tuned in and out of the chatter, though not at will. The first sip of the Bloody Mary had gone right to her head. She kept looking at Claire and thinking of Sin, glad now that he wasn't there.

". . . isn't large enough for a pool," Claire was saying, "but there's some sort of zoning problem with the swimming lane. Aubrey's working on that, though." She looked over at Aubrey appreciatively.

"Not in time for this particular summer," Aubrey said, "alas."

"We should all go to Ocean City," Rita offered. "To the beach. God, do I ever love the beach."

"I do too," Claire said. "But I can still hear my mother telling me that only *servants* swim in the ocean." She laughed. "Really. I always waited for her to fall asleep so that I could slip away and swim in real water instead of in our silly old pool."

"Oh yes?" Jessie said. "I hadn't realized you lived near the ocean."

"Only in the winter," Claire explained. "Palm Beach."

"Oh natch," Rita said, getting up and wandering into the kitchen, where she hoped Nick, at least, would commiserate. But Nick stood holding the glass that Claire had emptied as if it were Cinderella's slipper. "Oh no," Rita said. "Not you too."

"What?" Nick asked. "What's the matter?"

"Nothing." Rita walked back along the hallway and stood where she could barely be seen. Maybe the photo she had taken of Claire was an accident, a trick, an illusion, a fluke. Maybe, Rita thought, it wasn't the truth at all.

The Claire in the photograph wasn't at all assured. She was weak, small, reduced by placement and angle. The striation of the light, particularly as it crossed Claire's face, suggested imprisonment.

". . . A rug like this one," Claire was saying, leaning forward to let her hand rest on the weave. "Silk, like this one. But a runner, oh, about twenty feet long."

Aubrey was laughing as though he'd heard the story many times before. Laughing at what was to come.

". . . And it was beautiful, you had to admit," Claire went on. "Colors like stained glass. But the point is, she found it in some African bazaar and they wouldn't let Mother board the plane with the rug *and* me."

"And so she left Claire behind," Aubrey finished the story, "to follow on another plane. 'Well,' she told Claire's father and me, 'she *is* with a native girl. You wouldn't want me to let a rug like this slip through my hands.' "

"I was so young, of course," Claire said, "that it didn't seem at all odd to me." And everybody in the room laughed with her.

As though they're in orbit around her, Rita thought. And she's used to it, being the center of the universe.

Margaret, though, seemed removed. She was looking down at her lap, scraping the edge of a spot of hardened something on her denim skirt. Scraping it with her fingernails, which were surprisingly long, artfully shaped. Rita had a sudden vision of Margaret tearing through the roof of Claire's car with her fingernails.

"Here." Nick urged a glass upon Margaret. "I made this just for you."

"A Virgin Mary," Jay said.

Claire glanced at him. "And are *you* having one too?"

"Listen, everybody," Jessie interrupted. "I want you all outside. Outside, everyone." She picked up the Senator's drink and her own and headed toward the yard. "Nick? Bring everything down, won't you?" she said as she passed him.

Rita stayed behind with Margaret. "Hey," she said. "You're doing just great."

"What do you mean?" Margaret asked.

"With the Senator," Rita said. "I thought you'd be all—"

"Oh, *that*," Margaret cut in. "Honestly, I don't think he even remembers. I barely do myself."

"Yeah?" Rita said. "Well, for me it was quite a night."

"What was quite a night?" Jay appeared in the doorway of Jessie's bedroom.

"What are you doing in there?" Rita asked him. "Why aren't you outside with La Princesa?"

"Why aren't you?" Jay countered.

"Well, come on." Rita stood up. "We can't abandon Jess."

But when she and Margaret and Jay descended into the yard, it seemed they hadn't even been missed. Claire and Aubrey were chatting away, and Jessie was listening as if transfixed. *Really used to carrying the ball, those two,* Rita thought. *The old noblesse oblige.*

Aubrey was mopping his face with a handkerchief. It was easy to see that he would have been more comfortable inside. Jessie was looking directly at him. Rita expected her to suggest going in, but Jessie didn't.

"Did you know your house was once a funeral parlor?" Jessie asked Claire. "I thought of it now because they used to hand out little cardboard fans with their name imprinted on them. I still have one somewhere, I think."

157

"I could certainly use one," Claire said, though she didn't look it. She was just as cool and pressed as she had been in Jessie's living room.

Fresh and newborn, Rita thought.

"Hey, yeah, Jess," Nick said. He'd slipped out of his jacket and undone his string tie. Huge round wet spots began at his underarms and reached halfway down the sides of his shirt. "Don't you think it's kind of muggy out here?"

Jessie frowned at him, but didn't have time to disagree. A cloud passed in front of the sun and threw them all into shadow before she could speak.

"Oh! Just like before!" Margaret said, snatching up two of the pillows. "Quick!"

Everyone followed Margaret's lead. Drinks were guzzled and glasses laid on Nick's tray. Even Claire picked up a pillow. She and Jay almost collided at the foot of the stairs. Claire leaped back as though contact with him would sear her.

Rita put her hands on Jay's shoulders and held him back until Claire had ascended. "Tut-tut," Rita taunted him. "Pearls before swine."

He turned and glared at her.

"Jesus Christ," Rita said. "I'm sorry. I was only kidding."

The sky turned so black that Jessie had to turn the lights on inside. Then, as earlier, there was a brief, drenching rain before the sun came out again.

"It probably cooled things off," Jay said.

"Good. Then we can let some fresh air in here." Jessie switched off the air conditioner and threw open the windows. A breeze pushed at the curtains.

Nick stood in the doorway trying to get Jessie's attention. He was waving an omelet pan.

Then Margaret stumbled and Claire shrieked.

Margaret's Virgin Mary had landed on the floor beside Claire. The glass that had held it was cracked neatly in two. There was a splash, a blood-red sunburst, on Claire's leg. Claire wiped it with her hand. "What a close call," she said. She laughed to show that she wasn't upset at all.

Margaret, on the other hand, seemed semihysterical. Not screaming hysterical, but confused in a serious way. She told Aubrey, not Claire, that she was sorry. Not once, but three times. And then she stood there, staring at the spot on Claire's leg where the splash had been. There were still traces of it on Claire's stocking. And Nick had to actually move Margaret aside so that he could get at the red pool on the floor with a wad of paper towels.

Jay handed Margaret a fresh glass. "Here." He smiled at her. "You get a second chance."

Margaret took the glass and held it with two hands.

Jessie appeared with a dampened hand towel, and Aubrey hastened to take it from her. He knelt at Claire's feet but before he could use the cloth, Claire took it from him, saying, "Oh, Aubrey, please get up." She seemed more annoyed at Aubrey than at having been drenched with Margaret's drink, but she quickly laughed, as if to hide her annoyance. She handed Nick the towel when she finished with it and eased back into her chair.

Nick disappeared. Rita imagined him back in the kitchen, fondling the towel because of where it had been.

Everyone tried very hard to act at though the incident hadn't taken place, but things were even more strained now than they had been before.

Rita had never had a time like this at Jessie's. In the past, everyone had been completely relaxed, and that was the fun of it. Now—because Jessie had introduced the Senator and, especially, Claire into the group—everything was awkward, unnatural.

But Jessie couldn't be blamed. She had no way of knowing about Margaret's crush on the Senator, for instance. And at Jessie's age, she probably didn't perceive Claire as a threat. But God, Rita was really glad now that Sin wasn't there. Claire's good-sport routine had been, well, something Rita never in a million years could have pulled off. Rita looked across the room at Claire and watched as Claire pulled herself upright.

Rita heard it too. "The mad biker!" Rita shouted.

They crowded to the windows as the biker wound down the Row. "Hey, mirror-face! Where've you been?" Rita yelled at him, knowing her voice wouldn't carry over the motorcycle's roar. "He's the one," Rita said to the Senator, "remember? I told you about him."

The biker's appearance revitalized the party. They all laughed and joked and jeered before turning from the window to resettle into their chairs. When they did, they became aware of Claire, standing, clutching her slim white handbag. "I really must go." She smiled at Jessie. "Thank you so much for inviting me."

The Senator rose, startled, but prepared to accompany her.

"No, Aubrey, really. Really, don't." She backed away from him and toward the stairs.

Nick was pushing by with yet another tray. "What, are you leaving?" he asked her. "Hey, you can't leave. We got all this food. Tell her, Jess."

"Boy, if I were you," Rita told Jessie once Claire and Aubrey had gone, "I'd be so damned pissed."

"Maybe she got sick," Margaret said. "Don't you think so, Jaybird?"

"Sick," Jay said. "Sure."

"Well, even if she *was* sick," Rita said, "he didn't have to go too. What is he, some kind of puppet on a string?"

"Maybe he'll come back," Margaret said. "Maybe he's just seeing her home, making sure she's all right."

"Tucking her in," Jay suggested.

"If she's sick," Nick said, "maybe I could make up, like, a little tray of this stuff. You know, take it over to her."

"Yeah, and shove it up her rear," Rita said. "God, Jessie, I can't believe she would do this to you."

"You're all making too much of this," Jessie said. "We've had good times without her. We had good times long before she came."

"Without him, too," Rita said. "Except, I don't know, Jess. I couldn't help but think, when I saw you talking to him . . ."

Jessie stood up and gestured across the room. "Come on, Nick. Put that tray down. Come on, everybody, let's sing."

"I don't want to sing," Rita said.

"Oh yes you do," Jessie told her. She hummed to give them the key. "Come on, 'Sentimental Journey.' "

They looked at each other, shifted awkwardly, but for Jessie's sake began the song.

Aubrey was at Claire's side, though she walked quickly. Twice he attempted to take her arm, and twice she shook him away. She stopped walking abruptly, and when he reached for her she told him that if he so much as touched her sleeve she would scream.

"But what is it?" he asked, his arms where they'd frozen, midreach. "What happened? What's wrong? I can't think of anything, any reason . . ." He let his arms fall, then raised them again to gesture at the houses on the Row. "And those people. Margaret. Jessie. What must they think?"

"I don't care what they think." She started walking again.

"Where are you going?" he asked her. She had passed her own door.

"I don't know," she said.

"Claire. Really. We can't just walk the streets."

"No," she said, "I agree. *We* can't."

He pretended not to notice the word she had emphasized. "Well, then. Let's go inside. We can talk about whatever it is."

She cocked her head toward Jessie's house. She seemed to be listening. Then she laughed. "I do believe they're singing," she said. "You see? They don't think anything at all."

"Still, it wasn't . . ." He hesitated, not wanting to rile her. "Seemly. Our leaving that way."

"Seemly. Oh God, what a wonderful word. No, Aubrey, it wasn't *seemly* of me."

"Of us," he corrected.

"Of us. If that makes you feel better about it." She turned, headed back toward her house now.

"Claire . . ." He was perplexed, but he followed.

She stepped out of her shoes in the vestibule, and he picked them up and carried them inside. At the entrance to the living room, she dropped her linen jacket on the floor. She unhooked the clasp at her waist and drew her skirt down over her hips. She was wearing a white satin slip without trim of any sort.

Aubrey groped toward her.

"I told you," she said, "if you touch me, I'll scream."

She went up the staircase, and he wondered what he ought to do. Finally, he picked up her clothing, folded it, and laid it across the arm of a *faux bois* chair. He sat into the mate to it, opposite, and waited for Claire to reappear.

He kept an eye on his watch. When an hour had passed, he started up in search of her. His heart was thrumming. It was louder than he'd ever heard it.

On the second floor, he moved through each of the rooms, not daring to call her name. He felt that he soiled every immaculate space that he entered.

Then he climbed to the third floor, and then into the turret.

He found her there, amid cardboard boxes and packing crates. She was still wearing the simple white slip. She was kneeling in a sea of excelsior. Several trophies, heavy with tarnish, were arranged beside her.

Her fox-hunting gear was spread out on the floor in the corner. He walked past her, and stooped to touch the black melton coat, the bright canary vest and breeches. Her boots stood tall, patent leather tops gleaming.

It stirred him to see her garments laid out that way. He brushed the velvet of her hunt cap with his fingers, making streaks in the nap. He brushed again to erase them. "I remember all of this," he said. "The way Harnette would set out each of your things. I remember the way you'd inspect them, making sure they were all just so. Just so."

She didn't answer. She kept pulling blackened silver from the box. The excelsior made small, crisp sounds beneath her hands.

"Every season," he continued, "you would dream of being blooded. Every season you would say, 'This year will be the one.' "

Claire stopped what she was doing, remembering with him. Her fingers drifted to her throat. She could still feel Harnette's strong brown fingers there, winding the long white stock tie around and around. Jerking the ends of it into a proper knot. Chiding as she did so. "Blooded, huh? Well, that ain't likely, girl. They don't kill no foxes in this here part of the world, and if you ask me, tha's good. I don't want you coming on home like some cannibal, blood runnin' all down your face. Your Uncle Aubrey, he wouldn't like that neither."

Claire still dreamed of it: the mindless, flat-eyed frenzy of hounds swarming their prey.

In her childhood dreams, she had imagined the scarlet-clad huntsman reaching into that circle of snarling hounds, foaming jaws. Then the huntsman's hand, saving the blood-drenched hank of fur that had been the fox. Holding it high. In Claire's earliest dream, she would be blooded with ceremony. Would dismount and kneel on the dry, frozen earth and wait to have her forehead anointed with precious fox blood.

Steve had altered her dream, deepened it and made it ever so much better. He had told her how he would perform the blooding. She would still kneel. But Steve would wrench a fox's paw from the carcass that the hounds had torn. The bone, stained red, would be sharp, protruding. Steve would take the bone and nick her cheek so that her blood and the fox's would mingle.

It would be solemn and pagan and beautiful, and that way—Steve's way—she would wear the blood-badge not just for a day, but for the rest of her life.

But it hadn't happened, not in all the years she'd been hunting. Harnette had been right. She had never been rewarded with a kill. Had never been blooded, even with the tepid dab that some hunts bestowed when a fox did manage to die.

Claire forced the thought away and returned to the task of uncrating her prizes. But Aubrey went on, prefacing everything he said with a whispered "I remember . . ." She turned to see him fondling the lapel of her melton coat. She stood in one sweeping motion and walked over to where he squatted.

He looked up at her, his eyes glassy. "I remember . . ." he began.

"Stop it."

"But I do remember . . ." He looked away from her, turned his face so that he wouldn't meet her gaze.

She crouched down beside him, moving whenever he did, so that finally he could not continue to look away. "Aubrey," she said, "*I* remember, too."

"But you don't," he protested. "You were just a little girl. You don't know . . ."

She raised herself, laughed down at him. "I *remember,*" she said.

"You invented things," he answered.

"What things?"

"You imagined all sorts of . . . things."

"What things, Aubrey? What things did I imagine?"

"This is foolish," he said, staring at her ankle and shaking his head from side to side. "Foolish."

"What things?"

He looked up at her, and when he did, she slid the strap of her slip down her arm and over her elbow, exposing one breast. Then she reached across and began with the other strap.

"Don't do this," he beseeched her. "Please no. Don't do this, Claire."

"Don't do what?" she asked, doing to him precisely what he had, for so long, done to her. Whenever, as a child, she'd protested one of his fumbling advances, squirmed away from him with a whimpered "Don't do that," he would ask: "Don't do what?"

She was so young, and he was her Uncle Aubrey, her father's friend, her father's substitute, eventually. She was so young, and his question always confused her, always made her wonder if she had, in fact, given Aubrey's idle, innocent touch the wrong significance. She learned not to ask, even in later years, when she knew that she had not been wrong.

"Don't do what?" she repeated now, looking at him in a way that laid bare all of it.

Aubrey covered his face with his hands and sobbed.

She had expected to despise him openly if such a moment ever came. Now that it had, she felt a rush of sympathy, and not for Aubrey alone, but for herself, too.

"I don't know why I said you couldn't touch me," she told him. "It doesn't matter if you do. I don't feel anything when you touch me, Aubrey. I taught myself that. And I became very good at it. At feeling nothing."

Her words were harsh, but her voice indicated that she didn't mean them harshly. This made Aubrey weep.

"Oh, Aubrey. You were sweet and kind and gentle. And that's what did it, don't you see? When I grew up and met others like you, men who were gentle and kind, men who tried to touch me as you

164

did—softly, delicately—*I felt nothing.* I had numbed myself because of you."

"Claire, don't," he said, but it didn't stop her.

"Oh, don't misunderstand me," she went on. "Because I did learn to feel. The first man to make me feel . . ."

"I loved you, Claire. I never . . . I only . . ." He reached for her, for the hem of her slip, but she drew away. He continued to reach out toward her, even taking a few steps on his knees.

"It's no use," she said. "I can't comfort you. You'll have to find someone who can. Just as I have to. Again."

Claire lay in the driftwood bed and pretended to be asleep, until finally she heard Aubrey come down from the top floor and make his way out. He did not stop on the second floor to speak to her, and she was glad of that.

He had stayed up there long after Claire had walked out of the room. So long, in fact, that now it was almost dark outside.

She got up, moved to the window, and flung it open, wrapping her fingertips under the wide outside sill and arching back, as if it helped her to breathe. She listened to the night sounds, sorting them as she did so, searching for the one she most wanted to hear. She might have heard it—she wasn't sure.

She pulled the straps of her slip into place and slid her raincoat over it. She felt hurried. Something pressed against the tender underside of her toe, and she looked down to see what it was. A pearl from the strand that had broken, luminous in the half-light. She put it into her raincoat pocket along with one of her scarves. She felt along the floor, found her ballet slippers, and pulled them on, letting the elastic snap across her instep.

There.

She went out into the street.

In no time at all she was wishing that she'd worn proper shoes, because every uneven patch of pavement seemed to cut right through the slippers to her feet. She felt everything: cracked concrete, bits of stone or gravel, paper, sand, twigs. She worried about glass, but forced herself to keep walking.

Then her heart quickened. She heard the roar of the motorcycle somewhere in the distance. Behind her, yes? She hadn't meant to pause, but had to in order to let the thrill, the shiver, pass through her body. She made the pause seem deliberate, turning the collar of her raincoat up, retying the belt.

She was afraid that he wouldn't stop, would only hover near her, taunting her, and then drive on.

Closer.

The engine erupted beside her and then, just as suddenly, stopped.

She turned, and felt her mouth opening, but instead of words, her breath just caught. The night wind rose just then. She could feel it lifting at the edges of hair. She put a hand up, wondering when she'd let her hair down.

He let the bike tilt left until it came to rest, but he didn't dismount. He let one heavy boot fall to the pavement, that was all. She thought of her ballet slippers and how right they now seemed, feather-light and delicate and weak.

Then he laid his hands, black-gloved hands, on his upper thighs. She thought of her own hands, bare and slender, and her own legs, as thin as his were thick.

Ah, but his face! A secret face, a face behind a mirror mask, a face that could be anyone's.

He stood and humped down on the bike until the huge Harley growl came again. The tail pipes blew papers and dust down the gutter of the street. A shower of dust stung Claire's ankle as she straddled the bike behind him.

She turned her legs out as wide as she could, so that the underside, the tenderest part, would touch his clothing.

He reached back and slapped his palm against her thigh before straightening the bike, a slap that stung more than the whirl of dust had, a slap that would probably leave a mark. Claire smiled and ran her hands along the silky black fabric of his jacket. She leaned back to read what was embroidered there: VIETNAM atop an irregular design—a map of the country, she supposed. And beneath the map,

166

SOUTHEAST ASIA GAMES. She finished reading just in time. Her head snapped back as they broke forward, and her long, pale hair whipped and twisted as they gained speed.

She felt tipsy, drunk, though she wasn't. It probably seemed so, she thought, because of the way the lights on Pennsylvania Avenue blurred into a continuous carnival stream. Claire turned her head so that she'd catch sight of their reflection in one of the plate-glass storefronts, and briefly she thought she did, though for less than a second at a time.

She pulled the scarf from her raincoat pocket and held it at the corner, letting it billow out, like her hair, behind. She watched the windows for the long streak of scarf, but then the windows were gone.

Over the bridge, the Anacostia River black beneath them, Claire realized that she didn't have the scarf anymore, that it had blown off, free. She turned to look for it in the space between bridge and water, but they had reached the ramp now, and she settled against him, following his motion as he leaned.

She pressed her cheek against his back, her eyes closed. She nuzzled the embroidery. She tried to imagine how they looked together, she in white and he in black, both atop a thrusting chrome steed. There should be a moon, a bright full moon, to complete the scene.

The sound changed, and she knew they were over the water again. This time he cruised, so slowly that she marveled he could keep the motorcycle balanced. And then he stopped, but with the engine idling, beating like a drum.

They were alone on the bridge.

A wonderful fear coursed through her.

But then he nudged her with his elbow and she saw why he had stopped. He pointed at the pale silk monogrammed scarf she had lost. She scampered off the bike and retrieved it, then paused at the rail to fling the pearl in her pocket into the river. She held the edge of the scarf, prepared to trail it as before, but he took it from her, knotting in on the center post of the handlebars.

Claire climbed aboard again, giddy, and they took off, her head going *snap,* the engine blaring anew, the two ends of the scarf fluttering up his thighs like silk tongues. She could think of nothing but the way it would be: his black-gloved fingers closing over her naked shoulders.

She strained forward and bit at his jacket, holding the fabric tight in her teeth for as long as she could. When she let go at last, she smoothed her lips over the mark.

He revved and the front of the bike lifted, the verve of the engine shaking right through.

And now, home.

Jay was typing with a vengeance when the telephone rang, and now Margaret was glad of that. She held her free hand over her ear so that she could make out what the Senator was saying. His voice was bleary and his sentences were disconnected. It was clear, however, that he wanted Margaret to come to his apartment.

"Yes, of course. No, I don't mind," Margaret said. She tried to sound the way she might have at the office. She looked anxiously at Jay, but he hadn't noticed anything out of the ordinary. "No, really. It's no trouble at all."

When she got off the phone, she went over to her desk and gathered up some papers. She took anything she came across. She didn't look at Jay. She couldn't. "Some kind of office emergency," she said. "Bob Sandusky wants me to take him some things."

"Fine with me," Jay told her, still pecking away at the keys.

"We might . . . we might work through the night."

"I'll probably do that, too," Jay said. "Go right ahead."

She summoned the courage to glance his way and saw that he was reading what he'd written. He smiled at the paper and then put it aside. He rolled another piece into the machine. "Bye," he said, aligning the sheet.

But then, just as she'd gained the door, he called, "Margaret?" Her heart stopped.

He wanted to know if she had any more typing paper.

"No," she said.

"Then wait up. I'll walk out with you. I may as well finish this at my place."

It seemed to her he took forever to gather up his things.

"What's the emergency?" he asked when they reached the sidewalk.
"Oh, just some dumb speech."
"Well, be good." He kissed her cheek and walked her to the car.

Margaret's hands trembled and her palms were gummy as she drove crosstown. She found herself worrying about little things. Suppose she couldn't find a parking place. Suppose she had a flat tire. Suppose she fainted in the lobby of his building. Suppose he'd only called her as a joke.

But she knew it wasn't a joke when he opened the door.

"I've bought you some things," he said, indicating a roomful of gift-wrapped boxes. There were boxes everywhere, on the floor, on the tables, on the chairs. Small pastel-wrapped boxes and enormous striped ones. Oblong boxes and perfect squares. "Some presents for my little girl."

"But . . ." was all Margaret could manage.

"Here," he said, coming around behind her and laying his hands on her back. "I'll take your coat."

"Senator . . ." she began.

"None of the 'Senator' business," he said. "You just call me what you've always called me. Uncle Aubrey."

"But . . ."

"Come on over here and pick out the one you want to open first."

"I think . . ." She looked around for her coat, but he had hidden it away.

"How about this one?" he suggested. "I bought this one a long, long time ago. You'll like this one. It's very special." He nudged a package into Margaret's hand.

She started to open it. He came closer as she did. His breath came in short, thick spurts. He stood so close that his clothing brushed Margaret's. She stepped away and continued removing the wrapping.

"You always did take your time," he said. "I liked that."

Margaret took a bracelet from the box. Crystal circles joined by

169

silver links. Inside each crystal was a miniature fox head.

"Here," he said, taking it from her and fastening it on her wrist. "Now how about a kiss for your Uncle Aubrey." He offered his cheek, and Margaret let her lips tap at it.

He gave her another box, and she opened it to find a fluffy white angora cardigan. "There!" he said. "I knew you'd like that. Now, come on. Off with the one you're wearing." He undid the buttons of Margaret's blouse. She moved her shoulders so that the blouse would slide off easily. Then she moved her shoulders again to get into the sweater. He buttoned it up. "Oh, that's very pretty," he said, smoothing his hands back and forth across her bosom. "It fits you so well. Yes. Now, let's have another little kiss."

Margaret pecked at his cheek again.

"This time," he instructed her, "you pick one out. That'll be more fun."

She chose a medium-sized box wrapped in rose-colored tissue. It was tied with a curlicue bow.

"That's a very good choice," he said. "You'll like that one, little darling. Now, hold on. Don't open it too fast." He sat on the arm of an easy chair to watch.

Margaret pulled off the tissue, opened the box, and gasped.

"Hold it up, now," the Senator said. "Let's see."

She let the box and the wrapping drop and held up a tiny pair of sheer bikini underpants.

"Like those?" the Senator asked. "Here, let's try them on."

He knelt in front of Margaret and waited while she untied her wraparound denim skirt. She handed it to him, and he folded it. "That's right," he said. "We don't want it to get wrinkled, do we?" Then he stared at Margaret's cotton panties. "Oh, darling," he chuckled. "Oh, darling, how I remember those." He wrapped his arms around Margaret's legs and pressed his cheek against her knees. Then he drew back and tugged at the cotton. "All right, darling, let's just take these old ones off."

Margaret drew the panties over her hips, and the Senator caught at the elastic and took them down the rest of the way. She leaned a hand on his shoulder for balance when she stepped out of them.

He patted her tummy and kissed it. "I'm sure the new ones will fit. They might be a little tight in the back, though. Turn around, little darling, and let your Uncle Aubrey see."

Margaret turned with small, halting steps. He laid his hands and then his lips on her buttocks. "They'll fit just fine," he said. "Better hurry up, now. Lots more presents here to open. Lots more."

When the last gift had been opened and tried, Aubrey Denton sighed and settled wearily into one of the chairs.

The rug was littered with boxes, tissue, ribbon. Margaret knelt and began to refold the wrapping paper.

"Leave it," Aubrey said. "Harnette will get it later."

Margaret looked around for her clothes. She reached for her things cautiously, as if afraid to startle him back to reality.

She glanced at him from time to time, wondering what it was that had drawn her to him, ever. His position, she supposed. As if partaking of it might vindicate her own lack of it. But clearly, it was Claire Albritten and not Aubrey Denton who had power.

After Margaret had made the errant phone call to the Senator so many months before, she had turned to Jay as if to hide behind him. Turned to the fact that Jay—a man who cared for her—existed. But still she had yearned for the Senator, for what the Senator represented. It was the reason she hadn't then, as Rita suggested she should, resigned from her job.

Now, she would. Now, she could. Now, she was free of Aubrey Denton and—she glanced around the room—all this madness.

She took her clothing into the bathroom and changed.

When she came out, she shook his shoulder. "Senator?"

He had closed his eyes and dozed off. He awakened and focused on her. "Margaret." He patted her arm. He stood and looked at all the articles spread about the room. "I'll help you with these," he said.

Margaret wanted none of these things to remind her. She wanted only to get into her car and drive away. She wanted Jay and normalcy, their plans for whatever life they would have. She wanted Rita and Jessie and all of the people who before had never seemed enough.

But Margaret felt that she owed the Senator, who, after all, had not embarrassed her the night that she had telephoned him. The night that *she'd* been foolish. This would be their secret, she assured him, *And* she'd be leaving her job.

"What will you do?" he asked, as they worked to gather the gifts. It was almost as though they had given a party and now were clearing the debris. Even yesterday, a thought like that would have excited her.

"I've been wanting to go to law school," Margaret said.

"I'll write you a recommendation," he answered. "A fine one."

He drove her home. He hadn't remembered that she'd brought her own car, and Margaret couldn't bring herself to tell him.

The Harley whipped around the corner of the Row. It was bent so low that it seemed Claire's bare knee would touch the pavement. The edge of the foot pedal scraped the ground and threw sparks.

The biker stopped at Claire's front door with a lurch that almost stalled the engine. When he cut the power, the bike protested, raising and tossing and bucking. Claire lifted her arms out to the side and let her body follow the movement. When it settled, she climbed out of the vinyl saddle and leaned against it. Her legs felt as if they would not hold her. She spread her raincoat, lifted her slip, and rubbed at them.

Then she moved to the front of the bike and straddled the big front fender. She rested her arms on the handlebars and leaned toward the biker's visor, as if to penetrate the silvered layers of mirror.

He reached up, perhaps to reveal himself.

"No!" she said.

He dropped his hand.

The light from the streetlamp struck the mirror and reflected onto Claire's face. Her skin seemed lit from beneath, white on the bone, black in the hollows. She studied the eerie effect of the light in the visor and then reached forward to stroke it.

He pulled back sharply and slapped her hand away.

She laughed, grabbing the handlebars and arching back, letting her hair swing from side to side.

He braced his legs and grunted and pulled the bike from under her. Her coat tore and she toppled, but caught herself with a hand behind.

She examined the fingers of the hand that had saved her under the streetlight. They were bleeding. Her blood seemed black in that light. She laughed and jammed her hand up toward his face.

He leaped and came down hard, but the bike didn't start. Before he could try it again, she was back at him, her hands and her laughter threatening to snare him.

They scuffled, and he managed to push her away.

She stepped out of the circle of light that the streetlamp made and for a moment it seemed she had disappeared. Then she came at him again, her fingers all over his jacket. She was trying to wipe her blood on the cloth. He caught her wrists and held her off. Then he pushed her again, as hard as he could, jumping the bike with the same, huge effort. The engine caught.

"No, don't go," she screamed, rushing toward him. He whirled her around as he passed, and for a moment she spun there, a smear-white blur.

She started after him in confusion, not knowing why he had chosen to leave. She took several running steps and then stopped and sucked at her fingers as she stood in the street.

The sound of the motorcycle diminished and was replaced by clapping. Claire turned quickly. Yes, it was someone clapping.

"Bravo." Jay stepped out of the shadows to confront her. "That was quite an interesting show."

Rita got Sin's address from the Baltimore operator. Then, to keep from using it, she called Rosenberg and forced him into going to Wolf Trap. And now, after she and Rosenberg had sat on the lawn and watched some dancers who were so far away that they might have been inside a little girl's music box, she'd lured Rosenberg home with her, promising the leftover sausage pinwheels that she'd brought from Jessie's brunch.

But before they got inside Rita's place, there was Margaret, pacing the vestibule. She had obviously been waiting feverishly for Rita.

"Where have you been?" she asked Rita. "And where's Jay?"

"Not with me," Rita said, throwing up her hands. "I'm with this old geezer, see?", pushing Rosenberg forward, into the light.

"Oh God," Margaret said when Rita introduced him.

"Look, Rita," Rosenberg decided, "I'll just be on my way."

"No!" Rita ushered him inside her apartment. "I'm telling you, this isn't like her," she whispered in his ear. "You have to stay."

"You've got to help me," Margaret said. "I've got all these . . . things. And I have to get them out of here before Jay sees them. *You* have to take them, Rita. Really."

"What things?" Rita asked.

"Come up and see."

Rosenberg, meanwhile, had wandered back toward Rita's kitchen. "So where are these sausages?" he asked.

"Just a minute," Rita told Margaret, and then started the oven with a cache of Nick's pinwheels inside. She set the timer. "When this goes off," she told Rosenberg, "eat."

"I don't want Jay to know," Margaret said, as she and Rita took the stairs.

"Don't worry," Rita assured her.

"But he will. My car's there."

"Don't worry. We'll get your car. But where? Where is your car? What's this all about?"

The boxes were piled beside Margaret's coffee table. There were several stacks. Rita took the lids off a few and whistled. "Don't tell me," she said. "You've embarked upon a life of crime."

"Oh, Rita. You have to promise not to tell."

"I promise," Rita said, plundering some more. "So tell."

Together they carried the gifts out onto the landing and then downstairs. The smell of the sausages permeated the hallway. Margaret

174

gestured at Rita's door, reminded by the aroma, of Rosenberg. "What will he think?" she asked.

"Nothing. He's used to craziness."

"Well? Should we take them in?"

"No," Rita said. "Leave them here. You go upstairs and I'll take them in by myself."

She opened the door to find Rosenberg snoring away.

Late—or early—as it was, she tried to phone Sin again. She'd use what had happened with Margaret as an excuse. It was a good excuse, as good a one as any woman ever got to call a man, at that hour, anyway.

There was no answer.

"Is there a name for it?" Rita asked, when she had finished telling Rosenberg, in abbreviated form, all that Margaret had conveyed. "I mean, Christ! She said he even called her Claire. Made her sit in his lap. And those presents. He must have bought Claire something every week! Margaret said that he told her she could have them all. Every one of them!" She looked over at Rosenberg, but he seemed intent on his driving.

"So what do you think?" Rita persisted. "Does it have a name?"

"I think," Rosenberg said, "it's called 'a torch.' "

"Oh, come on. I mean a scientific name. God, they should make a movie. He could run for president, and his opponent could suspect and get somebody to break into his place and find all the stuff and then force him, at the last minute, to renounce the nomination. And it isn't that farfetched, either. Him being President. My God, he's a senator now! Jesus Christ, I didn't even think of that. Maybe we should tell somebody, like the FBI."

"Rita," Rosenberg said.

"Oh, I know, *you* can't, but why shouldn't I? He could have killed Margaret, her walking around his apartment, asshole that she is, dizzy, maybe even drunk. And him thinking she's Claire and then getting mad because she hasn't loved him back all these years. And then wham, just like that, Margaret *is* Claire and Senator Aubrey Denton is going to get even."

"But instead," Rosenberg pointed out, "he brings Margaret home with lots and lots of presents."

"Look, what are you saying? That Aubrey Denton's okay?"

"No, not that he's okay, but that your diagnosis is too ... cinematic."

"Well, you wouldn't give me yours. There it is, right there, the blue one." She pointed out Margaret's car.

He pulled alongside it. "You have the keys?"

Rita jingled them in the air.

"Good. I'll watch till you get started."

Rita was half out of the car, but she looked up at the building where the Senator lived and slipped back inside. "I didn't think of that. Maybe he's watching too. Maybe he's been waiting."

"Rita, it's almost dawn. The car is locked, but I'll wait here and you can check the back seat and the front seat and the glove compartment."

"All right," she said, succumbing to his sarcasm, "I'm going. But back up so I can drive away before you do."

Rita honked Rosenberg good-bye on the Southwest Freeway and then drove right past her exit. She didn't know why.

She did know. She was going to Baltimore, going to find Sin if it was the last thing she ever did. She rolled out Kenilworth Avenue toward the Baltimore-Washington Parkway justifying what she was about to do. *It'll help Margaret's story with Jay. It'll be easier for her to tell him I borrowed the car if I really did borrow the car.* And anyway, considering how infrequently she drove, it was a lot better to be out at this weird hour. No traffic. *And I have to know, I have to. Next to the crazy things Margaret does, this is nothing, this is minimal. I have to know.*

Jay shut the door to the racketball court and was instantly queasy. It seemed that he could smell every drop of sweat that had been spent here. What was more, the white ceiling, white walls, seemed to be closing in on him. A character in a Poe story. Which one? Margaret would know.

It had taken every ounce of courage for Jay to behave with such aplomb when he witnessed the tail end of Claire's scene with the biker. He wondered now at himself. Wondered how he had been able to do it—speak to her so condescendingly—when, in fact, he was wholly shaken by it. Even now, thinking about it.

But that was why he had come here, to exert himself in some healthy way. Exercise? No, exorcise. To be exorcised. He had a lot to get out of his system and was grateful that the Capitol Hill courts were run on an almost twenty-four-hour basis. Whatever it was that was troubling him, he knew, would have to be slammed, not coaxed, forth.

As soon as that thought came to him, he broke into a sweat. The same kind of sweat he'd experienced that night at Claire's. Not the sweat of physical exertion, but one born of fear, a clammy ice-hot sweat. It was as if he had a fever, a fever brought out by the cloying smell, or maybe the austerity of the racketball court. White, white on white, it reminded him . . . no, not like that, not like that at all. Clean white: the court was clean except for some places along the side wall where rackets had scraped.

And there was a ringing in Jay's ears. *Always a little ring in here,* he told himself. But no, this was different, this was the kind of ringing he'd heard a long time ago, a long long time ago, fourth grade, when they'd all made him spin around, spin spin spin. It was someone's party. They had blindfolded him. He'd heard that ringing exactly before his legs folded up underneath him, a high-pitched steady ring.

He was expecting no one, no partner. He had reserved the court, he said, to practice his serve. "Zee serve, I'll bet." The attendant smiled at Jay, stared at his arms as though measuring their power, their stroke.

"Right," Jay said, "the old zee."

"You didn't need no reservation," the attendant told him. "Not this early. Don't know why we're open this late. Guess you can't tell about people, though. You're here, I'm here."

Jay felt as though his collar was searing the back of his neck. "Get out," he told the attendant.

Jay bounced the ball and whacked it, watched it hit the front wall, then the side wall, and land in the left-hand corner of the back court. He didn't need to practice, he had the zee down pat. But he was still feeling queasy, sick. He needed to play more, get in here more. He hadn't played for such a long time, and he was good at it.

Now his hands felt as if they were shaking, but he looked at them, held them up in the cold white light, letting the racket twist and dangle from the cord attached to his wrist . . . *her wrist, her slender wrist, those pale, luminous pearls.* Jay's hands looked steady, no matter how shaky they felt.

Jay tried a straight serve and it was a dandy, channeling back no more than an inch or so off the side wall and landing just a hair from the wall behind . . . *her hair arrayed on the sheet, moon white . . .* "For you, Claire," Jay said, slamming the ball on its return.

Still queasy, still sick. *Fight it, fight it.* Hard to be patient, hard to wait for the ball to fall low enough for the sure kill. Jay waited, proving that he could. He killed and killed and killed, placing the ball on the front wall so low no opponent would ever have reached it. It sounded like rifle fire, the slam, slam, slam of the ball.

He felt a little better, not much, but a little. At least his legs weren't going to collapse beneath him the way they had that once.

The door to the court opened. "Hey," the attendant said, letting the racket cord wind around his wrist. "Looks to me like you need a partner."

"I don't know," Jay stammered. He was, suddenly and overwhelmingly, hungry. He thought he would be all right if only he could get something to eat. Steak. He wanted steak to keep from feeling so sick, so weak.

The attendant shut the door behind him. The smell of the court intensified, all that ice-hot sweat. "Look," the attendant told him, "we don't have to play a game or nothing. We'll just hit the ball around for a while." He served.

Jay automatically returned it.

The attendant examined him. "You been gettin' quite a workout in here, all by yourself." *Slam.*

Jay hit a kill shot that channeled so close to the side wall the attendant ought not to have tried for it. But he did, scraping his knuckles against the white wall and leaving a smear of blood there.

Jay felt the white room tilt and sway. Saw the attendant's face move in and out of focus. It reminded him of the time that Rita had let him look through her camera. Fisheye lens, Rita had said. The attendant seemed to recede, move farther and farther away, but no, it wasn't that, it was Jay who was moving, backing away toward the door, shaking his head, no, no, at the red streaks of blood on the white wall.

"Whatsa matter with you, man?" The attenadant was laughing. He closed his lips over his knuckles and sucked the blood away.

Jay didn't want a partner and wanted to say so, wanted to explain that he was queasy, sick. That he hadn't eaten, that he was sorry.

Words wouldn't come. The attendant watched Jay back out of the court and run away. "Takes all kinds," he said, trying to emulate Jay's swing. "Great kill shot, though."

Jessie was troubled, unable to sleep. She felt as if something ugly had invaded the very walls of her apartment. What could it be? Was it the animosity that they'd all begun heaping on Claire once she'd left the brunch? Had they only been waiting for an occasion to release it? Or was it the animosity that she, Jessie, herself felt?

Oh, she'd seen him, Aubrey, carrying boxes, gifts, from his car. She'd seen him. Paying homage, as it were. Paying homage to Claire.

It had seemed so promising, earlier. Jessie had been so delighted with him—with the stories he told, and especially with the way he'd examined the Biedermeier vitrine.

Edward had been like that, doing all of the things she thought men wouldn't—prowling out-of-the-way antique shops, for instance. Like the one where they'd found Jessie's bed.

"I could send a truck for it," Edward told her, "but you'd better think of a way to use it if I'm going to involve the store."

"Oh, I know just the way," she said, imagining the thrill of walking past what would certainly eventually be *their* bed on display. She'd have a mannequin bending over it, with an open suitcase—a leather-trimmed striped Oshkosh with tiny Yale locks. "She'll be preparing to pack The Tailored Woman's most splendid vacation array," she said to Edward. Jessie could envision the whole scene. Plans often came to her this way, perfect and complete.

"But the bed is so tall!" Edward protested.

"Ah," Jessie said, "that's why we'll have them place the bed beside the escalators. So the ladies can ogle all the way down."

Edward was nodding agreement in what Jessie guessed was his best conference-room manner. And then, quite out of the blue, he tried to lift her—right there in the antique shop, amid the urns and brass cupids and Tiffany shades—onto the bed.

He was off-balance when he started and he couldn't quite make it, almost dropped her, in fact. Finally, red of face, he let her slide to her feet, she laughing, and he stung by his failure. "Here." He reached for her again. "Let me get a better grip."

Several people in the shop had seen and were laughing, too.

Jessie sidestepped, afraid he'd fail again. Afraid, too, that she was somehow at fault. She pointed at the little stool beside the bed, the stool that was next to it even now. "I think that comes with it."

Later, at his place, she poured him a brandy, smoothing his temples. "Edward, Edward, silly. It's not important."

She might have told him the truth. That no man had ever attempted to lift or carry her. That her whole's life's emphasis had been on doing things by and for herself. That she hadn't yet mastered the skills that being with a man required, skills that no doubt even the store clerks already knew. She might have assuaged whatever unmanly things Edward was feeling by confessing her own unwomanliness.

Had that been where it turned?

Before Edward, Jessie had believed that something essential was missing in herself. She couldn't lay her finger upon whatever it was, and after a while stopped pondering and accepted it. *Knew* it. And knowing it, Jessie had, at the expense of all else, pursued her career.

It wasn't that she consciously turned from men. She just assumed she had nothing in her that they might want.

Until Edward. Without his having realized how cataclysmic the event was, Edward had come into her life and tapped a reservoir she'd always thought dry. Waiting for him in the yard she'd built for display, her dreams had run so rampant she could no longer will them away. Edward.

But in the end, he'd chosen a girl twice as assured as Jessie, though half her age.

Jessie had managed to forget the way it all had ended.

Earlier today, with Aubrey Denton sitting in the yard she'd re-created, it had been easy to pretend that she was his hostess and Claire and the others their guests. When Jessie had looked out her window and seen Aubrey's car on the Row, she had for a wild moment thought he was coming to apologize for leaving so abruptly. Then, when she saw the boxes, the gifts, she knew it wasn't so. Paying homage to Claire. Claire, who had wrenched him away. Claire, who had halted Jessie's rush of daydreams, hopes, happiness. Claire, who kept forcing Jessie's mind back to Edward.

Back to the day she'd spent in the Carnegie Museum, hoping to chance upon just the right backdrop to suggest a new display. She'd lost herself in the task, moving from room to room with her sketch pad in hand.

She returned to the store to find Edward in her office. She had forgotten all about his invitation until she saw him there.

"It's all right," he assured her. "Miss . . . Chadwick, is it?", looking at the girl for confirmation. "Miss Chadwick has been entertaining me."

Jennifer Chadwick was a student at Carnegie Tech who had joined Jessie's crew for the summer. She was talented enough, especially considering her youth. She had been sitting on the edge of Jessie's desk, and now slid to her feet. She was smaller, lighter than Jessie. She looked waiflike in her faded dungarees, her oversized sweat shirt. Her long blond hair was tied with a workman's bandanna.

Jessie smiled and waited for the girl to exit.

"You won't forget?" Miss Chadwick said to Edward.

"No, of course not," Edward said.

"Forget what?" Jessie asked when they were alone.

"Oh, the girl had some idea for a winter window."

"Why would she tell you?" Jessie asked. "Why wouldn't she bring it to me?"

Edward laughed. "I suppose she will. But meanwhile, I was here and you weren't. And after all, I *am* the boss."

Jessie dismissed the incident, but a few weeks later she was halted by Edward Moring's secretary as she left the office. Miss Chadwick had left some fabric swatches behind. Would Jessie pass them on to her?

Jessie carried the samples downstairs and dropped them on Jennifer Chadwick's worktable. "You left these," she said, "upstairs."

"Oh, did I?" Jennifer Chadwick looked up at Jessie in wide-eyed innocence. She hadn't tied her hair as usual, Jessie noted. It framed her face, coiled at her shoulders.

Days later, Edward had watched with Jessie when the tall bed they had found in the antique shop was moved into place beside the escalators. Then Jessie's crew came, bearing the items that Jessie had requested.

They were clowning, as they usually did when arranging a display. Jennifer, somehow, seemed separate from the rest. She was diminutive beside the bed, and Edward eyed her perhaps too intently, Jessie thought.

And had Jennifer winked at Edward, or was it Jessie's imagination?

Was it imagination that Edward had begun to mention the girl's name at every turn? Had Miss Chadwick had a hand in the beach wear display? Weren't the fabrics in the Oliver Avenue window those Miss Chadwick had suggested? How was Miss Chadwick coming along?

Jessie was glad when the fall semester began and Jennifer Chadwick was safely back in her college classes.

It seemed a preposterous memory when Jessie chanced upon a playbill on Edward's desk. It announced an upcoming production at Carnegie Tech. The date of opening night had been marked in red— not with a circle, but with a small heart.

Jessie read the credits and, to be sure, the sets had been designed by none other than Miss Jennifer Chadwick.

Jessie made a point of asking Edward to dine with her on the evening the play was to open. And he, of course, demurred.

Jessie watched from a corner of the lobby as Edward arrived at the play alone.

He did not leave alone.

Jessie went directly to his apartment building and waited. Several hours later—after a leisurely dinner, she presumed—he and the girl arrived. Jessie waited through the night. The girl emerged looking far less polished, far less beautiful than she had the night before.

Our Miss Chadwick.

A chill brought Jessie back to the present. It shivered through her body, and she knew that she'd have to give up all thought of falling asleep. There was, indeed, a residue of hatred here. She went into the bathroom and emerged with a steaming, soapy bucket and a sponge. She rolled the sleeves of her nightshirt and busied herself, for what remained of the night, in an attempt to wash the residue away. She began in her own bedroom, with the smudge she had made against the wall. The one marking Edward's height.

Sin's street, Rita thought, absolutely reeked of money. More of an avenue, wide and quiet, with grass strips flanking the sidewalk and huge, spreading trees. The houses were alike and finished to perfection, so impeccable she knew at once they weren't divided into apartments.

These were homes.

Homes for smart young couples, up-and-comers. He'd be a stockbroker and she'd be a lawyer; no kids. Twice a week he'd cook gourmet, and the other three nights she'd scare something up. The rest of the time they'd eat out, and they'd talk about all the great Baltimore restaurants they had yet to discover.

Are you making fun, Rita asked herself, *or are you jealous?*

The morning light was bright enough to let her read the addresses. She pulled to a stop in front of the house that was Sin's.

It was what she would have called a brownstone. But someone— was it Sin?—had told her there were brownstones only in New York. Nonetheless, she looked at the house and thought that inside she might find Nero Wolfe and Archie. Then, in an awful flash, *Sin and . . . who?*

Her next thought might have been beamed in from Rosenberg: *Get out of here. Go home.*

But did she?

She pocketed the car keys and tugged the rearview mirror to the left, the better to examine herself. Then she ransacked her bag for lipstick and a comb. *A little better, but not much.* She pursed her lips at herself, then dabbed some lipstick on her cheeks and smeared.

What she hoped, in the brief seconds between the car and Sin's front door, was that he hadn't looked outside and seen her. But why? Wasn't she about to ring the bell?

One bell for the whole house. More proof that this was no swinging singles' paradise.

When no one answered, Rita felt as if she'd just gotten away with something. But instead of leaving, she sat on the top step and waited.

You're really going to do it to yourself. You really are.

Eventually, people started coming out of the other houses. She was right, for the most part, about the inhabitants, too. She counted the Louis Vuitton portfolios and the Coach bags. Then the Monday-morning back-to-the-office traffic thinned.

Still, Rita waited.

She watched a mail jeep come around the corner. Then the mail-man, wearing Bermudas and a pith helmet, got out and started up the block. When he got to her, Rita reasoned, he would either (a) say hello and hand her the mail or (b) say hello, hand her the mail, and call the police.

He said hello and stepped past her. He stuck the mail, half in, half out, in a shiny brass slot. She waited until he'd driven the jeep away to retrieve it.

Sorry, Sin, just junk for you, Rita thought, flipping through the magazine offers and other ads, all addressed to Martin Sinclair. But then there was a picture postcard, too. Rita ignored the photo and turned it over. It was addressed to Mrs. M. Sinclair.

Rita started to read the message, but her eyes clouded at the salutation: *Evelyn!* Just like that, with an exclamation point. The *Mrs.* was no mistake, no slip of the pen.

Okay, she told herself, you asked for this. Now put the mail where it belongs and get out of here. And when Sin comes tonight, have Margaret tell him you've moved, and then do that, move. Arizona, China, Antartica. But first, get away from *here*.

But she didn't, couldn't. She just sat.

I'll just sit here till I die, Rita decided. Moss can grow up over me. He can find me here, like an old monument. Pigeons on my shoulder, pigeon shit on my shoes. No, not a monument, a tombstone. Tombstone is better, because this is it, I quit.

There were cutoff points for everybody, Rita reasoned. Places in their lives where they'd had one hurt too many. Places where they figured that they might as well pack it in. She didn't mean suicide, though maybe they were dead from that point on. She meant stopping, giving up.

It was just as she'd told Rosenberg, *Jessie knows, Jessie's got the secret.*

Get up right this minute, she told herself. Go home. But still she sat.

"What are you doing here?" Sin asked, coming wearily up the steps. Full daylight now.

Oh, another all-nighter, Rita thought. *I wonder with whom?* He and Evelyn must have some *arrangement.* "Thinking about how my ass hurts," she said, standing, stiff, her knees feeling as though they might crack and her back as if it already had.

"Well"—he had a key in the lock by this time—"come inside."

"Are you mad?" she asked him, hating herself for asking, too.

"No. I'm not anything," he said, walking over the mail.

Their footsteps, hers behind his, sounded hollow. She bit her tongue to keep from asking, *Isn't Evelyn at home?* She followed him down the wide hallway and into the kitchen, then watched him pour himself a glass of milk.

"Want one?" he asked.

She shook her head to say no.

He gulped it down and then leaned against the refrigerator door.

Rita looked around the room. *Microwave, Cuisinart, every appliance known to man.* "My mother would have an orgasm in a kitchen like this," she told him. "Probably her first."

Rows and rows of spices in pottery jars with little cork stoppers, spices she hadn't known existed. Hand-hewn wooden utensils, copper pots. Lots of cookbooks, too. *So Evelyn cooks. Or maybe he does, gourmet, twice a week.*

He pulled a skillet off the overhead rack and lit a burner on the stove. It looked like a restaurant stove. "Can I interest you in some breakfast?" He said it without turning around.

"No, I don't think so," Rita said.

She paused a beat and then told him, "I'm going to look around, okay?"

"Suit yourself." Sin was whisking eggs in an oversized pottery bowl. He still hadn't so much as looked at Rita, really. But he didn't say "Don't go here" or "Don't go there."

"It's really okay?"

"Yes," he said, "it's really okay."

She thought of *Jane Eyre. No tower, Sin, where Evelyn is chained? No reaction to my being here, Sin? Nothing at all?* "Well," she said, "you just go on with your eggs."

She didn't like anything about this. Wasn't he afraid? Damn, *she* was afraid. Maybe he *wanted* her to find whatever it was. Maybe he figured she was here and it was just too late. Maybe Evelyn was up there, too. Maybe he even thought the three of them could play games.

Maybe shit. Maybe she could just hear her mother yapping at her while she walked through someone else's house: *You be careful. If something turns up missing, who do you think they'll blame?*

She went upstairs. *Their room,* she thought. Huge. Pink marble fireplace, pink marble sills. Pale pink silk on the bed. *He probably wears a smoking jacket, like the Thin Man. And she wears one of those long, elegant satiny things. They sit here and they sip champagne.*

That dressing table, God, kidney-shaped and mirror-topped, with dozens of little crystal bottles, all shapes, all colors, almost every one of them with an atomizer or a glass stopper. *Yes, like the Thin Man, that era. He probably finds them for her in out-of-the-way Deco places, and she tells him he shouldn't have, calls him darling.*

Rita walked over to the dressing table, planning to treat herself to a good, long farewell sniff and squeeze. And then she saw it, an official-looking document. *Johns Hopkins University Hospital. Department of Pathology.* With *Hand Carry* stamped in red at the bottom.

Rita bent to read the part that was typed. The name, *Evelyn Emery Sinclair.* And then, *Diagnosis: Melanoma.*

Sin came up behind her before she knew he was there. He caught her waist and she straightened with a gasp. He circled her with his arms from behind, and she looked up to see their reflection in the mirror.

"She keeps it there," he said. "I could never figure out why. Whether to remind herself or whether to remind me."

"Where is she?" Rita asked.

"The hospital. She went in—to stay, I mean—just last night."

Rita's head ached, everything ached. It was like a soap opera, only happening, real. Still, he should have told her, should have *said.*

And worse than that, he was nuzzling at the back of her neck. Right here, in their *bedroom.* It was repulsive. "Sinnie"—she pulled away from him—"come on, don't." She knocked a couple of perfume bottles over and then quickly set them right. Then she watched behind her, in the mirror.

"Rita, when I'm with you, and only when I'm with you, *this* isn't happening. All *this* goes away."

That was it, the worst thing he could possibly say. "How goddamn *nice* for you, Sin." She spat the words out at him. "How nice that you can do that, make it all go away." *Let me out of here,* she was thinking, if she was thinking at all.

She whirled and made a move toward the door, and he blocked her path. "That didn't come out right," he said. "That isn't what I mean. Please, Rita, don't go. Please, listen to me." He guided her toward the bed and made her sit and she did, but far enough away.

"I'm listening," she said, staring down at her lap.

"I didn't know, at the Corcoran. When I met you, I didn't know. *She* knew, but she hadn't told me. She told me that night. When you, when everyone, had gone away."

"She was *there!* While you were in that office with me, she was *there!*" She looked at him now, looked hard. She couldn't believe it.

"Well, of *course* she was there. But I didn't know she was dying. I didn't even know she was sick."

"Sinnie, you made out with me with your *wife* in the next room? And it was okay, because you didn't know she was sick?" She got up, or tried to, but he grabbed her wrist and jerked her back.

"My wife?" He started to laugh or cry or something, both. He kept hold of Rita's wrist, though, even as she struggled, yanked, and pulled.

"Let go of me. I just want to get out of here, okay?" She thought about really socking him with her free hand, but didn't. She finally stopped fighting him and stood there. "Fine," she said. "Say what you have to say."

"Evelyn Sinclair," he told her, "is my mother." He dropped her wrist at last.

"Oh," Rita said. Her emotions started somersaulting. First she was glad, then sorry to have been glad, then just sorry. "Oh," she said again, putting her arms around his neck and pressing against him.

"Should we," she later asked, "be going out as if nothing's happening? Going out when your mother is . . ."

"Yes," he said, "I think we should."

"But—"

"Because if we don't," Sin interrupted, "I'll go nuts. Oh, look, Rita, don't misunderstand this, but I've been trapped by all this. By her illness. That night . . . that night at the Corcoran . . . oh Jesus." He turned away to face the window, and Rita walked up behind him, running her hands across his shoulders, his back. She was afraid he'd stop talking, but he didn't.

"Even while she was telling me," he said, "I was thinking about you. I heard her, but it didn't sink in. She was telling me, and there

I was, looking right past her and thinking about what it had been like when I took you into that little office. I think I must have even smiled while she was telling me, and finally, when I looked back at her and saw the expression on her face . . ."

"Oh, Sinnie," Rita said.

"She asked me to move in with her. Up here. The first thing I thought was, no, I won't. I didn't want to, Rita. I know how bad that sounds, but—"

"No." Rita stopped him. "Really. No. It's natural. And it makes it matter even more that you did it when you *didn't* want to."

"I never even liked her," Sin said. "I mean, I loved her, but she was always after me to be somebody else. She never understood about photography. About why I'd chosen to do it."

"Yeah," Rita told him, "my mother too."

He looked at her. "You never talk about your family," he said.

"Yeah, well, I don't know. Past a certain age, it seems kind of stupid. But my mother, she's sort of the blue-collar version of yours, I guess. And my father's dead. I think that's what Rosenberg is to me, really. Not a shrink, but a father substitute. But don't tell him that."

"Tell me about your father," Sin coaxed her. He put his arms around her and stood there swaying with her, back and forth.

"What I remember—the way I remember him, I mean—sounds really dumb."

"Try me," Sin said.

"Well," she began, laughing a little, "my father had this fixation about running out of toilet paper. Also soap. When our stock at home dwindled to something like thirty rolls or twenty-five bars, he would rush out, you know, to replenish the supply.

"To look at my dad, you wouldn't think of him as tidy. His face was . . . florid. And he sweated a lot. He had, you might say, a pretty messy look, overall. But oh, I'll tell you, he was much if not overly concerned with matters of cleanliness. He would rail if he found a hair stuck in the soap, or a Pepsi bottle that hadn't been rinsed before being placed in the return carton."

She was quiet for what seemed a long while, and then she continued. "I remember when we studied *King Lear* in school. The prof did like twenty minutes on Lear's rage. He kept using the word *excess,* over and over again, and giving examples from the text. I kept looking around the room, and there everybody was, busily writing, their heads going up and down because they agreed.

"*Christ,* I thought, thinking about what it would have been like for Cordelia if she hadn't rinsed out a Pepsi bottle. Or if she'd put her sneakers on without drowning them first in Dr. Scholl's.

"Now don't get me wrong. My dad wasn't a highfalutin guy. He didn't say things like 'Convey into her womb sterility' or anything like that. He usually gave me a simple 'Of all the lousy, no-good, rotten, good-for-nothing—' " She broke off, laughing.

Sin waited, hoping she'd go on, and she did. "Christ, *King Lear.* My father wrecked it for me. After he died, I could see my father out there on the heath, flushing and sweating and shaking his god-damn fist at—what did the prof call it?—oh yeah, *Raging Nature.* Anyway, there's my father, see, on the heath. One hand is the fist and the other hand is keeping the towel around his waist together. And he's yelling his head off at me, saying 'Is it so bloody hard to rinse the soap off before you get out of the tub?' "

She had Sin laughing with her. He kissed her sweetly, damp lips on her cheek, her nose, her eyelids. "I love you," he said.

"Sinnie," Rita whispered, over and over again. Goddamn, but she should have been with him, right beside him, in those awful hospital corridors. Goddamn, but she *belonged* with him.

But later, she had a momentary resurgence of inadequacy. "Do you think your mother would have liked me?" she asked.

"Does it matter?"

"Not a whole lot."

"Well, wait a minute," he said. "What would your folks have thought of me?"

This made Rita giggle. "As a matter of fact, my father always told me I should marry a beer distributor," she admitted. "They'd have hated you, probably."

"What are you telling me?" he teased her. "That I'm some sort of Ivy League type?"

"Actually, that was what I liked about you right away," she said. "That if I were casting you in a movie, I could make you either a street punk or a spoiled rich kid. Really, you could go either way."

"Comforting." He laughed.

"But, see? I couldn't. Go either way."

"Rita," he said, pulling her into his lap, "I like you fine just *your* way. This way. Okay?"

PART SEVEN

AUGUST

"Can you believe this?" Rita bubbled at Rosenberg. The opening of her photo show was under way. The bank's community room was bright and airy, and best of all, there was enough space so that people could stand back and get a good look at the pictures. It was also festive, made so by a champagne punch and several platters of tiny crustless sandwiches. "Even the Senator is here," she said.

"In a manner of speaking," Rosenberg answered, "the Senator is here."

Aubrey Denton had come into the exhibit alone, and had stationed himself in front of the blowup of Claire. His attention was so fixed that Rita imagined that if Claire herself were to approach him, he would turn away from her, turn back to the image on the wall.

"Well, I knew it was good," Rita commented, "but I must say, I didn't think *that* good."

"The hell you didn't," Rosenberg said.

"What I like," Rita noted, "is that people actually look at it. They don't just breeze past. It actually stops them in their tracks."

Jessie, for instance, had stood in front of the picture for at least five minutes, pondering. It had made Rita nervous, wondering what Jessie would say, because Jessie's opinions always sounded, to Rita, like those of a full-fledged art critic. She had stood beside Jessie, trying to read the expression on her face.

Finally, "I really like the way you've trapped her," Jessie began.

"Trapped?" Most people would have said *caught*. In fact, it always infuriated Rita that photographic moments were spoken of that way, as if by accident. At least *trapped* sounded deliberate.

Jessie pointed at the blowup. "Trapped. Trapped by all the angles. Everything—the doorway, the long hall, all of it—funnels the eye there." She made a stabbing gesture at the portion of the print where Claire appeared. "And the shadow of the railing," Jessie went on.

"I know," Rita broke in, delighted, "it's like bars on a cage. But it suggests bars, it's not real obvious, the way the bars in *American Gigolo* are, like, every time you turn around in that movie, you get bars."

She was in turn interrupted by Jay, who patted her head and then

195

her shoulder and addressed Jessie. "How do you suppose Rita would communicate if movies hadn't been invented?"

Rita was glad to see Jay being more or less his old self again. Earlier, she'd confided to Rosenberg that the Faye Arensberg book was turning Jay into a recluse, or worse. Today, though, he seemed more or less okay.

Still, Jay didn't say diddly-shit about any of Rita's pictures, not even the one of Claire. As a matter of fact, he hadn't even looked at the picture of Claire, even when he was standing right on top of it.

Relax, Rita told herself, *what do you care?*

Jay could be jealous, Rosenberg said, of Rita's current success. People get that way, he reminded her, citing as an example Rita's own behavior the night Sin's exhibit opened.

Rita smiled at the memory. God, she'd been jealous of everyone under the sun. Did Rosenberg remember the time she had driven herself crazy by peeking at Margaret's W-2? Now Margaret would be church-mouse poor. At least, she'd called Rita at Sin's to say that she had quit her job and was planning to go to law school. It would be up to Jay to support her. Turnabout, she said. It was only fair.

Turnabout. So Rita knew at long last what Margaret had been doing with all her money. But what made her think she could rely on Jay? Was he turning over a new leaf? Would he actually produce?

But Margaret also said that law school would come next year. Meanwhile, she'd taken a temporary assignment with the Senate Foreign Relations Committee. So Jay wasn't on the hook just yet.

Rita pulled Rosenberg's cuff back so that she could see the face of his wristwatch. "I'm worried about Sin," she said. "He should have been here by now."

"His mother, is she still hanging on?"

"Yes," Rita said.

Rita had been wanting to talk to Rosenberg about Evelyn Sinclair, but there didn't seem to be time for anything like that anymore. When Rita wasn't in transit between Washington and Baltimore, she was working, shooting an assignment or casing a location, or processing her film. But the deathwatch she and Sin maintained was getting to Rita in a number of ways.

For one thing, Rita had never been around anyone who was actually, day by day, dying. When Rita's father had died, it was bang, like that, a heart attack. This was awful and frightening, and sometimes Rita left the hospital sure that the smell of death was all over her. Dogs would turn away and cats would climb trees and even birds wouldn't come near either of them ever again. It was stupid and crazy, but she felt that way.

And why was Evelyn Sinclair still alive? It had to be because she wanted to be, but why would she *want* to be?

Evelyn Sinclair looked dead already, but the sound of her breathing—long deep breaths followed by long deep silences—said she was alive. Sin would sit there and talk to her as if she could hear. And maybe she could. Who knew?

One time, when Sin had paused in his bedside monologue, Rita saw Evelyn Sinclair try to form a word. At least, she pursed and then spread her lips over and over again. Her lips were dry, cracked, more white than pink. And no sound came out, no voice, none.

Rita—this was maybe the lowest of all—found herself thinking of the photograph she could have made of that. Evelyn Sinclair's chapped, broken lips and Sin bending over them. She hated herself for having such a thought at such a time. Callous bitch, she called herself. She didn't even dare tell Sin. But oh, she wanted to talk to Rosenberg about the whole thing, all of it, wanted to.

"Hey, sorry I'm late." Sin's voice behind her.

"Ah. My two favorite men in all the world get to meet at last," Rita said.

"A pleasure." Rosenberg pumped Sin's hand.

"It isn't every day," Sin said, "a fellow gets to meet his girl's psychiatrist."

Rosenberg laughed. "Did she call me that? Her psychiatrist?"

"Actually," Rita butted in, hugging Rosenberg, "as the good doctor is so fond of reminding me, I never once paid him, which makes him a friend instead of—"

"Rita, that reminds me," Rosenberg interrupted. "There's something I've been wanting to mention."

"Oh no!" Rita said. "You're going to send me a bill!"

"No. But I am going back into practice. I've made up my mind. Being retired, it was making me old before my time. But don't worry," he teased, indicating Rita's photographs and the onlookers they had drawn, "you'll be able to afford me now." He patted Rita's shoulder and walked off in the direction of the punch bowl. His step was jaunty again, Rita noticed, the way it had been when she met him. She watched him hustle a brunette with a poodly haircut. The brunette laughed and turned around. Rita clutched Sin's arm. "That's Margaret," she said.

"You told me she was dowdy," Sin complained. "She doesn't look dowdy to me."

And she wasn't. She had even done her eyes. Before Rita could even introduce Sin, Jay came over and draped his arm around Margaret, establishing territorial rights.

"Don't sweat it, Jay," Rita felt like saying, "Sin's got *me*." She felt that way—as if she truly were a prize.

Rita had finally realized the extent of her pretense. It wasn't just a matter of charging things she couldn't afford, or imitating Jessie, or wishing she could change places with Claire. Rita had pretty much gone all the way, never talking about her past, never admitting her background to anyone. That day with Sin—when she'd found out about his mother and when she'd talked, once and for all, about her own parents—she'd broken some kind of barrier. She didn't want to be anyone else and she didn't assume that Sin would want anyone but her. She was glad to be Rita Puleo, and she'd keep that name, she'd decided, even if she and Sin married.

And all of this showed. It showed in her face and it showed in her work and it showed in her relationship with Sin. Rita didn't have to prove anything. She, herself, was the proof.

"You know who's missing?" Rita looked around the room. "Claire."

"Tsk-tsk-tsk," Jay said. "Such a loss."

"Why do you have it in for her?" Rita wanted to know. "She never did a thing to you."

"And I," Jay said, "never did a thing to her."

"Nick!" Rita said, looking past Jay. She left the group to embrace Nick. "Oh, you came!" she told him.

"I coulda done a lot better than these sandwiches," he said, pulling a mangled one from his pocket. "A lot better."

"Oh, Nick, I'm so glad you're here. Come on, meet Sin."

"Miss Puleo?" A woman on the staff of the bank approached her just after she'd finished introducing the men. "There's someone outside who'd like to see you."

Rita told Nick, Sin, and anyone else who could hear that she'd be right back.

She stepped outside and looked up and down the street. There were people, but no one who seemed to want to see her. She was about to go back in when LeGrande stepped out from one of the doorways. She looked for his macho friend, but apparently he was alone.

"You got your pictures up in there?" he asked her.

"That's right," she said.

"You got that one up? Of me and Denise?"

So that was it. "Yes," she told him.

"All right if I come see it?"

"Sure."

"All right if I bring Denise?"

"Hell, yes. Bring your whole family. Your mother, your grandmother, your aunts, your uncles." She would have invited LeGrande if she had thought he'd be interested. His seeking her out to ask her made Rita's whole day. It was pure—the way Nick's appearance was pure—because it wasn't tainted by any feeling of how he *ought* to be there. He *wanted* to be.

Claire was the last to arrive. It was amazing to watch the way she changed the motion in the room. At first there was a dip in the noise level—more whispering and less actual talk. Then, as though she were drawing them in some mysterious, moonlike way, people, even strangers, began to move in her direction. Not obviously. Initially, they seemed to lean toward her. Pretty soon, they'd taken one, two, or a few steps. Finally, the side of the room where Claire *wasn't* had been virtually deserted. It was Sin who pointed all of this out. "Interesting," he commented.

"They ought to use her in high-school gym classes," Rita added.

"You know how those teachers were all the time harping about posture. Watch the way people stand when they're talking to her."

Men, especially, stood taller, but she had a noticeable effect on the carriage of women, too. It went beyond stance. Everyone seemed eager, more animated in Claire's presence. They vied for it.

"Look at Rosenberg," Rita said. "He's lit up like a light bulb."

"Probably professional interest."

"Oh, come on. Claire needs a shrink like I need"—she snatched up another handful of sandwiches—"more calories. Should I introduce them?"

"What makes you think Rosenberg is looking for somebody?" Sin asked.

"I think," Rita said, "we're all looking for somebody. Whether we know it or not. Whether we admit it or not."

But now came the moment Rita wanted and yet dreaded most. Claire Albritten was standing in front of the photograph of herself. Rita had asked Claire to sign a blanket permission form just after the photo session at Claire's home. Claire had, but with no knowledge of the existence of this particular shot. There was little Claire could do if she didn't like the picture. Nothing she could do, in fact. But Claire's reaction was important to Rita.

Rita walked over to stand beside her. Claire reached for Rita's hand and squeezed. She didn't seem able to speak, she was so moved.

"I'm real glad you like it," Rita said, sounding far more matter-of-fact than she felt. "I have a copy for you. I had it framed and everything. Do you want Sinnie to put it in your car?"

"Please," Claire said.

Claire was still in front of the photograph when Sin and Rita returned from the street. She seemed unaware of all but that picture. Unaware, for instance, of the way so many in the room were riveted, watching her. Nick, LeGrande, Jessie, Aubrey, Margaret, Jay. Each of them watched from somewhere in the exhibit room.

After Claire left, everyone else began to go. Now Rita and Sin were alone except for someone clearing up dishes and glassware and ashtrays.

Sin touched the frizzy edges of Rita's hair with his fingertips. "It was great," he said. "A real triumph."

Rita giggled. "You sound like a newspaper. Speaking of which, I don't know. Maybe I shouldn't have said all that stuff." But when the Capitol Hill reporter approached her, Rita was simply carried away. Even Sin, at his Corcoran opening, hadn't been interviewed! Rita had gone on and on about the way photographers got typecast in Washington, stuck either in the commercial camp or in the art camp. And, of course, how there wasn't any money in art. "Oh God, Sin," she asked, "did I badmouth anybody?"

"As a matter of fact," he told her, "you badmouthed everybody."

"Oh no," she said, "who?"

"Candice Bergen, Caroline Kennedy, Gina Lollabrigida, Susan Ford . . ."

"What did I say?"

"That they used more than their eyes to get ahead. And that you were better than all of them put together."

"I didn't!"

"You did."

Rita thought for a bit. "Well," she decided, "at least it's true."

It was still early when they got back to Rita's place—just turning dark, in fact. Sin grabbed the newspaper and started through it, tossing all but the movie guide aside. This he held up, making it into a question.

Rita felt like dropping into bed and staying there. But "Sure," she said. "Only I don't want to see anything that's *moving* or *intelligent* or *deeply meaningful,* okay?"

"Agreed. How about a revival?"

"What's around?"

"*Polyester,*" he read, "at the Circle."

"No thanks."

"*Dona Flor and Her Two Husbands?*"

"I've seen it three times. But maybe. Where is that?"

"Inner Circle."

"What's at the Biograph?" Rita asked.

"*The Woman in White.*"

"Shit. You just saw it."

"I did?"

"Well, not *just,* but not that long ago. First time you came here, remember? I joked around about watching it on TV, and you said you just saw it."

"Oh, that. Well, I was sort of joking, too. What I saw was—see, now I even know who—Claire. *A* woman in white."

"What are you talking about?"

"The first night. When I pulled up, to see you, she was standing there, at the curb. Claire. All dressed in white. That's what I meant when I said that. You just never let me get around to explaining."

"My God," Rita said, "when you got here it was the middle of the night."

"It was pretty late."

"And she was *standing* out there? God, she must be out of her head."

"Make up your mind," Sin said.

"Well, basically, I don't think she needs a shrink. I just think she doesn't know shit about the city and so sometimes the things she does seem, I don't know, odd."

"I meant, make up your mind about the *movie.*"

"Oh, the movie. *The Woman in White,* of course."

"Say, baby, what's happening? You ain't done no talkin' lately about the Planet Claire."

LeGrande had finally told Claude about that. He told Claude the truth now, too. "I don't want to talk about her, man. The chick is some kind of weird." It was a conclusion LeGrande would rather not have reached. Now everything was twisted in an odd sort of way, his thoughts, his feelings.

"Bad weird or good weird or what?" Claude asked.

"Jes' weird," LeGrande said, sitting down on one of the wino benches in the park.

"I thought she was your fox, LeGrande. I thought she was your white-tailed fox."

"She ain't my fox," LeGrande told him. "She ain't my nothin'."

He could not believe that he had once dreamed about a whole planet full of girls like Claire. It was just too much to contemplate. He felt better thinking there were only two: the Claire everybody else saw and the one he knew about. He saw truths about her everywhere, like even in that picture they had up of her there at the bank. Damn, but that picture troubled him.

He started getting mixed up about her after he'd found out about that mousy dude going there, the night the biker chased that girl down the street. Man, that night had put him through some changes.

He'd still gone over to her place afterward, still said "Miz Albritten" and all like nothing had happened, still worked for her.

But it wasn't the same.

And what about those things of hers, all her underthings and nightgowns and stuff? Stuff she'd worn, too. He could smell her on those things like she was still in them. She'd started leaving them out for him to find.

He told Claude all of this, even about the day she had him come up to her room, her just wearing that white robe and spreading herself out all over the bed.

But Claude didn't seem surprised. "Yeah," he told LeGrande, "and that ain't all. I hear she rode on that bike, too. The Harley."

That made everything else seem of a piece. And LeGrande didn't want to believe any of it, but especially not that, Claire with her legs spread and her hair flying on the back of that bike. "That bike ain't been around," he said.

"That's right," Claude insisted, "but it ain't been around 'cause she rode on it. Give it some kind of curse is what I heard."

"How do you know?" LeGrande asked.

"I just know, that's all."

He found himself following Claude. He knew from the way Claude walked that there was some goal, some purpose. He had not expected Claude to lead him to the motorcycle. It was in the alley back behind the market.

Claude pulled a board back so that LeGrande could see into the garage where the big chrome machine rested. It was like seeing some deadly jungle beast asleep in its cave. "That is one mean bike," LeGrande said. "I wonder why he ain't ridin' it."

"Go on, boy." Claude shoved LeGrande toward the opening with his knee. "You can fit yourself through there."

"Yeah, but s'pose . . ."

"Just go on," Claude said.

Then LeGrande was looking at the motorcycle in the garage gloom, and examining, too, the pale silk scarf tied to its handlebars. No mistake about it, LeGrande had seen the scarf before. And anyway, it carried her initials. "I can't picture her riding this thing," LeGrande said, though, by God, he could. "I can't picture it. He musta stole that scarf." He put his head down and rubbed his eyes, trying to erase the picture of her riding that thing. Why did that bother him so much? Supposing that she did?

When he looked up at his friend, Claude had slipped into that black, shiny jacket. "Aw shit, Claude," LeGrande said, "you ain't tellin' me that the biker is you."

"Naw," he said. "Biker is this cat named Zabo. I do a little dealing with him now and then. But I'm tellin' you, he said the chick fuckin' attacked him. Like she was crazy or somethin'. It must have been wild, man." He pointed at the helmet on the floor in the dank garage corner. The mirror visor was ruined, cracked clean through.

"She do that?" LeGrande asked.

"No, he did it. Right afterward. He come back and threw the thing. But on account of her, though."

"You see him do it?"

"No. He told me about it. He said he'd give me a real good price on the Harley, if I wanted it."

"You gonna buy it?"

"Well, I got some bread saved. But I don't know. Seems like she put a curse on this machine or something."

They both stared at the bike. It seemed to have lost a lot of its gleam. "Anyway," Claude continued, "after that night, Zabo, he won't ride the thing, and he won't deal no more. Said he was going back to just making deliveries or something. He said everything seemed like it was too close after that. Like he had too much to lose. Wife and kid and all."

"He white?"

"Yeah."

Claude watched LeGrande, and then he said, "We could fix her if we wanted to. We could fix her good. See, I been thinking about coming up with something, like a plan. I don't know how it goes, exactly, but I do know how it ends."

"How?" LeGrande could not help asking.

"With you and me not ever having to work for nobody no more."

After Rita's photo show, Nick had thrown out all the snapshots he'd taken. They weren't much good, anyway—just girls in the Laundromat. And because he'd taken them from above, you couldn't even tell, really, who they were. You couldn't see the things they were folding, either, the underwear and so on. They were no damn good, the pictures, not even the ones of the sniffer, because there was no way of telling what it was she was doing.

Nick knew what he wanted a picture of, and it had nothing to do with the girls who did their wash downstairs. He wanted a picture of Claire Albritten. A picture of her that would be his very own. He might even tack it up beside the statue of the Virgin, because that way he could light his candles for the both of them. It would be the last picture he'd take.

He picked up his Polaroid and went out for a walk along the Row. He just might get lucky and see her going in or out.

It scared him, though, being there with his camera and all. He walked as quietly as he could so that he could keep on listening all around. This time of year, it wasn't easy. There was a night wind blowing. Scary, the wind, the way it pushed the street grit along. It sound like someone skipping. More than once Nick almost dropped the camera so that he could run.

All her downstairs lights were on, but she wasn't in any of the rooms that he could see into. He couldn't go right up to the windows and look in, but because the panes were long and wide, by moving around on the pavement Nick could see in. He had to be really careful, though. If someone were to see him, they would know right off. They might start asking questions, even going back to Faye. Nick didn't want questions. Questions made him stutter. Stuttering made him sound as though he wasn't telling the truth. He'd made a novena after Faye so they wouldn't ask him questions. The Virgin had granted what Nick asked. But supposing he had to ask again?

"Watch where you goin', dude."

Nick had been turning around and around, listening, making sure no one would see him with his Polaroid. He'd backed right into Claude. He looked up now into Claude's unsmiling brown face.

"You hear me?" Claude said. "Get out' my way."

"I wasn't takin' no pictures," Nick said. "I wasn't."

Claude was about to say "Who said you was?" But then he saw the way Nick kept glancing up at Claire's windows and he knew, pretty much, what Nick was up to. Zabo had told him a couple of things, too, about how the guy was all hung up and weird. "Yes you was takin' pictures," Claude said. "I know all about your pictures."

Nick started sweating. He thought real fast. "No," he said. "I'm sellin' this camera, see? Know anyone who wants to buy it?"

Claude took the camera from Nick and rolled it over and over under the streetlamp. He held it up to his face, looked through the viewfinder. "Is it hot?"

"Naw," Nick said.

"Five," Claude said.

"All right." Nick held out his hand. "Five."

After that, there was nothing for Nick to do except go home.

PART EIGHT

SEPTEMBER

Rita had just entered the neon-and-chrome interior of Macchia-velli's when she spotted Jessie on the far side of the room. When the little restaurant on Pennsylvania Avenue had first opened, she and Jessie had come here together at least twice a week. After a while, when they'd sampled just about everything on the menu, they'd eaten here less often. Somewhere in the course of time, they'd stopped coming altogether. Rita wondered about that now. "Holy cow," she said, helping herself to a chair at Jessie's table. "If you knew you were having dinner here, why didn't you call me?"

"I thought you'd be with Sin," Jessie said.

"I'm not always."

"You could have fooled me."

I *would* have to sit here, Rita thought. But it was too late now. She tried to change the subject by gesturing at the room. "They should get rid of these lights," she said. "Everyone looks Martian in here."

To her astonishment, Jessie laughed. "I always thought it looked like the inside of a jukebox," she said. "As a matter of fact, I've been trying to use that idea in one of my displays. I haven't really boiled it down yet."

It was so rare for Jessie to talk about her work. Rita loved it when she did, especially when she talked about her concepts for display. So original, always. But instead of continuing, Jessie asked Rita if she'd like to split a bottle of Chianti.

"Sure," Rita said, not daring to ask how big a bottle. But at least she didn't have to panic about what it might cost. She was selling her photographs steadily now. In fact, an art director had actually called *her* to ask if she would be doing the interiors of the Claire Albritten house. One of the reasons Rita had told Sin to go on back to Baltimore alone was so that she could drop by Claire's place and set up an appointment for what Claire called the after pictures.

"*After* pictures," Jessie repeated, as if it were the lowest form of photographic assignment she could imagine.

Rita bristled, wondering why Jessie, who had always seemed supportive of Rita's work, should now turn critical. But Jessie had changed. She had always been sarcastic, but now her remarks often had a decidedly bitter edge. Rita chose to agree with Jessie, side-stepping all possibility of argument. "I know," she said. "I hate to think of myself doing that kind of thing. But the way I figure it, I owe Claire. If I'd told her I was only interested in those moody shots of her prowling around an unfinished house, she'd have thought I was nuts and said no. So I let her think I was doing before and after stuff and got what I wanted. And those pictures of her—especially that one—really established me. So I owe her the after, right? Anyway, it won't kill me."

"Those pictures of yours," Jessie said, recalling Rita's show, "they were truly extraordinary."

I'll be damned! Rita thought, glad now that she hadn't made an issue of Jessie's implied comment on the after shots. "Well," she said, "Claire's extraordinary. And that place of hers! The whole time I was shooting over there, I kept thinking about what's her name—Faye Arensberg. I could *feel* what happened there. I think it's in the photos, too."

The wine came, and Jessie poured for both of them. "We should drink to something," she told Rita, with her glass held high in the air. "The photographs."

"Those," Rita said, "plus whatever comes next. For all of us."

After the toast, she and Jessie lapsed into silence, as though both were wondering what whatever comes next might be. Finally, Jessie said, "I should get everyone together again. Once more, at least. Before everyone's gone."

"Before everyone's *gone*." Rita laughed. "Wait a minute here. Who's going?"

"You have, in a way," Jessie said.

Rita immediately became defensive. "I spend some time here and some time in Baltimore with Sin. It's only natural. You know about his mother."

"I'm not disputing whether or not it's natural," Jessie told her.

"So who else is going?" Rita asked. "Me and who else?"

"Margaret and Jay are looking for a bigger place. They'll probably get married."

Something in Jessie's voice—perhaps Jessie's struggle to sound so matter-of-fact—alerted Rita to the knowledge that this must have happened a dozen times or more in Jessie's life. A dozen people must have come to the Row, only to get themselves together and move on. The Row was like that. Why did Jessie remain?

"Why don't *you* go, too?" Rita asked. "Some big high-rise someplace. Really. Why don't you?"

"Oh, Rita." Jessie waved a hand dismissively.

Rita knew better than to pursue the subject. She flailed mentally for something that would keep the conversation going. "I haven't seen Margaret in ages," she said. "It used to seem as though every time I turned around, there she was. God, she drove me crazy."

Jessie smiled.

Rita continued. "No kidding. Worst, though, was when she started pulling that *we* shit. That just about drove me out of my skull. It seemed so goddamned pointed, but maybe that was just because *I* didn't feel like a *we* at the time. I saw her one time, in the drugstore, buying cough medicine, and she told me, '*We*'re sick.' "

Rita had expected Jessie to laugh, but Jessie didn't. "I hadn't noticed," Jessie said. "Perhaps I'm used to it."

Another too-long pause.

"What about Claire?" Rita asked. "Will you invite her? What's going on with her anyway? Is she still seeing the Senator?"

"I won't invite her," Jessie said. "And I have no idea who she's seeing."

"You know what would be terrific?" Rita offered. "Something on Halloween. Like, how about having dinner on Halloween? It's not so far away, and it's on a Sunday this year. We could all pitch in for the food, and all you'd have to do is cook it. God, we could have turkey, and that mushroom-and-chestnut stuffing that you make. I have been telling and telling Sin about that stuffing. And we could have wild rice. And those apple pies that you put whiskey in."

"Jim Beam Apple Pie," Jessie said. "Well, fine. Halloween sounds perfect."

All the lights were on inside Claire's house, but no one answered

211

when Rita let the knocker fall against the cypress door. She tried a few more times, then walked around back to see if Claire's car was there.

It wasn't. Rita was just about to leave when tires squealed and headlights flooded the alley, freezing Rita in their glare. They turned out to belong to the Jaguar.

"God," Rita said. "When you came around the corner I felt, I don't know, like a deer. I felt like hollering, 'Don't shoot!' " Claire had the roof of the Jaguar open, which surprised Rita, since the nights had already grown quite cool. "Aren't you freezing?" she asked Claire, noting that Claire was wearing a blousy white leather jacket over a turtleneck.

"I had the heater on," Claire said.

"Do you mean you haven't had that thing fixed?" Rita was incredulous.

"I will," Claire said. "I just haven't had the chance."

Rita didn't believe her, but decided it was none of her business. For all she knew, it had to do with insurance. Why would she assume that there was something pathological about it? Rita chose, then, to drop the subject of the Jaguar's tattered roof and followed Claire inside the house. "I want to set up an appointment to take the after stuff," she explained, whirling around to take in all of the kitchen. Claire had gone ahead with the Allmilmo that she'd shown Rita in an ad so many months before. "It looks great," Rita said, but in fact, it looked unkitchenly. It was too spare, too clean. "Do you actually cook here?" she asked.

"Salads," Claire said, "toast. That kind of thing."

"Yeah," Rita said, "that's about my speed."

"And cocoa!" Claire added. "That's one of my specialties. I can fix us some right now, if you like."

"Terrific," Rita said. "And while you're slaving over a hot stove, I'll just wander around, okay?" She smiled at Claire and moved off into the other downstairs rooms.

All that white-on-white. Rita thought of *2001,* one of the last scenes, where the camera seems to tumble through the womb-white setting. *Fresh and newborn.*

Rita wanted most to see the room with the huge stone mantel. The room where Claire had said she'd hung the photograph of herself. Indeed, she'd said that Rita's print was the showpiece of the room, if not of the house itself. And considering the house, Rita thought, that was quite a compliment.

Rita shut her eyes and propelled herself toward the mantel. She wanted to feel the effect of the photo all at once. But when she stood still and opened her eyes, she caught her breath and felt the sudden rush of adrenaline through her body. And then she felt the long, slow pull of it draining away. It was dizzying. Rita leaned against the arm of a chair to regain herself. She shut her eyes again, hoping that when she opened them, what she'd seen would be gone, a trick of her vision, a mistake.

She looked again. No mistake.

The photograph, like the roof of Claire's Jag, had been slashed. Three diagonal gashes. But as if that were not enough, the figure of Claire had been entirely obliterated. It had been hacked at so many times that only a hole remained.

Rita forced herself over to it. The plaster of the wall behind had even been chipped away. Rita looked down at the floor and saw the gray tufts of photographic paper and backing that had once been an image of Claire.

Claire musn't come in here, Rita thought. *Mustn't see.* But when Rita turned, Claire was there, behind her with the silver tray. She had already seen. She was staring at the photographs with too-bright eyes and an all-too-radiant face.

She's about to be hysterical, Rita thought, *and, Jesus, I don't blame her.* "Sit down," Rita said, and she took the tray away and set it on a side table. "Come on." And sure enough, Claire did become hysterical, laughing, laughing, as though she couldn't and wouldn't ever stop. "Here." Rita urged a cup of cocoa in her direction. It was pale brown, with a dollop of whipped cream and dark chocolate shavings on top. "Here, come on, drink some of this."

Rita wondered what she ought to do next. Offer Claire her own apartment? She was clearly unsafe here. Maybe whoever had cut up the Jag's roof had done this, too. And, worse, had to come in here— *into this room*—to do it! "Claire," Rita said, "I think maybe you'd better call the police. Really. This is just too much."

"No," Claire answered. "No, I won't." Her voice was breathy. Her eyes still had that glitter.

"Claire, listen," Rita said, everything rushing in on her so that she didn't know what to mention first. It was, she thought, as if some crazed projectionist was mixing reels. In a flash, Rita saw the Claire she'd captured in her photograph, the Claire who hadn't had the roof of the car fixed, the Claire who didn't mind having things smeared all over her door. Claire, the victim, actually getting off on these things. But if Claire only knew what they might mean, where they might lead!

Rita knew she had to warn Claire, and warn her so utterly that she would leave this place, leave the Row. Rita felt that if she could make Claire see what all of this was pointing toward, she could save Claire. "Maybe I shouldn't tell you this," Rita began, "but I don't see what else I can do. It's about this house. It's about something that happened right here. Right here, in this house. . . ."

It took Rosenberg forever to come to the door, and when he did, he was in his bathrobe, with striped pajama bottoms showing below his knee. Socks instead of slippers.

"Are you in bed already?" Rita asked.

"Touch of flu," he explained. He sat on the sofa and pulled a plaid wool coverlet over himself.

Rita laid a hand against his forehead and then his cheek. "My God," she said, "you're burning up."

"I'll be fine," he said. "Now, tell me what's up."

"Nothing's up," she lied. She had hoped to tell him about Claire— about how she was sure Claire *knew* about the house, about Faye, about the murder, and how she wasn't afraid. Far from it. Claire, if anything, seemed to groove on it and all the rest, the car, the photograph. "You get into bed," she said. "Did you take any aspirin? How 'bout juice? Did you drink any juice?"

After she got him settled, she flipped through the Yellow Pages.

"Who are you calling?" he asked, his voice shivery and weak.

"A private-duty nurse," she said. "I can't leave you here like this."

Rita knew she would never get through the night on the Row after what she'd seen at Claire's. She would take a train to Baltimore, she decided. She didn't even have to call Sin, she could take a cab from the train station. She would tell him all of this, and cry, and make him hold her until she stopped crying. If that was being a baby, well, so what? Wasn't it wonderful to be able to be a baby if she felt like it? Wasn't it wonderful to have someone to be a baby with?

While she waited for the nurse to show, Rita called Jay. "You know all about Faye Arensberg," she said, "so you tell me. Is Claire in any danger? Like, is the person who got Faye likely to be after Claire?"

"Well, I certainly hope so." Jay laughed.

"I'm serious," Rita said. "Somebody cut up the roof of her car, and somebody actually got inside her house and—"

"I'm serious, too," he assured her. "Then I could write a sequel."

"Jay? Fuck you." She hung up, then ransacked Rosenberg's bookshelves. She was reading about a murderer named Ted Bundy, who killed girls with long hair parted in the middle, when the doorbell rang.

The nurse was gorgeous.

"Great," Rita said. "When he wakes up and sees *you*, he'll think he's died and gone to heaven."

The nurse laughed.

Then Rita trudged off in the direction of Union Station.

PART NINE

HALLOWEEN

Although Claire was not a member of the Potomac Hunt Club, she had been invited to the opening of its formal fox-hunting season. Because the day designated was October 31—Halloween—there would be, instead of the customary hunt breakfast, a gala costume party held that night. Claire knew what she would wear—not a costume exactly, but something so out of character it would serve as one.

The meet would begin in just over an hour. Claire called the stable to make absolutely certain that Illuminating had been meticulously groomed. The stable girl told Claire that she was about to load the horse into the van that would take him to Valhalla, where Opening Meet would be held. Yes, she assured Claire, his coat had been clipped, and yes, his mane and tail had been tautly braided.

Claire apologized for pestering about it, explaining that she'd always been able to observe and oversee hunt preparations herself. Having her horse boarded out and away from her made her more than a little nervous.

The stable girl laughed, saying that she understood. "Valhalla at two o'clock sharp," she confirmed.

"Two o'clock," Claire repeated.

Then she went upstairs to get into her formal attire—the melton coat, the canary breeches made of cavalry twill, the woolen vest, the tall black boots with gleaming patent tops. Claire climbed the steps to the third floor two at a time, feeling that familiar prehunt thrill. It was just as Aubrey had said that day: Every season it coursed through her, the propelling belief that this year would be the one.

It was far less likely that she would be blooded at Potomac, where foxes had to be coaxed into the territory and hand fed by the hunt staff so that they would stay. Still, there was always the expectation, always the chance of a kill.

She picked up her breeches and gasped. They were cut as though with scissors, particularly at the crotch. The fine yellow wool hung in tatters there. In addition, Claire noted as she turned them this way and that, long, razorlike slashes had been made along the portion of cloth that would have stretched along her thigh.

She tossed the breeches aside and picked up the satin-lined wool vest. It, too, had been mutilated.

Then she examined her boots, pushing her arm down into the length of leather that would have rested against her calf. There were long cuts. Even the flesh of her arm showed through.

Aubrey! she thought, remembering the day she had left him alone up here with her riding things. Aubrey! that terrible day.

It had to be Aubrey.

Claire rushed to the telephone. She tried to call his office and then realized that on a Sunday he would be at home. She called his apartment and reached his answering service.

Her hands were trembling and she was certain that her voice was trembling as well. She tried to calm herself without success. She told the operator only to say that Miss Albritten had called.

Then she rushed about, attempting to put together an outfit that might be suitable for Opening Meet. It was no use. She'd brought few of her hunt things with her and Aubrey had destroyed them all. She couldn't try to borrow things, because there was no time. And since it was Sunday, she couldn't buy them. Opening Meet was the most formal hunt of the year, and therefore she couldn't appear in anything less than the proper, tradition-sanctioned garments.

She phoned the stable and learned that Illuminating had already been sent in the van on his way. Thus, Claire had no choice but to drive to Valhalla.

Before she left, she called Aubrey's apartment once again. "That's right," she said, "*Claire Albritten.*" As though her name alone constituted a significant threat.

There were tall, sleek horses everywhere, and riders in immaculate attire. Most of them wore black coats with Potomac's colors blazing on the lapels, but here and there were men in scarlet. The Master. His staff.

Claire saw the van from Illuminating's stable and drove as close to it as she could get. The stable girl was talking to someone, but Illuminating stood between the girl and whoever it was. Claire mar-

220

veled at the horse's beauty as she approached, his gleaming coat, his long, flat muscle. The picture they would have made! Damn Aubrey! Damn him!

The stable girl started when she saw Claire in street clothes.

"It's very silly," Claire began to explain, "but my things have been . . . stolen. Too late to do anything about it. I phoned, but you'd already . . ."

The person to whom the girl had been talking stepped around Illuminating's fine muzzle and into view.

He smiled at Claire. "Looks like we're both shit out of luck," he said. "My horse came out of the trailer lame." It was Steve.

Claire must have reacted powerfully, because the stable girl giggled uncomfortably and backed away. Illuminating stomped and snorted, threatening to break his leather tie. Steve laid a gloved hand on the gelding's shoulder and quieted him.

Claire had never seen Steve in formal riding garb before. He looked magnificent, broad-chested, slim-hipped. He seemed to realize she was assessing his appearance and stepped back so that she could get a better look. "Brand new, all of it," he said. "What do you think?"

A shame to let it go to waste, Claire thought. "Ride my horse," she said. "Ride Illuminating."

Just then, a petulant female voice called at Claire's back, "Stevie." Claire opened her mouth as if to protest, but before she could, Steve was introducing them. He called Claire "an old friend," and explained to Georgia Talbot, his companion, that Claire had just offered him the chance to ride the big bay horse they had earlier been admiring.

"Why that is just too, too sweet of you," Georgia said, barely looking at Claire at all. The horse Georgia was mounted on threatened to jump out from beneath her. He was all nerves and pent-up juices. Georgia patted his neck and laughed. "I've got to keep him moving," she said. "He's such a silly thing." She trotted off and called back over her shoulder, "See you in a bit, Stevie."

"I assume you'll be taking Georgia to the party tonight," Claire said, giving the girl's name just enough emphasis.

"That's right," Steve answered.

"I'll see you then *before* the party," she told him. "Just a minute.

221

I'll give you the address." She ran to the Jaguar and produced a scrap of paper upon which she wrote.

"Claire . . ." he said.

"How lucky for you that Illuminating was here."

Steve glanced to where the other riders had gathered around the Master. Hounds were about to be released. "Lucky, yeah," Steve said, pulling the stirrup irons along their leathers and readjusting the buckles so that they would suit the length of his legs.

"Tonight," Claire said.

Though it was early, Jessie set the table for her dinner party that night. She'd chosen a fawn linen cloth and matching napkins and simple brown earthenware dishes. In the center of the table she'd heaped Indian corn. She topped that with a pumpkin she'd carved that morning. She lowered a fat orange candle into its hollow and stood back, as if already seeing the eerie Halloween glow that it would cast.

Then she realized what she had done. She had set six places instead of five. Wrong, she knew. Still, she reviewed: Margaret and Jay, Rita and Sin. Five, counting herself. Two couples, and herself.

Jessie began to take up the extra place setting but then thought better of it.

Why not call someone? Aubrey. It was late, but there was always a chance that he might be free. He hadn't been round to Claire's in a very long while, and he might very well be lonely. If she didn't call, she would never know. Indeed, Aubrey might be waiting for her call, hoping for it. She would lie to him, she decided, and say that she'd only just decided to have people over. A spur-of-the-moment thing for Halloween.

Aubrey.

She dialed his home number and then almost hung up when the ringing stopped.

But it was an answering service, not the Senator.

"Oh," Jessie said awkwardly, thinking that she ought not to leave a message.

"One moment, please," the woman who'd answered said, leaving the connection dead behind her.

Jessie waited, perplexed, not knowing why the woman had left the line. Perhaps it meant that she would be connected with Aubrey after all.

But another voice—another woman—came on the line. Her voice was punitive, and she asked, "Is this Miss Albritten again?"

Jessie hesitated and then said, yes, it was.

"Well, Miss Albritten, the Senator called in just a few moments ago and we did give him all of your messages."

"Oh," Jessie said, "thank you." And she was genuinely grateful, feeling she'd been spared unbearable embarrassment. Aubrey would have no need of her. Not with Claire calling him. Not with someone as young and lovely as Claire offering herself and leading him on. *Offering herself.*

It was already getting dark when Rita parked Sin's car in front of the Baltimore town house. She'd been shooting at Harborplace all day. She was glad they would be going to Jessie's, where she could wear old clothes, take her shoes off, and relax.

Odd. Not a single light inside.

Rita felt a little twist of fear. *She died,* Rita thought, *Evelyn Sinclair died and he's at her bedside all by himself.* She considered driving to the hospital, but decided not to, on the off chance she was wrong and when he got back from wherever he had been, she wouldn't be there.

She unlocked the door with the keys that he had given her, and when she went inside she saw a note: *Gone to newsstand. Look on coffee table, living room.*

Newsstand? Whatever for? Coffee table?

She went to the table and picked up what was Evelyn Sinclair's scrapbook, a collection of clippings from newspapers and magazines. Social bullshit about Evelyn, and, of course, stuff about Sin.

Rita flipped through the pages and saw that Sin had pasted in the Capitol Hill newspaper's item on Rita's opening. Right in the same book with all this family stuff.

"Hey," Sin said, when he found her there, "you're not *crying?*"

"Yes," she admitted, "a little bit, I am."

"Well, don't drip on these magazines," he said. He had just brought home a fortune's worth of them.

"What do you have?" Rita sniffed.

"The stuff you shot for *Washington Dossier*."

"Let me see." She had done the spread so many months ago she could barely recall it. And there was no way of knowing what they'd selected from what she'd turned in. But these assignments and others had pulled Rita out of the hole. Sin still didn't know any of that. The way she'd carried on, for instance, when an announcement for a fur sale at Saks had come in the same mail with a threat from Visa or American Express. *But I was in the hole in a lot of ways back then.*

"Here's something I did for *Smithsonian*," Sin said.

"When did you do that?"

"Last year sometime. They finally got around to using it."

"Ah, but here," he said, opening Rita's illustration for an article called "Let Her Know You Care."

Rita looked at it and smiled.

"God, those props," Sin said, pointing to the dozens of gifts that surrounded the model. Angora sweater. Bracelet with fox heads embedded in crystal.

"Why are we doing this?" Rita asked.

"Just to kind of round things out. We'll put them in the scrapbook, okay?"

There was nothing in the scrapbook like that. Things *about* the Sinclairs, not things *by* them. Rita laid her hands atop his, and his were quaking. He pulled them away.

"When, Sinnie?" she asked him. "When did it happen?"

He leaned back against the sofa, leaned so hard that Rita was afraid that it would tip. He sounded as though something jagged had stuck in his throat. "Just . . . right after you left."

Rita thought, *Jesus*. "We can't still go to Jessie's," she said. "I'd better call her."

"No," he said, "I want to go."

"Sin . . ."

"I want to."

They were still on the sofa, still not touching, not even holding

224

hands. And so clearly separate, Rita thought. Horribly separate. Arguing. Actually arguing. Maybe not shouting, but differing, and at a time like this.

"We can't go," she insisted. Weren't there arrangements? Didn't they have to do something? Sign papers? Order a coffin? Something? But Rita didn't dare ask.

"Rita," he said, "I've got to get out of here. Let's go to Jessie's right now."

"We can't yet," Rita said. "I told her later than this."

"Let's go somewhere then. Please."

"We could drive around," she said. "It's stupid, but it's all I can think of."

"Let's go."

"Sin," she said, the minute he had started the car, "I really don't think this is such a great idea."

"Why not?" He hit the lights, released the emergency brake, but didn't pull away from the curb.

"I'm not sure," she said.

Some costumed kids walked down the street past the car, oblivious to them.

"We could go trick-or-treat," Sin offered.

Rita laughed, but it sounded awfully like a smirk.

"Fuck it," he said, "let's go inside and get drunk." He turned the ignition off, doused the lights, reset the hand brake.

"That's stupid too," she said. Rita felt so sad, not just about Sin's mother, but about this, about the way that they were being with each other, both of them.

"It *is* stupid," he agreed, and started to laugh.

"Clue me in," she said, surprised by the angry edge of her voice. It was there because his laughter didn't include her. And because laughing, now, seemed wrong.

He kept on laughing nonetheless, even had trouble stopping. "I can hear her now," he said. "My mother. Giving us a little pat on the back. Telling us to buck up, carry on." Still laughing. "She did

225

that when my father died. Told me that. Even read me some little poem about how life goes on. Completely out of character."

Rita expected him to go on, but he broke off there. She followed him into the house.

"Well," Rita said, once inside. "If we're going to get drunk, I'm going to get comfortable." She eased out of her shoes and wiggled out of her panty hose. She'd meant to change into jeans, but hadn't.

She padded to the liquor cabinet, poured herself a drink. She didn't even look at what, just took the first bottle that came to hand. "How about you?" she asked him. "Anything special in mind?"

He came up quietly behind her. He didn't touch her, but stood so close that she could feel his erection through the fabric of her skirt. She leaned back against it, but involuntarily. Voluntarily, she was telling herself, *No, no, this is wrong. Not here, not now, this is wrong.* But the Rosenberg voice she had internalized kept saying, *Ah, but he's connecting with you again. Connecting with you at last.*

"Sin," she said, with barely any voice at all. She set the glass down.

He had his hands on her hips now, and she moved them aside to fumble with her clothing, lift her skirt, push at the waistband of her panties. She wanted his hands on her flesh, and as quickly as she could get them there.

He had his hand down inside her panties now, and she moved against him, wanting to reach back and take his zipper down, but no, not wanting to stop for even the second it would take to do that.

"Sin, oh, Sin," she said, her voice soft, softer, even, than the sticky, sucking sound where his fingers were. "We can't stay like this," she whispered, but wanting to.

He took his hands away, the one that had been rubbing at her streaking wet across her belly, and wet still, when she turned to look at him, along her cheek and her nose and in her hair. She caught at his hand, kissed at his fingers.

He stepped back far enough to uncouple his belt and the button of his trousers. She thought she couldn't wait, couldn't, and reached for him when he had his trousers and his underwear down around his knees.

She dripped saliva into her hands and ran one hand along his penis, the other under his testicles.

These clothes, these layers and layers of clothes. But she couldn't be apart from him long enough to take them off. Wouldn't be apart.

They were both still wearing everything, more or less. Sin even had his shoes on, she realized, her bare toes scuffing up against them.

"This is better than drunk," she said, freeing a hand to yank at his shirt buttons, and wondering how she would ever get her sweater over her head. Kissing him the whole while, too. "Much better than drunk."

"Wait a minute," Sin said, breaking away from her and lowering himself to the carpet. Almost falling, because of his trousers, but making it and untying his shoes.

Rita slipped her panties off, watching him. He had one shoe off when she pushed his hand away, made him lie back against the floor.

"Your minute's up." She lifted her skirt and slid herself as slowly as she could along his penis.

The lights in the room were on and none of the curtains were drawn and any trick-or-treater in the whole wide world could have looked inside, but Rita just didn't, didn't care.

"Mmm. I would like to squoosh myself right up next to you, like a teenager," Rita said, as they rolled down the Baltimore-Washington Parkway.

"Go ahead," Sin said.

"I know, suit myself."

"Right."

"You mean sit on the console? Oh, damn bucket seats."

"Designed by a Puritan elder," Sin said.

"You stole that line," Rita told him. "I don't remember the movie, but I remember the line."

"It wasn't a movie," he said. "It was a rerun on TV."

They were quiet for a while and then Rita said, "Did I tell you about Rosenberg?"

"No."

"Well, I called him and—"

"Is he better?" Sin interrupted her.

"Is he better? Let me tell you how *much* better." She went on to say that Rosenberg and the private-duty nurse Rita had hired were practically engaged.

Sin laughed. "My little matchmaker," he said.

Rita did sit on the console for a while. "We must have looked ridiculous," Sin mused, with a silly grin on his face as he said it.

"I know," Rita agreed. "I thought about that, too. Not the whole time, but every now and then. I had this picture of you with your pants around your knees, and me with my skirt up. Did you?"

"Not during," he said. "For me, it was total mind blot."

Then Rita asked, "Do you think it was ever that way for your mom and dad?"

"Hell, no," he said.

"I don't think mine either, but how would you ever know? I mean, it might be like this for everybody, Margaret and Jay, and Claire and whoever."

"Let's hope so," Sin said.

"I don't know," LeGrande said, turning the camera over a couple of times. "Don't seem like no pictures'll come out unless you get up real good and close."

"I will get up close," Claude said. "Just like we said. I'll get up there right on the ledge of the window. You make sure I'm there before you go inside."

"Suppose she see you?" LeGrande asked.

"Shit. It's up to you, boy, to make sure she don't see. It's up to you to keep her occupied." He continued with glee. "You sure you can do that now? Keep her occupied?"

"Yeah, I'm sure."

"I'm telling you"—Claude picked up on how LeGrande was fast running out of steam—"you and me, we won't have to work no more. And it ain't like you got to do nothing. You jes' act like you gonna, so I can take some good pictures. You jes' get her to undress. This chick see these pictures and she gonna pay us money for a long, long time."

"Yeah, and maybe she won't. Maybe she call the cops the minute I come through the door."

"Shit. She won't call no cops. Not if all this stuff you been sayin' about her all the time is the truth."

"It's the truth," LeGrande said. "You know it, too."

"You call her one of them names. Call her *bitch* or *slut* or something. I tell you, LeGrande, you call her that, she gonna melt right in your arms."

"I don't know," LeGrande said. "Mama and Denise, they never spent a Halloween in their whole life without me being there."

"You *will* be there, my man. You *will* be there. This thing with this white chick ain't gonna take all night. This thing, you wait and see, ain't gonna take no time at all."

Claire put her mother's diamonds on, the earrings and then the necklace. She stood back, admiring herself in the many-mirrored room. Mother had sent the diamonds as a random gift, with a note saying, *Here, you need something, darling. Something nice.* Claire remembered them well, remembered thinking what a waste they were on Mother, how they called attention to the creases in her face and on her throat.

Claire had bought a shimmering black dress, strapless, with a long slit on either side. The only black—save for her riding coat, the thick melton—she had ever owned.

It set off the jewels wonderfully—set off, too, Claire's hair. She'd swept her hair up, but loosely, and dreamed about the way it would come undone.

Steve would approve. She could almost feel his fingers tugging at her hair, her shoulders. Claire was exultant in her mother's diamonds and her long black dress, awaiting Steve.

The champagne was downstairs, chilling in the big silver ice bucket she had won so long ago. A challenge trophy. She had retired it. Her name was engraved in flowing elaborate script on the silver surface.

"Challenges are few," Claire had said when she was given it, and everyone had applauded her.

She decided to go down and get the trophy, bring it here, beside the bed.

Claire glided down the staircase, barefoot now, but planning, when Steve came, to wear thin-strapped, impossibly high-heeled shoes. She barely paused in her descent when she found LeGrande at the foot of the stairs.

That was the moment that LeGrande had feared most: when she found him, unbidden, in her house.

"Why, hello, LeGrande," she said, walking past him.

LeGrande held out his hand, but stopped just short of catching at her arm. His motion, however, made her turn and regard him. She said nothing, only looked. She was admiring him, he thought.

He got all of his courage together and spoke to her. The sound of his own voice made him brave enough to add the appropriate gestures. What he heard sounded insolent. "Miz Albritten," he said, taking a bottle out of a brown paper bag and unscrewing the cap. "I bought us some wine. Now you just go get us some glasses, you and me. All right?" Then he eyed her up and down and added, "Unless you got some other dude coming by."

For a minute she looked as though she might laugh at him, but in the end she didn't. She just stood there, a smile in her eyes, LeGrande thought, and let him look her over. And then she said, "All right."

She walked past him, and just the whiff of her perfume made him bold. "Make 'em big glasses," he said. "Great big glasses." And then, with the wine bottle open, he dashed upstairs, taking the steps, not two, but three at a time.

He hit the light switch and made the room dark. Not all dark, but silvery dark, because of all the white and all the mirrors. He could see Claude out there on the ledge, plain as day. He cut the lights on again, and it worked, Claude was gone. Leastwise, LeGrande couldn't see him anymore.

He walked around the room thinking about how easy it had been. Just the way Claude said. All he had to do was keep the light on, get her naked, and Claude would take the pictures and they'd be fixed for life. For *life*.

She came in, with two teeny little glasses, though.

"Woman," he said, "you call those big?"

She did laugh now, but not at him. She held the glasses out, waiting for him to pour the wine.

He managed to do that, and without spilling any, too. And then he said, "You gonna like this. It's real sweet." He clinked his glass up against hers the way people did on television.

She took a sip and a little bead of the wine hung on her lip and started down toward her chin.

He reached up and wiped it off. The first time he'd ever touched her. Man, his cock, it did stand up and *salute!*

"You got a radio?" he asked her.

"Downstairs."

"How about if I get us a little *soul?*"

She put her wine down and went over and sat on the edge of the bed. He took that to mean yes, and then he went downstairs and found a station that was playing Kool and the Gang. He turned it up real loud, so they could hear it good.

He wondered, would she take that dress off while he was down there? But when he came back into the room, she was right there, just the way she was when he left her.

"I like to groove while I make love," he told her. Never mind that he never before had. "How 'bout you?"

"LeGrande," she said, and her voice was just as sweet and thick as maple syrup. And then she leaned back on the bed, put her legs up on it and all, and stretched her arms out.

He came over and sat on the bed beside her. But before he could think of what to do next, she rolled over, face down, ass up. He looked at the long zipper that ran down the back of her dress and he started to pull on it.

She didn't say anything. She just lay there, more and more of her white skin showing until he was all the way down around her ass. But to get to her ass, she would have to scoot up some, so he could pull the dress the rest of the way off. Did he have to ask her, or what?

He looked over at the window, but he couldn't see a thing. He knew Claude would be out there, though. Even knowing Claude was watching, LeGrande had a hard-on that was *fierce.*

She rolled her face over to the side and looked at him all hurtlike. "LeGrande?" she said. "Aren't you afraid I'll get away?"

"What do you mean, get away? Don't look to me like you goin' no place."

"That's not so, LeGrande. If you don't tie me, I'll get away. I will."

231

She rolled halfway over and gave him a good long look at her tits. He did look, too. And she laughed again.

"What am I gonna tie you with?" he asked. Sounded pretty senseless to him.

"Just look in the drawers, LeGrande." She rolled back over. "I'm sure you'll find *some*thing." When he turned back to the bed, she had arranged herself facedown again.

He used a brassiere to tie her left hand and another brassiere to tie her right. She groaned like he was hurting her the whole time. It did something inside him, he wasn't sure exactly what, but he grabbed a handful of that hair of hers and snapped her head back. "This is what you want, ain't that right?"

"Yes, oh yes," Claire said, almost crying.

He hiked her dress up far, so that he could tie her legs, too, each at the ankle. He used her stockings, and tied them to the frame of the bed. He wasn't thinking about Claude now, not one bit. "All right," he said, staring at that back of hers, "you try now. You just try to get away." Of course, he still had to get the rest of that dress, now like a big wide band around her waist, off her.

She wriggled like she was trying to get away. Then she stopped. "One more thing," she said. "Under the pillow. My mask."

"Your what?"

"*Get* it," she shouted at him. LeGrande lost his hard-on just like that, the minute her voice was raised against him. But some other, more potent, feeling replaced it. He calmed himself down some and then said, "How'm I supposed to get something that's under your pillow, with your head on it and all."

Claire laughed. "Cobra," she said, arching back despite her bonds. "Cobra."

LeGrande watched her in amazement and then he slid his hand underneath the pillow and pulled the white mask out. He pulled it over her head and adjusted it so that it would blot her vision.

"LeGrande," she said, like a little girl now. To make up for shouting at him, he figured. "LeGrande? Do you have your knife?"

It scared him, her saying that. He wished he didn't have it, but all the same, he took it out of his pocket and let the blade of it click out. He held it just beside Claire's ear.

She made a noise and coiled herself up as much as she could with the way he'd tied her.

"What you have in mind with this knife?" LeGrande pushed the blade back in, then clicked it out again. "Is it, like, some kind of cock to you, or what?"

She didn't answer.

He leaned over her, the blade beside her shoulder. Even though she couldn't see the blade, she knew that it was there. He could tell, watching the way her shoulder tensed when the blade came near. The way the skin where the knife had passed turned into little goose-bumps. Some kind of weird.

He put the blade down in front of her mouth. "Yeah," he said, "that's what it is. A big, cold, shiny cock. You want it in your mouth, don't you, honky bitch. Ain't that what you want?" He wanted her to say yes, wanted to put the knife in there. He thought of how warm the blade would be when he pulled it out again.

She stuck her tongue out and tried to reach the blade with it. LeGrande watched her tongue seek. "Girl, you like a snake," he said.

She swallowed. "Cobra," she said.

"Cobra, yeah." He watched the way that she was breathing. He thought about giving her a slash. He wanted to, he realized, because it was what *she* wanted. It scared him, knowing that she could sway him that way, actually give him thoughts. If he stayed there, she'd make him do more and more.

He thought he'd better cut her loose and get out of there. He looked over at the window, like maybe he ought to signal Claude. He turned the light out in the room so he could see the sill where Claude was stationed.

When he did that, just like that, the radio downstairs went dead.

He should have known, man. He and Claude weren't gonna get her, she was going to get them. She had somebody coming, somebody who was here already, somebody who was gonna put his and Claude's ass behind bars.

LeGrande listened.

Then the phone started ringing. He walked over to it and yanked the cord out of the wall. It went on ringing, though, in the other phones. Everywhere, in the bathroom, upstairs, and down.

LeGrande stuck the knife in her face. "You tell me who's down there."

She didn't answer, except to laugh like this was funny.

The ringing stopped. Then LeGrande heard a door slam back against the wall. Like somebody was coming and that somebody was good and mad.

LeGrande dropped the knife and went to the window, ignoring Claire when she begged him to stay. "It's all right, LeGrande," she whispered. "It's someone I know. A friend. Stay, LeGrande. It's all right."

LeGrande opened the window and shoved Claude. "Come on, nigger," he said.

Claude said, "Shit," and dropped the camera.

They both jumped at once, and it was a long, long way down. LeGrande thought both his legs would break, because he hit all wrong, hit with them stiff instead of bent, the way they were supposed to be.

"We gotta find that thing," Claude said, rooting around the yard.

"Fuck it, man, there's someone in there." He pointed at Claire's window and started to yank Claude away. He was limping, but moving anyway. "You want that thing, you come back some other time," he said, and went along just as fast as he could.

Strapped to her bed, Claire called out to the footsteps on the staircase. "I had a wonderful surprise for you, but, alas. He got scared and ran away."

The footsteps walked across the bare wooden floor and stood beside Claire's bed.

"Untie these things and take this mask away, darling," Claire said. "I want to turn and look at you for a while."

When there was no response, Claire laughed. "All right. All right to whatever you want to do."

Still not a word.

"Say something, darling." Claire's voice took on an impatient edge. "How on earth do I know what you're thinking?"

Claire's body gleamed in the half-light, gleamed like silver. She was so still that it seemed she would dissolve into the pallor of the bed sheets, fade quite away.

She was breathing heavily, excitedly.

The bed sheets would be damp beneath her body.

So beautiful, Claire in the half-light.

"Do something," she said, "for God's sake."

The knife beside Claire glinted, the blade long and slender and inviting. The killer chose the knife LeGrande had left behind, fingers closing knowingly around its hilt. The killer's own knife would not be needed now, not this time.

Slowly, gently, the killer brought the blade down along Claire's spine, taunting the silvery flesh without actually touching it. Yes. The killer knew that Claire's young skin would rise and prickle to acknowledge the blade, knowing without seeing. Just as Faye's had.

"Mmm," Claire said, "lovely."

Blade across her shoulders, blade glistening along the pale wispy hair at the nape of her neck. Blade along her arms, first the left and then the right, loving, appreciative blade.

Claire and her killer began breathing the same thick rhythm.

Blade down Claire's long white back again, piercing slightly now, tracing a soft and delicate blood-black line until the knife reached fabric. Then the killer held the fabric free of Claire's flesh and cut the dress away.

"My back burns," Claire pouted, squirming so that the thread of blood moved. As if her blood itself were alive. The killer rubbed a palm across the blood line to smudge it.

Claire squealed. "I *told* you," she said, "it burns."

The killer grabbed Claire's hair, snatching it so fiercely that Claire's sudden inhalation caught in her throat. The killer placed the blade there and let the edge slide, as a razor's edge might, into Claire's thin, lucent flesh.

The killer's breath came faster, watching Claire's black blood dapple the pale white sheet beneath her. The blade had only drifted in.

Nothing had been forced, or severed. Nonetheless, Claire seemed unable to speak. She hissed, "St . . . St . . . St . . ."

Too soon. Over to soon. Not yet, but it would be. Soon.

The killer turned the blade to Claire's bonds, cutting free the right ankle, the right hand. Then the killer heaved Claire's body so that she hung face forward over the edge of the bed. She seemed limp, dangling by the bonds that remained.

The killer walked around the bed to face Claire, snatching, removing, Claire's mask.

Claire's eyes grew so enormous when she saw, so huge, that the killer laughed. And then, even as she hung suspended there, Claire laughed, too, jerking her free hand up toward her forehead.

She laughed, thinking of all the men, all the men in procession, Steve, and the Cobra, and her Mystery Man, all the men, all that she'd ever wanted. It seemed to Claire so right that she be blooded now, at last. She searched for her own voice, to tell the killer to blood her, start the ceremony she'd dreamed of, hoped for. But she couldn't speak. She could only jerk her free hand toward her forehead.

The killer brought the blade forward experimentally, drew it softly across Claire's breast. Claire shook her head, no, and continued fluttering at her forehead with her free hand.

Blood, in short, thin spurts, fell from the neck wound.

Claire's gray-silver eyes sought out the eyes of her killer, pleading. But not to live, the killer knew. It was something else that Claire wanted.

Then Claire became aware of the soft fall of blood on her chest. She smiled as if in gratitude and rubbed her free hand through it. She looked at her hand in the dimness and then smeared the black blood in a circle on her forehead. She was still smiling, nodding her head now to signify yes. She even tried to say the word, the killer thought.

The killer brought the blade down toward the blood spot Claire had made, and Claire turned to avoid the blow. The blade sliced through Claire's eyeball with a small sucking sound.

The killer left the blade there and backed away, watching.

A glaze was falling over the eye that was intact, even as the killer observed it. Soon the eye was flat, dead, like the button eye of a toy.

Toy, yes. The way she dangled there. Like a doll that had been cast away. The image pleased the killer, who stepped back for a last look. To admire it, remember it, the room bathed in silver light.

Was it also blood that pooled at the base of the great white bed, or merely what had been Claire's shimmering black dress?

"Who's all coming?" Rita asked, counting the place settings.

"The usual bunch," Jessie told her.

"Who?" Rita insisted. "Sin, me, Margaret, Jay, you, and who else?"

Jessie busied herself scattering ashtrays around the room, straightening pillows and piles of newspapers, doing, in short, all the things people do when they want to avoid the subject at hand.

"Come on," Rita pushed, "who?"

"Edward," Jessie said.

"Edward? Who the heck is Edward?" She looked over at Sin, but he seemed to think this was a normal conversation. Hell, maybe it was. Rita examined, briefly, the way she'd been carrying on, and then shifted her approach. "That's just great, Jess. God, really, that's great. That takes care of everybody, too. You, Rosenberg, everybody." She proceeded to repeat for Jessie the tale of Rosenberg and his private-duty nurse. She was about to ask Jessie for details about Edward when Jay and Margaret arrived, letting themselves in.

Jay seemed to gallop up the stairs. He had two boxes with him. "Ta-da!" he said, handing one to Jessie and one to Rita.

"What's this?" Rita asked, taking the top off and seeing a stack of pages inside.

"My book," Jay said. "I finished it."

"Well, fine," Rita answered warily, riffling the pages and stopping here and there to scan, "but don't you have to sell it, too?"

"Rita," Margaret said, "he *will*. The important thing is that he got it *done*."

"I guess so," Rita said. *And for your sake,* she thought, *I hope so.* After all, in less than a year Margaret would be looking to Jay to support her through law school.

"Thanks very much," Jessie said, putting her box of manuscript atop an end table. "I look forward to reading it." She smiled. "I really do." She excused herself and went into the kitchen to continue preparing the meal. Wonderful smells emanated from the direction of the kitchen. Sage and cinammon above all.

"Who else is coming?" Jay asked, counting the place settings. He whispered so that Jessie wouldn't hear.

"Edward," Rita answered.

"Who the fuck is Edward?" Jay asked.

"Hey!" Jessie's voice carried down the hall. "I could use a hand in here."

Sin and Margaret jumped up simultaneously, almost colliding. "I'll do it," Sin said. Margaret looked at Rita, as if to ask if that would be all right.

"He loves cooking and shit," Rita said, seconding him. "Really." She wished that she could tell them that Sin's mother had just died, but she and Sin had agreed on the drive down that they wouldn't. They decided that if they were to tell, it would put too much of a strain on everyone. That no one would feel free to laugh or have a good time. Actually, Sin had decided that. Rita had only reluctantly agreed. "It's like pretending that it hasn't happened," she'd protested. "It's wrong, holding something like that in." Up until Sin went into the kitchen to help Jessie, Rita had kept watching him as if he'd crack—start crying or something. *Too much TV*, she thought, *too many B movies*. Sin didn't appear to be anywhere near breaking down. It was, indeed, as if his mother's death hadn't occurred.

"Oh, Jaybird, look." Margaret reached for the Sunday paper, which was stacked beside the couch. The magazine section was on top and there was a picture of somebody playing racketball on the cover. The type superimposed on the photo said that a review of court facilities would be found inside. "Show me the club where you play," Margaret said.

Rita looked knowingly in Jay's direction, but he didn't so much as glance her way. While he and Margaret went through the article together, Rita opened her copy of Jay's book and began thumbing through it.

She wanted to get to the murder. She scanned each page, looking for a telltale word: *blood, stab, death, killer*, something like that. On one of the pages, the word *bed* jumped out at her, and she began to read. As she read, Rita actually became afraid, could feel fear, climbing like *The Tingler* along her spine. She kept looking over at Jay, but he seemed unaware that Rita was even going through the book.

"I know that guy," Jay said, pointing at something in the magazine section. "*Great* kill shot!" Rita felt almost dizzy, as though Jay's words and the sounds coming from the kitchen were miles and miles away. She was in a long hollow tunnel and there was a ringing sound in her ears. She read on, the walls of the tunnel narrowing, the ringing getting louder, louder, like an alarm. . . .

The killer was coming nearer. Climbing Faye Arensberg's stairs. Faye sat unaware, brushing her long blond hair. Unaware, sitting in the center of a huge white driftwood bed. . . .

Rita must have made some sound, because when she stopped reading and looked up, Jay was staring at her.

Rita thought: *You bastard. You slept with Claire. You were in that room.*

Margaret, meanwhile, was at the window. "Look," she said, "the Senator is here."

Rita looked outside and saw the BMW, exhaust pluming from it. Seeing it somehow dissipated the anger she'd felt toward Jay. "I remember when Claire moved in," Rita said. "I thought, 'There goes the neighborhood.' No shit, I figured there'd be Rolls-Royces and Mercedes-Benzes all over the place. Big parties. Servants. The whole bit. And all we ever got was one lousy senator. With a BMW yet."

"Can't have everything," Jay said.

They continued talking, filling each other in on things. Rita was talking about Harborplace, extolling it.

Jessie had come into the room for the tail end of Rita's speech. She glanced out into the street and frowned.

Rita wondered when this Edward was going to arrive, but didn't ask. She had a funny feeling that he wasn't going to show. That he'd stand Jessie up. What would Jessie do? Would she cry the way Rita cried whenever it had happened to her? Or would she just serve dinner and pretend the other place setting wasn't there? *We're all so full of shit,* Rita thought. Margaret pretending nothing had happened with the Senator, and Jay pretending that he was faithful to Margaret, and Sin pretending that his mother hadn't died. Rita felt as though she just might scream, and for a moment thought she *had* screamed—but it was something else, something outside.

They all moved to the window and watched.

An ambulance had parked immediately ahead of Aubrey's car. The back doors of the vehicle had been hurled open, and several white-clad attendants had carried a stretcher into Claire's.

Then several—not just one or two—police cars came. Two cops jumped out of an unmarked car and began roping off the pavement in front of Claire's house.

The door to the BMW was open, and Senator Aubrey Denton sat in it. He'd swung his legs toward the pavement and stayed that way, half in and half out of the car.

Two patrolmen, one with a clipboard, came and crouched at his feet. Aubrey gripped the doorframe of the BMW on both sides.

"I'm scared," Rita said. "This is something big."

Claire's front door had been ajar, Aubrey told the police, and he had pushed at it. He had known, he said, even then. He walked from white room to white room until finally he'd found her. Walking from room to room downstairs, he had known, he told police, where and even how she would be found.

The police treated him with deference. It wasn't so much his position, though they took note of that, as his sorrow—so thorough, so real.

"She called me," he'd kept saying at first. With such amazement that they'd thought he was referring to some occult experience. Thought he was claiming that Claire's dying voice had reached him across the city.

It seemed to LeGrande that the two cops arrived at his home just minutes after he himself had. They had his knife inside a thick plastic bag with a label on it and the one cop kept waving the thing in his face. The blade was open. LeGrande had scratched his name onto the blade, so they knew it was his. Or did they know? They kept asking him, was it his?

Even with the bag waving and the plastic so thick, LeGrande could see that the blade wasn't clean like he'd left it. But Claude had been there. Claude knew what went down. Claude would tell them that he, LeGrande, hadn't dirtied that blade with her blood. "You talk to my friend," LeGrande kept saying, half crying at first and then, because of their attitude, almost growling the words out.

And then he heard his mama, home with Denise from trick-or-treat. That made him feel a whole lot worse than everything else.

"You got my boy in there?" he heard his mama say. "Somethin' happen to my boy?"

The detective in the alley found the camera and bagged it. He was about to carry it inside Claire's house when he spotted Nick. Nick seemed drunk, seemed to stagger, though he didn't, the detective noted when he got that close, *smell* of alcohol.

"It ain't mine no more," Nick kept repeating. "You gotta believe me."

It took the detective more than a little while to figure out that Nick was talking about the Polaroid that had just been plopped into the evidence bag.

Back toward the front of the house, the detective could hear the crowd starting to gather. How did they know? The way this guy knew. Was it instinct, or had they all been waiting for it? The detective had been on the force for a long time. He had been here for Faye Arensberg.

Better cuff this guy and read off his rights, the detective thought. The guy didn't seem like he was going anyplace, but with people milling around like that, you never could tell. He could just get into the crowd and disappear.

Jay looked across Jessie's living room at Rita. She was holding the manuscript box right up against her chest. Everyone else in the room was looking down into the street, but not Rita. She was looking right at Jay.

241

"I think we'd better go down," she announced.

"I'm right behind you," Jay said.

The stretcher that came out was completely shrouded. They all knew what that meant. They'd been talking, but now they all stopped.

It was a fair-sized crowd, with a sprinkling of kids in costume. Someone dressed as a skeleton, for instance, was in the closest row. But even those who weren't dressed for Halloween looked eerie, touched by the red, whirling bubble lights.

"Rita . . ." Jay moved toward her the minute they'd gained the street, but Rita kept moving away. Jay looked alternately at her and at the policemen, who seemed to be everywhere.

Rita was looking for Sin, with no way of knowing how she'd lost him. She'd thought he was right behind. She'd heard his voice, hadn't she? She felt like a child lost in a department-store crush. Faces everywhere, but none familiar. And where was Margaret? Rita knew that Margaret had been right behind Jay. And where was Jessie?

Jay grabbed at her, pinching her arm through her jacket. "Rita, please . . ."

It was surreal, viewed from above this way, all of their faces red for a moment and then black again. Everyone seemed extra animated, Jessie thought, hands flailing, heads nodding. Jessie raised the window to add sound. She somehow expected everyone to turn and look up at her when she did, but no one noticed, no one at all. Jessie might have stayed there, watching, but the timer went off in the kitchen, signifying that dinner was ready to be served.

"Rita."

"Jay, if you touch me, I'll call a cop."

"But why?" Jay asked.

"*Why?*" She hugged the manuscript box as though he might try to wrench it from her. "The driftwood bed in here, that's why."

"Rita, all it means is that I was in there. So what?"

"Don't tell me that. You slept with her. That bed. It's in there. That bed, and—"

"I did not sleep with her," he said. "You didn't read the scene."

Rita hadn't. She'd skipped a few pages and found, even more to her horror, that Faye had supposedly had a photograph of herself, and that the photo had been mutilated. "Funny coincidence, isn't it," she told Jay.

"I added that," he said. "You told me about it on the phone and I put it in."

"You added it pretty quick."

"So what does that prove?"

"That you murdered her. *Murdered* her. And I'm giving this to a cop."

She tried to turn and shield the box containing Jay's manuscript, but he grabbed her arm and began to twist it. Rita didn't holler, couldn't make herself holler. All those cops, all those people, what could he possibly do to her? But, in addition to twisting her arm, he was pushing her along toward his apartment. "I'm not going anyplace with you," she said. She kicked his shin and he went "Oof" and broke his hold.

"Then listen to me," he said. "Stand still and listen."

Where was Sin? Rita wondered. And Margaret? And Jessie?

Jessie laid the turkey on the oval earthenware platter and snipped the stitches that held the stuffing inside. She scooped a great deal of it into a bowl and then carried it to the table. Now the yams and the wild rice.

Meanwhile, she put the pies she had baked into the open oven so that they'd be warm when the time came for dessert.

"How can I believe you?" Rita asked Jay, but she felt her hold on the box of manuscript loosening. She had thought of it as evidence, thought that Jay had been pursuing her to retrieve it. But it was evidence, wasn't it? Or maybe Jay was telling the truth about how he'd used Claire as a model, but that it was, or had seemed, innocent.

But then she remembered that Jay wasn't innocent, wasn't innocent at all, only looked that way, took pains to look that way.

"Rita, if you give the police that manuscript, it's what they'll think, too. It's what everyone will think. Rita, look at me. Is that what you believe?"

Rita looked hard. She remembered all the times she'd been alone with Jay. He couldn't be a killer, she'd have seen some sign. But wasn't that the way it always turned out when a killer was caught? Everyone would say they never would have guessed, he was so quiet, so innocent, never said a harsh word.

And then Rita thought of Jay in a scene, much as she thought of her father as King Lear. She remembered Jay, standing in her own apartment, with his hand clasped over his heart. "Sex . . . for me," he'd dragged out in his phony French accent, "ees a matter . . . of . . . domination." Would a killer clown around like that? On the other hand, that domination business and the sex club . . .

Jay repeated, "Rita, is that what you believe?"

"No." She handed Jay the box.

Jessie had come outside without her coat. Rita listened to her in disbelief. Jessie actually expected them to come inside and eat. Was she crazy?

"I didn't go through all this trouble for nothing," Jessie said. "Now get the others."

"I don't know where they are," Rita told her, indicating all of the onlookers. The ambulance had gone, but the crowd still grew, probably because of the cop cars. And probably, too, because of the rumors that were starting to spread. Just before Jessie had come out, Rita had heard Aubrey Denton's name, and also Faye's. There were already two television crews setting up outside the house.

"Find them." Jessie went back the way she'd come.

Rita looked at Jay, and Jay said, "Christ. And you think *I'm* weird."

When they filed back into the apartment, Jessie was at the head of the table in the pumpkin's glow. The shadows reminded Rita of the statue she had seen at Nick's: the Virgin. An eerie thought. She tried to banish it. She'd heard someone say that Nick had been taken away, but only as a witness. She decided to carry on, just as Jessie wished. Why not? Before Claire's death had been discovered, she and Sin were already pretending that his own mother's hadn't happened. "Mmm," Rita said, "smells yummy."

Jessie looked at her and smiled. Rita sat on Jessie's right. Immediately across from Jessie was the empty place setting. Rita wondered about this Edward character, half envying him for not being there.

Jessie stood to carve the turkey. "My carving knife," she said, feeling around the table for it. At the very word *knife,* they'd all tensed. Was this, Rita wondered, the way it would be forever after? They'd been through two murders together, after all. Or would it go away, after the police had finished trying to figure things out?

"I'm glad we weren't here while all this was going on," Margaret told Jay.

"What do you mean?" Rita asked.

"I mean I'm glad that—"

"Where were you?" Rita demanded.

"We were at the photocopy place. Getting Jay's book copied."

"Both of you?"

"Well, I said *we,*" Margaret told her.

Rita and Jay looked at each other, and Jay rolled his eyes. "An ironclad alibi," Rita said, laughing. She hoped she wouldn't have to explain why. It was really silly now, to have accused Jay when all .the while he'd been someplace with Margaret. And the crazy thing was, he hadn't even thought to tell Rita that. He hadn't remembered.

Jessie was still standing. She hadn't begun to carve.

"What's the matter?" Jay asked her.

"I don't have my carving knife," she said.

"Here it is," Sin said, edging it along the table. Rita took it and passed it on. It had a long, triangular blade and a thick ivory handle. It had been in Jessie's family forever, Rita knew.

Going on with this dinner is a big mistake, Rita thought. *We're all a little whacko.* She looked over at Sin, who hadn't said a word for the longest time, except when he'd found the knife. Rita was about to ask him something, just to get him to talk, when somebody knocked on the downstairs door.

"It's probably the police," Jay said. "I'll get it."

Seconds later, Jay and the officer were framed in the door. Jay pointed at Jessie. Still holding the carving knife, Jessie took a few steps backward, almost walking into the vitrine. The glassware inside rattled just slightly, like wind chimes.

"*She* lives here," Jay said. "The rest of us are only here for dinner."

"That wasn't too bad," Rita said, when the officer had gone. "I mean, considering."

"Well," Jay said pointedly, "it isn't as though any of us are suspects. They just wanted to know if we saw or heard anything."

"Like last time," Margaret said. They all sat in silence for a moment.

It was Sin who tried to lighten things. "I'd bet on the Senator," he said.

"It could have been anyone," Margaret defended. "Nick. Or LeGrande. Anyone."

"Not LeGrande," Rita said. "LeGrande is secretly a pussycat." From the corner of her eye she saw Sin getting their coats. Rita stood. "We'd better hit the road. Long drive. Jessie?" She turned toward Jessie, offering a hug.

But Jessie moved past Rita to stand directly in front of Sin. "But you can't go," she said. "There's no reason to go." Her voice was low, almost seductive. She reached up and put her arms around Sin's neck.

"Wait a minute," Sin said softly, holding her away from himself for just a moment so that he could drop the coats on the floor. "Here." He took Jessie into his arms.

Jay, Margaret, and Rita stood rooted, watching. Watching as Jessie yielded to him, seemed to grow smaller. She buried her face in his lapels and her shoulders shook. "Let me help you," Sin said.

"Could you? Oh, could you, Edward?" Jessie's words caught. "Could you lift me up and carry me? Could you lift me up and put me into bed?"

Sin stayed in the bedroom with Jessie for the longest time. Rita and Margaret and Jay didn't quite know what to say as they waited for him to emerge. "Leave it to Rosenberg," Rita quipped, "to leave town when we need him most."

"Jessie's just afraid," Margaret said, "and you can't blame her."

"But it did seem sexual," Jay offered. "The way she—"

"Oh, fuck off." Rita cut him short, but she knew as well as he that it had seemed that way. She relented. "Jessie called him 'Edward.' So it has to do with this Edward guy. Mister no-show."

"I wonder where she met him," Margaret said.

"I wonder if he ever hugs her, or holds her, or, you know, all the stuff we need. I wonder if he ever . . ."

"Carries her to bed," Jay finished.

"Stop making this into a joke," Rita protested. But she knew that her own Rosenberg remark was meant to make light of the episode. How handle it otherwise? God.

"Do you suppose that they're—" Jay began, but Rita interrupted him.

"I know you're kidding, Jay, but so help me, if you say it, I'm going to punch you out."

"I can't believe how jealous you can be. At a time like this," Jay said, "all you can think of is that she is in there with your boyfriend."

"I'm not jealous," Rita said. "I just don't like you making fun that way because, really, think about it, you're making fun of Jessie."

They all sat silently now. Then Margaret voiced what they all were thinking. "One of us, at least, should stay over with her," she said.

"Sin's mother died tonight," Rita told them matter-of-factly. "So we can't."

No one responded to her statement. They just accepted it as a very routine thing to say.

Sin emerged with a shrug. "She's sleeping," he said, picking his and Rita's coats off the floor. No one else had thought to.

"That's all you have to tell us?" Rita demanded.

"What's to tell? She was shook, that's all, and now she's fine."

"Well, what was it?" Rita asked. "Was it this Edward, telling her he'd come for dinner and then not showing up? Was it, you know, what happened to Claire? What was it?"

"I don't know," Sin said. "I guess it was a combination of both."

PART
TEN

TWO YEARS LATER

The Row was now all but indistinguishable from the rest of Capitol Hill. The house that had been rubble had been cleared away, and the lot where the mess had been was a small city park now. It sported tulips in spring and holly berries in winter. The other places in the Row had, save one, been similarly improved.

The house in which LeGrande lived, for instance, had had its proud pink covered with a stately gray. Its new residents had begun the renovations the very same day that a ramshackle truck had come to cart away the black family's possessions. LeGrande, vindicated by Claude's statement to the police, had never been charged with the crime. Still—perhaps because no one had been charged—he and his mother and Denise had moved away from speculation, to one of the urban-renewal projects, it was said.

Claude, who'd returned of his own volition to clear his friend, had, in that act, cemented his tie to LeGrande and to a more or less legitimate way of life. The two, on Claude's meager savings, had managed to purchase a truck and now ran a small hauling business.

Jay and Margaret had married and now lived in Cleveland Park. She was clerking for a smart Georgetown law firm, and he was still busily revising his book, this time to take Claire's death into account.

Jay's old basement apartment was inhabited now by an artist, a long-haired blonde whose craft was evident by the paint-spattered smock she always wore.

The place that had served as apartments for Rita and Margaret was a single-family home now. The porch had been removed to reveal a structure that might have been Georgian. The elegance of the couple who lived there was immediately apparent: Morning and eve, they walked a haughty trio of borzois.

Rita was in Baltimore, living in the house that had belonged to Evelyn Sinclair. She and Sin had recently done a book of photographs together—of stained-glass masterpieces they'd managed to track down in unlikely places all over Baltimore and Washington. These works of art—transoms and windows and door panels—were the early creations of an artist of some renown, and so the book was well received and they were guaranteed other, similar projects. Rita, as she was quoted in a recent interview, didn't want to photograph people, ever.

Nick, who, like LeGrande, had been questioned and released, could still be found in the Market. He was a married man now, though, and had moved from the flat above the Laundromat into a duplex out near Andrews Air Force Base. It was a long commute for Nick, but he didn't mind. His wife, Angie, owned a car, and after Nick dropped her off at the nursery school where she worked, she let him drive it into D.C. He'd sing along with the radio, happy, very happy, at last. They, along with Zabo and his wife, bowled twice a week, and occasionally the two women would go off to a bingo together.

Claire Albritten's property had been donated, with all of its furnishings, to the Master of Foxhounds Association. Claire would have approved of what they'd added: a long row of taxidermic trophies—hardwood plaques bearing fox masks and fox paws, visible from the street.

Senator Aubrey Denton had, of course, seen to all the details of the transaction. Then he'd retired from politics and moved back to his home state. For reasons of health, he'd told the media in what was to be his last television interview. Those watching were appalled by the amount of weight the Senator had lost.

Jessie still lived on the Row. She had gone as far as she could go at her job, except for cost-of-living raises. She didn't care enough about her house to alter anything further. The yard had been a major step for Jessie, and it was enough.

Jessie didn't think about the others who had lived on the Row. Rita, Margaret, and Jay had each called her, but she never attempted to contact them in return, and eventually they stopped.

Jessie didn't think about the murders, either. She spent her days at the store and her nights at her window.

Jessie watched the Masters of Foxhounds come and go. Many of them were older men—tall, austere, gray. She wondered if she would ever build enough courage to ask one of them to join her for a drink in her little, flower-bedecked backyard.

That would be nice.

That would be safe.

Unless, of course, the one whom she'd selected would later chance to visit the long-haired blonde in the paint-stained smock. Jessie would hate that. She would hate to have to kill another of those girls.